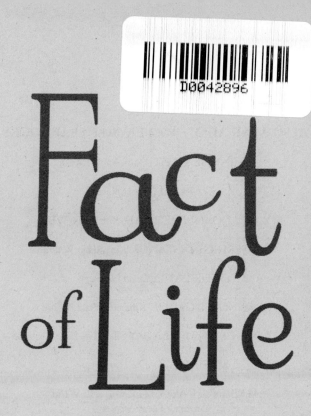

Fact of Life #31

D0042896

ALSO AVAILABLE FROM LAUREL-LEAF BOOKS

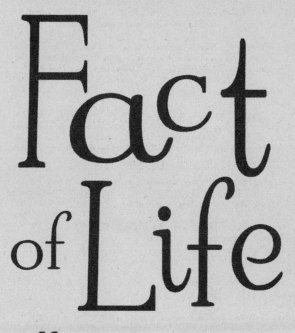

Fact of Life

of Life

#31

Denise Vega

LAUREL-LEAF BOOKS

Copyright © 2008 by Denise Vega

All rights reserved. Published in the United States by Laurel-Leaf, an imprint of Random House Children's Books, a division of Random House, Inc., New York. Originally published in hardcover in the United States by Alfred A. Knopf, an imprint of Random House Children's Books, a division of Random House, Inc., New York, in 2008.

Laurel-Leaf and the colophon are trademarks of Random House, Inc.

Visit us on the Web! www.randomhouse.com/teens

Educators and librarians, for a variety of teaching tools, visit us at www.randomhouse.com/teachers

The Library of Congress has cataloged the hardcover edition of this work as follows:
Vega, Denise.
Fact of life #31 / Denise Vega.
p.   cm.
Summary: Sixteen-year-old Kat, whose mother is a home-birth midwife, feels betrayed when a popular, beautiful classmate gets pregnant and forms a bond with Kat's mother that Kat herself never had.
ISBN 978-0-375-84819-3 (trade) — ISBN 978-0-375-94819-0 (lib. bdg.) — ISBN 978-0-375-84957-2 (e-book)
[1. Midwives—Fiction. 2. Pregnancy—Fiction. 3. Mothers and daughters—Fiction.] I. Title. II. Title: Fact of life number thirty-one.
PZ7.V4865Fac 2008
[Fic]—dc22
2007049654

ISBN 978-0-375-84309-9 (pbk.)

RL: 7.0
Printed in the United States of America
10 9 8 7 6 5 4 3 2 1
First Laurel-Leaf Edition

To my niece, Sarah Elizabeth Perkins,
who continues to make a difference in the world

First Trimester

*During this wonderful first phase, things are happening already!
You can expect all kinds of new and interesting changes in your
body—changes in breast size and tenderness, feelings of fatigue,
nausea and vomiting, frequent urination, and many more.*

*The baby starts as a cluster of cells before moving quickly to
having a heartbeat. It has reflexes and the ability to move those
teeny-tiny limbs. Backbone, spinal column, and nervous system
are also forming!*

1

911.

The numbers seemed to pulse on my pager, quickening along with my heartbeat. Abra only used the pager for emergencies, because sometimes I didn't answer when she called my cell. I jammed my headset into my cell and dialed her number.

"Katima, thank God." Her voice was soft but the words were quick, anxious. I rarely heard Abra sound anxious. "Where are you?"

"On my way to school," I said. "Where are you?"

"I'm at Linda's," Abra said. "She's in labor."

"Is everything okay?" Linda was one of my favorites of Abra's mothers. I had been working two afternoons a week at Abra's Midwifery for over a year and had gotten to know a lot of the women. Linda and I had hit it off, sharing a love of rocky road ice cream and a hatred of reality TV. I had helped her plan her birth—the music, atmosphere, different birth options. I didn't want her having complications.

"She's doing beautifully," Abra said. "But I'm not. Marion

broke her foot, Sarah is at another birth, and Carmen isn't picking up any of her phones or responding to my page." Abra sucked in a breath. "I have no one to assist me."

I eased down on the brakes of my Honda hybrid as I came to a stop sign. "Um, okay. But you've delivered lots of babies without an assistant."

"I know. But Linda wants one, so I need you to get to her house as fast as you can."

"Say what?" I hit the gas too hard, jerking the car forward.

"I've excused you from school," Abra said. "This is life experience, Katima. A transcendent experience. You won't get that in any classroom."

My hands shook on the steering wheel. I turned down a side street and pulled over, shutting off the ignition. I didn't know if I was pissed at her for assuming I'd do it or excited that I might actually get to see a live birth.

But what did I know about assisting?

"You're out of your mind."

"Well, that's highly possible," Abra said, "seeing as how I've exhausted all of my usual assistants and I'm calling a sixteen-year-old high school student who's worked at the Midwifery for a year." She chuckled. "If I'm not out of my mind, I'm clearly a little desperate, Katima."

Clearly. "Is it all right with Linda and Wayne?"

"Of course," Abra said. "I would never do something like this without asking them." There was a pause before she spoke again. "Actually, Linda is the one who suggested it."

"She did?" A grin spread across my face. "Tell me how to get there."

• • •

I pulled up at Linda's house about thirty minutes later. It was in a new development—big gables and dormer windows, small trees, new sod. I was shaking with nervous excitement. I'd never seen a baby emerge like an oversized Otter Pop except in that movie we saw back in sixth grade. The idea thrilled and petrified me at the same time.

I glanced around the car. I had no idea what I might need, but I knew there would be times when we would just wait. Unzipping my backpack, I flipped through textbooks and notebooks, pulling out the Rocky Mountain Women's Triathlon brochure I'd been reading. Then I grabbed my sketchbook and some pencils before heading into the house.

"Kat," Linda said when I arrived. "I'm so glad you're here." She was wearing one of her husband Wayne's oversized T-shirts, her nipples poking through the fabric. Her maternity underwear hugged her butt.

"You sure you want me here?"

She made an "are you kidding?" face. Then she quickly sucked in her breath.

"Another one?" Wayne asked, rubbing her back.

Linda nodded, letting out her breath slow and even. Abra once told me that for some women, labor pains are menstrual cramps times a few hundred—for some, times a thousand or so. Yikes. But Linda's face wasn't all pinched up in pain. It was calm; her eyes focused.

I turned and watched Abra as she moved between tasks, so fluidly she hardly seemed to be moving at all. I thought of that phrase "She was in her element." But here in this room, with the shades drawn and a few candles flickering, Abra was more than that—she *was* the element. I'd seen her at the office, but never at a birth, never like this—a person who moved with grace and perfect timing, anticipating, checking, doing. Always doing the right thing.

"Slowly, Katima," Abra said as I hurried over. "You want to create a calm environment." She motioned me next to her. "Help me with this." I stepped around the large layer of plastic spread out on the floor beside the bed. "Your job is P-I-E," Abra whispered. "Physical, informational, and emotional support."

"I'm not a doula, Abra," I said. "I'm your receptionist and occasional office visit assistant."

Abra smiled, but I knew what she was thinking: *You don't have to remind me that you are a lame excuse for a birth assistant.*

"Just do what I tell you," she said. "You'll be fine."

Like I would know how to do anything except what she told me. But at least she had some confidence that I could help out.

"Hold the sheets up," she said. I did, and she put plastic beneath them. We smoothed the sheets back down and fluffed the pillows.

"All right," Abra said, surveying the room. I could tell she was taking a mental inventory, making sure everything was in its place. She had a table with all of her supplies at the ready; the birthing ball and birthing stool were resting in a corner in case Linda wanted to use them.

I wasn't sure what she needed me for. It looked like she had everything under control. I glanced at her as she stood out of the way, her eyes resting softly on Linda and Wayne.

Abra. The best home birth midwife in the Rocky Mountain region.

Abra. Practically perfect in every way.

Abra. My mother.

2

It was quiet except for Linda's and Wayne's soft steps across the carpet. Linda had told me she didn't like it too quiet. She liked a little noise, no matter what she was doing. But maybe now that she was actually here, in the middle of labor, she didn't want anything at all. Still . . .

"Would you like some music, Linda?" I cringed as my voice grated against the silence. "I'm sorry," I said. "I just remembered you said—"

"Music would be wonderful, Kat."

"The iPod system is over there." Wayne pointed to the dresser.

I wasn't sure where Linda was in terms of her labor stages, but she was still engaged in conversation and walking around a lot, so I selected the fifth song in our First Stage list and pressed Play. Nineties rock pulsed through the speakers.

Abra stepped forward. "I don't think—" she started to say, but Linda raised her hand. "It's perfect," she said, swinging her hips. "I know it's going to be worse later and I may not be able to do this." She waved me over to her. "Let's dance, Kat."

Wayne smiled as I joined her, shimmying to the music. Abra slipped into the bathroom and I heard her turn on the tub faucet so Linda could labor in warm water.

Halfway through a shimmy, Linda gripped her belly: "Oh, dear." She breathed through the contraction, clutching Wayne for support. I took the chance to peek into their bathroom. It was huge, practically another bedroom. The tub was way at the opposite end, surrounded by sea-green tile. Abra trailed her fingers in the water, humming to herself.

"Kat," Linda said, "could you get me some ice?"

"Sure." I turned back to the bedroom and scooped a few small cubes from the cooler into a cup and brought them to her.

"Thanks." She pressed her other hand into her abdomen. "I think I'd like to try the tub."

Linda and Wayne went into the bathroom while I switched the music to something softer. I lit the candles next to the bed; they were lilac-scented, something Linda and I had talked about during her visits.

Abra poked her head out of the bathroom. "Get the birthing ball, please, Katima."

I rolled the large ball across the room, stopping at the bathroom doorway. I had no desire to enter a bathroom where at least one adult would be naked, possibly two. Another of Abra's mothers had told me how her husband stripped down and joined her in a large portable tub. Apparently the husband had knelt tall beside his laboring wife, his family jewels clearly visible through the water.

I'd prefer that the jewels stay in the box, thank you very much.

"Could you bring it all the way in, Katima?" Abra's voice interrupted my thoughts.

"It's right here," I said, giving it a nudge. It rolled about a foot and stopped.

"Katima." Abra was using her "enough nonsense" tone.

"Okay." I lifted the ball in front of my face so I wouldn't see any naked bodies. That was a mistake. I stumbled on my next step, the ball flying from my hands. Horrified, I watched it bounce off Wayne's back (fully clothed, I had time to note with relief), then ricochet off the mirror before smacking me off balance.

"Oomph." I fell back into the bedroom, clutching the ball to my chest.

Wayne's chuckle made my face burn. I stood shakily, lowering my eyes as I rolled the ball toward them. Then I fled to a corner of the bedroom, Abra close behind me.

"My goodness, Katima." She squatted in front of me. "Are you all right?"

"Fine."

"What was that all about?" she asked. "And why were your eyes closed?"

I sighed. I knew I was supposed to feel the joy and sacredness of the human body, to relish the beauty of Linda's pregnant one on full display. But I couldn't. I just felt embarrassed for her, and for me for seeing her that way. "I was just trying to respect their privacy."

Abra smiled. "There is no privacy in childbirth, Katima. We're all one. It is us and we are it. We're all naked and we're all fully clothed."

I crossed my arms over my chest. I didn't need a cosmic Zen lesson right now.

For the next hour or so, Linda labored in the tub, Wayne and Abra assisting her. I pulled out my sketchbook and stared at a

9

blank page. Nothing. I drew a few lines but it wasn't flowing, so I set the sketchbook aside and sat by the bed, squishing the soft wax gathered at the bottom of the candles.

Linda and Wayne appeared at the doorway. Linda was wrapped in a towel, clutching Wayne's arm. "I think we're close."

I looked around. Should I sit in a corner, out of the way?

"Change the music, please, Kat," Linda said.

"Right." Okay, she was near the end of her labor—time to pull out the big diapers. I clicked through the playlists. Gone were the rock and pop; in their place I spun Native American flute music, gentle and natural.

"Almost there, Linda. You're doing beautifully." Linda was on the bed now, and Abra spoke in a soothing croon in rhythm with Linda's breathing, as if her voice was a part of Linda's breath, a part of her.

I stood next to the iPod system, feeling completely useless.

"Pat her face with a damp cloth, Katima." Abra nodded toward a shallow pan of water and a washcloth. I nodded, grateful for something to do.

Linda moaned and breathed through the next contraction. I blinked in the dim light, basking in the almost cavelike feel, the glow of candles flickering in time to breath and movement, the rumpled earthiness of the blankets forming natural hills and valleys.

Shifting uncomfortably, I was suddenly aware of my thin arms, the bony elbows poking out as I flipped the cloth over on her forehead. I felt out of place next to Linda's full, rounded body and wondered if Abra noticed the stark contrast at this end of the bed.

"Breathe in deeply, Linda. That's the way." Abra rubbed Linda's thighs. "Exhale through an open mouth. Imagine your cervix dilating, growing wider to allow the baby to come through."

I looked down at Linda. I knew she was thinking about what Abra had just said. I squeezed her hand. "It's getting bigger," I intoned, like a hypnotist putting a client to sleep. She chuckled, just before the next contraction.

Abra glanced up, surprised. "You laughed."

"Kat made me," Linda said.

Great. I'd screwed up again. Maybe there was some rule against laughing during a birth. But what did she expect? I was a last-minute replacement, completely untrained.

Twenty minutes later: "I feel the urge to push," Linda gasped, sitting up taller.

My heart thumped. It was time. It was time to see the baby come out. Without waiting for instructions from Abra, I headed for the iPod, scrolling through the songs. I pressed Play and *The Lion King*'s "Circle of Life" filled the room. I glanced at Linda. She probably didn't even notice the song. Her eyes were closed as she moaned softly to some internal rhythm. It was clear she was somewhere else, somewhere deep inside herself.

"I can see the head, honey!" Wayne's voice startled me. He was staring at the mirror positioned at the foot of the bed, eyes bright with excitement. As I turned to look, my hand caught on the sound system's power cord. The system flew off the dresser, smacking my thigh before hitting the carpet. The iPod popped out of its cradle and dropped to the floor, silencing the "Circle." I scurried to pick it up, slipped on the plastic, and fell into Abra, sending her sprawling. My hand reached out instinctively toward

11

the baby's head—to catch it, protect it; to make sure it didn't fall into the empty space between the bed and the floor.

But the baby wasn't coming out yet, and I landed with a thud.

Abra pushed herself up and knelt in front of Linda, hardly seeming to notice the lump that was me next to her.

"Are you okay?" Wayne asked both of us.

Abra nodded. But I was not okay. I had to get out of there. Crawling across the carpet, I opened the door with one hand, slinking into the hall before pulling the door shut behind me. Could the floor please open up and swallow me?

Slumping against the door, I sighed heavily. Why had Abra called me? Because she had to. Why had I come? Because I had to. Not just because Linda had wanted me, but because I really, really wanted to see a baby born.

Linda moaned on the other side of the door and I bit my lip, tears pricking my eyes.

"Oh, God. Look at that hair!" Wayne's voice. I wondered if Abra even noticed I was gone, had slunk out like a cat who'd just knocked over the sugar.

I covered my ears with my hands. I wanted to run. Down the stairs and out the door, and keep running until my lungs burst open. But my butt was superglued to the floor.

Linda cried out. I drew my knees up and buried my head between them, my sobs rising. I swallowed hard, ignoring the pain in my thickening throat. I heard the baby's soft cry, then a "Thank God" from Linda and an "I love you" from Wayne.

The baby had been born, and I'd missed it.

Several minutes passed before the doorknob squeaked. I scooted away, looking up at Abra as I wiped my cheeks.

"It's a girl," she said, smiling. Then she pushed the door wider. "Linda asked for you."

I dropped my head down again. "I can't go in there."

"Yes, you can." I felt her hand on my head and ducked down. Why did her touch feel like fire to me when it seemed to console everyone else?

"They hate me."

"Nobody hates you." Abra tapped the wall behind me. "They want you to come in."

I sighed deeply. I could either stay in the hall or go in and try to make things right.

Seconds slid by.

I took a deep breath and stood up.

Linda sat in bed, naked from the waist up, the baby nestled between her breasts. The umbilical cord was still attached, snaking out from under the blanket that was wrapped around the baby. Wayne sat beside Linda, his arm curving around her shoulders. The smell of sweet sweat mixed with the lilac candles pulsed around us, but more than that, the very air vibrated with life.

"Meet Claire," Linda whispered, kissing the baby softly on her still-bloody forehead.

"Hi, Claire." I knelt beside the bed, reaching out a tentative finger to touch the tiny fist next to the baby's face. "She's so beautiful," I said. Then I sniffled, hardly able to look at Linda. "I'm sorry I screwed up. I hope I didn't ruin it for you."

Linda reached out and squeezed my hand. "You'd be amazed how much you don't notice when you're in labor. The outside world sort of disappears." She smiled. "Besides, you made Wayne laugh with the whole ball thing. He needed that."

I smiled and placed my hand gently on Claire's back, watching my hand rise and fall in time to her breathing. Tears sprang unexpectedly to my eyes, and I let them slip down my cheeks.

Abra crossed the room, rolling up the soiled plastic mat. Her bare feet made no sound across the thick carpet; her straw sandals had been tossed, forgotten, in a corner. She glanced at me and smiled. I managed a slight smile back.

I gave Claire another pat, then got up and followed Abra, holding the garbage bag open as she stuffed the mat into it. I snuck a peek at her as she blew a wisp of hair off her face. For a moment she looked old. Tired. But then she tossed her ponytail over her shoulder and turned. Her eyes were bright, happy, filled with joy and the knowledge that she'd just done something worthwhile, meaningful. Something that mattered.

I wondered if I'd ever feel like that.

I ran. In the dark of a Colorado Friday night. In the silence. With each inhale, I left behind the image of the flying iPod. With each exhale, I let go of myself curled up outside the door, missing the birth I had wanted to be a part of.

I ran for nearly four miles before my legs rubberized and my lungs ached, forcing me to slow down. I turned around, jogging back toward the rec center's parking lot. I felt each breath, each muscle stretching and contracting; heard the soft pat as my shoes hit the dirt; smelled the cool September air filled with moist grass and leaves and the slightly sour scent of the canal, recently drained in anticipation of winter.

When I reached the trailhead, I cooled down, walking back and forth. Stretching out on the bench, I breathed deeply, closing my eyes and picturing little Claire in my mind, her soft cries and snuffles murmuring like a lullaby in my ear. The experience of seeing her small, breathing body washed over me again.

I opened my eyes and stared up at the few stars that had muscled their way out from under the glare of city and street lights. If I stared long enough without blinking, the stars seemed to pulse and spin, coming alive in the blackness.

The night sky made me feel like there was something much bigger and better than myself, an entire universe doing its thing without a lot of help from me.

It soothed and depressed me at the same time.

When I got home, I headed for my room, plopping down on the window seat in the dark. I turned on my cell phone and saw four text messages from Christy Buchanan, best friend extraordinaire. I had called her on the way to Linda and Wayne's to tell her about the assist. She thought the whole midwife thing was "cool and funky," and the messages were no doubt pleas for "the full story."

But I didn't feel like talking about it. I stared out the window into the night. As lights from a passing car lit the street, a picture came, fully formed, into my mind. I leapt off the window seat and turned on the light. Grabbing my sketchbook, I drew— Linda, Wayne, and Claire snuggled together on the bed, the umbilical cord winding its way around all of them, like a ribbon tying up a package. I used my pastels to add color, smearing a golden yellow with orange so the light was muted and warm.

It was just as I'd seen it when I'd come in after the birth—the three of them, separate but connected, pain and love and hope swirling around and through them.

I'd drawn it because it had come to me and demanded to be put on paper. Now I didn't know what to do with it.

Sighing, I put the picture in the back of my closet and covered it with an old shirt.

3

"Watch out!" A shoulder rammed into mine. I spun sideways, reaching out for support. Lockers slammed. Heavy perfume and BO mingled in my nostrils. I blinked in the stark lights of Tabor High School Monday morning. Alien territory, even though I'd been here since I was a freshman.

I turned to see who I'd collided with, but he was already barreling down the hallway, shoulders rotating in linebacker fashion, ready to knock other unsuspecting bowling pin humans out of the way.

Slipping in and out of the flow, I made my way to my locker. The door groaned as I heaved it open, sounding like I felt. My run Friday night had only been a temporary fix. Humiliation and embarrassment had a way of prodding you again and again.

Abra had tried to make light of it on Saturday afternoon. We were in the kitchen, cleaning up after lunch. "Linda's happy, Claire is healthy. Don't worry about it." Easy for her to say. She did everything perfectly.

"You just need more experience," my dad had said, tapping

17

me on the shoulder as he passed me to put away the condiments. "Just wait till next time."

Like there would be a next time. I doubt Linda was going around bragging about my wonderful birth assistant skills. *Want a birthing ball thrown at you? Call Kat. Want to birth your baby with no one to catch it? Kat will be sure to knock the midwife down so nobody's there.*

Yeah. The invitations to assist would come pouring in.

Abra's face didn't tell me how she felt about a possible next time, but I could guess. She'd be against it.

"I'm not coming back to the Midwifery," I said suddenly, there in the kitchen. It was a bold statement. An impulsive statement.

A stupid statement.

Abra washed an organic apple, not looking at me. "If that's what you think is best."

I bit my lip. That wasn't what I had expected her to say, what I'd wanted her to say. Where was the surprise? The disappointment? The protests? She was playing the oldest parenting trick in the book—calling my bluff. Now I was stuck.

"I'll need a few weeks to find a replacement," she said, placing the apple in a bowl.

"Why? A monkey could do my job." A hamster could do it. We'd put one of those little running wheels on the desk so she could exercise when things weren't busy.

"A monkey could not do your job, Katima." Abra looked at me. "If you're serious about this, then please stay at the Midwifery for a few weeks until I can get someone else."

"Fine." I had rolled my eyes, but secretly I was relieved. Even though part of me was embarrassed to go back, the thought of not being there depressed me.

The first bell rang, bringing me back to the Tabor hallway. I sighed heavily. I'd had a disastrous first birth assist, had quit the best job I'd ever had, and now I was at school, where I felt completely incompetent.

Closing my eyes, I assumed the yoga Mountain Pose—feet close together, back straight, shoulders relaxed, hands at my sides. Then I moved my hands into prayer position, bringing them in front of my heart, breathing deeply. When I felt calmer, I opened my eyes. Two girls were walking by, giving me one of those "she's so weird" looks. Whatever. I felt better.

Glancing over my shoulder, I saw Libby Giles and Mitch Lowry walking down the hall in my direction—so perfect together, the perfect golden couple. His arm was draped around her shoulders like a scarf. Her hand was up, fingers interlaced with his, as she whispered in his ear, bringing a smile to his face.

Libby and Mitch were seniors to my junior status, both athletes. Libby had lived in my neighborhood, about three blocks over, since I was in fifth grade. But it might as well have been thirty miles, for all we saw of each other.

Now, I try not to make assumptions about people because I hate when they make assumptions about me. Like, I'm tall so I must be a good basketball player. (I am, but that's beside the point. It's the assumption that pisses me off.) And my parents have always told me not to take things at face value, not to "judge the depth of the ocean by the color of its surface."

And I really try not to do that. But for some reason, when it came to Libby Giles, I couldn't. Maybe because she was so completely opposite of me. I don't know. I do know that when I saw her the first day of my freshman year, it was like someone had shined one of those glaring spotlights at us and said, "Look:

Beautiful sophomore girl over here, freshman freak of nature over there." And I guess if you judged by usual standards, it was true.

Libby	Kat
Strawberry blond hair— with a lot of help from Clairol	Oak Express desk—brown locks
A nice, normal five foot five, 118 lbs. (spied on her using the scale in the locker room)	A towering five eleven, 160 lbs. (But I work out and I'm not done growing. Besides, it's mostly muscle)
Hourglass bod	Grandfather clock
C cup	Barely B, but again, I work out. Abra says breasts are mostly fat and if you don't have a lot of fat, you don't always have a lot of breastage. Sometimes you do, though, which is totally not fair. Of course, it doesn't help that the women on both sides of my family are less than well-endowed. "Bigger doesn't mean better," Abra says. "If you want to have kids, what matters is your milk supply. Any size breast can give good milk." Moooo.

Of course, Abra would hate that. "Never compare yourself, Katima," she often said. "You are unique, exactly who you are supposed to be, created for a divine purpose. Comparing is a waste of energy better spent understanding that purpose and living it out."

I had no idea what my divine purpose could possibly be, except maybe to inform the Divine Creator that when it comes to the diversity of the human race, she could have been a little less lopsided when handing out social natural and social misfit genes.

I watched Libby and suddenly wondered what the chart would look like if we judged by unusual standards, instead of the usual ones.

Kat	Libby
Tall, like a tree waving in the breeze	Short to average height, like a bush squished against a house
Able to perform yoga positions in crowded school hallways	Able to apply mascara without a mirror
Invisible to most people, thus possessing quality alone time in which to develop a deeper sense of self	Always surrounded by adoring fans, leaving no room for quality alone time, thus unable to develop any sense of a meaningful self (but has lots of admiring fans, so doesn't notice this lack—so it doesn't really matter, does it???)
Full breast would fit completely in average guy's cupped hand (assessed scientifically, not from personal experience, unfortunately)	Large breasts spill out of average guy's hand, forcing him to scramble for the best possible grip, possibly spoiling the entire experience

Yeah, right. Screw comparison charts. At least I was doing something cool like the triathlon. Libby's athletic prowess didn't extend beyond the volleyball court.

Organizing my books in my arms, I closed my locker. I watched Mitch and Libby, remembering one of Christy's reports.

Buchanan Field Report: ML & LG
- Mitch and Libby—first date—June
- Libby usually dates for 1 mo, but sometimes longer
- Prediction: Summer fling. Libby and Mitch will break up before school starts

It seemed to me that Libby liked to try out different guys, kind of like how you try on different clothes. To see if they fit okay. So far, she hadn't found her size.

But this was one prediction Christy had gotten wrong. Mitch and Libby had gone out all summer and now it was September—over three months.

I looked down the hallway. Libby and Mitch had broken free of the group and were now only a few feet from me. She was wearing tight jeans and a V-neck shirt stretched over her C cups. Her eyeliner was heavy, rimming her eye before curving dramatically up toward her brow.

I wondered if she'd notice me. I wondered why I just wondered that. Why I cared. But I did. Because there was a difference between being anonymous (my choice) and invisible (someone else's choice). Libby Giles made me feel invisible. And not even just your average, everyday, you're-a-little-bit-transparent-but-I-can-still-see-your-outline invisible, but completely obliterated. And the weird thing was, she didn't even do anything to make me feel this way. She just had this power to invisibilize me.

I tried to catch her eye as she got closer, but she only had eyes for Mitch Lowry. They kissed as they passed me. I watched. Hey, if you're into PDA, you must be expecting an audience. Other people turned away, I guess to give them their privacy. *It's our hallway, too,* I wanted to shout.

But I just watched. And wondered what it would be like to kiss a guy in the middle of the hallway for everyone else to see.

4

"So?" Christy grabbed my elbow as I headed for Spanish. "Was it amazing or what?" She was wearing her Monday hat—a white straw fedora with a red satin band. Her blond hair was braided down her back and she was wearing a green lace blouse, black jeans, and low heels.

"Muy elegante," I said, nodding at the hat. Christy loved hats. And not just your ordinary baseball cap. No, she liked ladies' hats of all kinds. What I called old-fashioned and she called vintage. Christy shopped eBay for hats.

"Merci." Christy was taking French. "So why didn't you call me?"

"I'm sorry," I mumbled. "I was—"

"Exhausted, I'm sure," she said. "But how exciting! Your first birth. I mean, wow." She squeezed my arm. "But you must speak to the press. I've got deadlines, you know."

Christy was an all-around Knower of Information. Not like a nosy, gossipy person who always asked questions and listened in on conversations. She was more like a magnet, because she didn't go looking for news—it just seemed to be drawn to her.

"I don't want to be late for class," I said.

"You mean late for Manny." She grinned. I scowled.

I'd been in love with Manny Cruz since seventh-grade Spanish class when he said, *"¿Quiere que decir* 'I love you' *en español?"* We were paired up for the dialogue and he was reading from the textbook, but I didn't care. I was convinced that he was sending me a coded message; he just didn't know it yet.

"I've got editors breathing down my neck for this story," Christy said.

I laughed. "What editors? You write status reports on the love lives of various members of the student body, and besides yourself, you have a readership of one—me. And guess what? I already know this story." I bent over the water fountain and took a swig.

Christy frowned. "But I don't. And I'm supposed to be your best friend."

I straightened up.

"See?" she said, holding out her empty hands, "I'm not even pulling out the notebook. Strictly off the record."

Smiling, I felt tears unexpectedly prick my eyes. Christy was the only one who knew that my mom was a midwife and that I worked with her. Well, her boyfriend, Glen Martin, knew, too, because I would sometimes forget he was there and start talking about it. But he never said anything. Half the time I don't think he was even listening, because talking about women and pregnancy kind of freaked him out.

"I missed it," I said finally. "Things . . . happened. I wasn't there when she was born."

Christy's face fell. "Oh, Kat, I'm sorry," she said, patting my arm. "I knew something was up when you didn't call." She raised her eyebrows. "Is there anything I can do?"

I shook my head. "But thanks." We started down the hall again.

"Okay, then."

I loved this about Christy. She was dying to know more, but she dropped it because she knew I wasn't ready to talk about it.

Pulling a pencil from behind her ear, she reached for her notebook. "If you're in the mood, I have some news that should cheer you up."

She obviously had a new scoop on Manny. I wiped my mouth. Right now, listening to stats on the guy I'd been crushing on since seventh grade and who barely knew I existed seemed depressing and pathetic beyond measure. This was what my love life was reduced to. No actual guy, but information about him, information that did nothing except keep my hopes alive or dash them, depending on whether he was dating anyone or not. It was stupid. Ridiculous. It sucked in the biggest way possible.

And it was all I had.

I sighed heavily. "Tell me."

Christy tapped her pencil against her teeth as she flipped the pages, and I felt a little surge of adrenaline. Getting a Buchanan Field Report (BFR) was a little like getting your report card. The teacher says it's good, but is her definition the same as yours?

"No girlfriend," she said. "Dating here and there. Told Mitch he 'needed a break' from relationships."

I nodded. Even though Mitch was a senior and Manny was a junior, they were really good friends. According to the Buchanan Field Report, they had played Little League together and had stayed friends all these years.

The bell rang.

"Oh, man, I'm late." Christy gave me a quick wave before hurrying away.

When I got to Spanish, Manny was helping a girl pick her notes up off the floor. He was so nice, he didn't realize she had probably dropped them on purpose so he would help her.

I slipped into my assigned seat, directly in front of him. You would think this proximity would have created some kind of connection between us, but alas, we were still stuck in what Abra referred to as Level 1 communication—polite talk only when necessary. Like now.

A single tap on my shoulder.

Manny: "Did we have homework?"

Señora García-Smith: *"Por favor, Manuel, en español."*

Our teacher said his name like she was blowing the tops off dandelions. *Mawn-well*.

Manny: (raised eyebrows at me, as if to repeat his question)

Me: *"Sí."*

Manny: "Did you do it?"

Do I want to do it with you? Sí. *Well, maybe not the whole "it," because Abra gave me the whole truth and nothing but the truth, and I'm deathly afraid of STDs and pregnancy and not feeling good about myself after. Oh, wait. That's not what you were ask-ing, was it?*

Señora García-Smith: *"Manuel."*

Another eyebrow raise.

Me: *"Sí. ¿Y tú?"* And you?

Manny: *"Dios mío."*

Señora García-Smith: *"¡Manuel, por favor!"*

Manny: *"Estaba en español, Señora."*

It was in Spanish. I laughed. So did the rest of the class.

27

Señora García-Smith smiled. *"Sí. Estaba."* She turned to face the class. *"Por favor. Página veinte y dos."*

I opened my book and felt another tap on my shoulder.

"That would be page twenty-two," Manny said.

"Gracias," I whispered.

"De nada."

When he asked to borrow a pen—*una pluma*—I grinned and handed him my favorite Pilot pen. Everything is better in *español.*

5

I worked at Abra's Midwifery Tuesday and Thursday afternoons, when I only had morning classes. On this Tuesday—my first day back after the birth-assist failure—I felt naked, exposed, and incompetent. But I also felt a little bit of relief that I was still there, even if only for a few more weeks. I already regretted quitting. But I couldn't take it back. It would be too humiliating.

When I stepped inside the Midwifery, I was nervous. But as I hung up my jacket and flopped down in one of the chairs, I felt better. I could almost feel the joy of the new mothers, hear their laughter and excitement. It was like they left a part of themselves behind and it lived in the walls, in the very air around me.

The Midwifery wasn't like a traditional doctor's office. The small outer reception area had two comfortable overstuffed chairs and a table between them. The reception desk stood just opposite—the first thing you saw when you walked in, along with a picture of the Fate Goddess on the wall behind it. In the far corner was the toy section, with a LEGO table, lots of LEGOs, and other assorted toys in a box.

I had painted the walls light blue and green, blended together in places to create a warm, comfortable mood without transitioning into comatose boredom. To the right of the desk, closest to the chairs and above the LEGO table, was the Babies on Parade—BOP—wall, completely devoted to photographs of proud parents and the babies Abra had caught. I had painted a huge mural of a parade scene, and the pictures were scattered along the parade route. I'd embellished them with balloons and hats, with some babies riding floats.

The parade scene was already about a fourth full, which was pretty amazing, considering most of the photos were four by six. When you saw them, it made sense that Abra's name meant "mother of many" or "mother of nations" in Hebrew—at least according to babynames.com. She'd picked it herself when she was eighteen. She had been born Carrie Jane Bernard, but said Carrie meant "melody or song" and she couldn't sing worth a baby's first poop. And Jane meant "gracious and merciful," among other equally daunting things and "how could I live up to that, for heaven's sake?"

Names and their meanings were a big thing with Abra. She was just Abra, no last name, which didn't seem to bother my dad. They went ahead and gave us kids—me and my sister, Lucy (Lucinda, which means "beautiful light")—his last name, Flynn, because Abra said it was too hard to go through school without a last name and the computers might go into cardiac arrest.

When I asked her why she didn't want to call us Bernard, she said it was out of a sense of duty for our survival.

"I did not want to see a repeat of St. Bernard dog jokes, Bernardo Retardo, and all of the humiliation I suffered," she told me.

I could see her point and wished she had applied this reasoning when she named me Katima. Teachers always mangled it on the first day of school and were relieved when I said, "Just call me Kat." They could never remember which syllable to emphasize (the first one, like Fátima). No one ever pronounced it right, and even if they did, they looked at me like I had a fisheye in the middle of my forehead. "What kind of name is that?" For the record, it's a combo of Fátima and the Japanese name Kana. It means "powerful daughter." Like I'm going to try to live up to that. And why did it have to be powerful *daughter*? Why not just powerful *woman*, without having to connect back to a parent, which felt like connecting back to Abra—which made me feel two inches tall?

Kat, which is also short for Katherine, suited me better. Katherine meant "pure and virginal." I didn't know about the pure part, but I had the virginal thing down.

Abra refused to call me Kat, and Lucy was always Lucinda. " 'Kat' doesn't do you justice," she said when I asked her once. "It's too harsh and short."

But Dad understood. "She wants to be called Kat. She didn't get to choose her name. At least let her choose her nickname."

"I just can't do it," Abra said. "It feels blasphemous."

Whatever. I was just glad most people called me Kat.

I heard the elevator ding down the hallway. A minute later I glanced up from my American Government homework as Abra pushed through the main door. Her cheeks were flushed, her ponytail tangled over her shoulder from the wind. Abra rode her moped or bike just about everywhere. When she attended a birth, had lots of groceries, or needed to transport someone, she used Dad's hybrid car.

She stopped in front of my desk. "These are for you," she

said, dropping two things next to my textbook. One was a bent, water-stained spiral notebook, the wire unraveling on top. The other was a brand-new journal, a picture of an earth mother on the front.

"What are they?"

"This," Abra said, tapping the wrinkled notebook, "is my doula and midwife bible. And this," she said, pushing the journal toward me, "is going to be your own bible."

"Huh?"

She picked up the old spiral notebook, holding it gently in her hands. "I know it doesn't look like much, but this is my notebook from both my doula and midwifery training. It has everything I learned about the process, as well as some of my own thoughts about what I would do differently." She placed the notebook beside me again. "I'm sure you'll see how I struggled to find my way."

Right, Abra. I'm sure I'll see lots of evidence of your incompetence in there.

I opened the notebook casually, as if I really didn't care what was inside.

The first page was neat, Abra's handwriting large and loopy.

Observation #1: The doula's role is to provide P.I.E.—physical, informational, and emotional support to the mother.

She went on to list several things a doula does, like recognizing the sacredness of the birth and how the doula should be a protector and nurturer of the mother's experience and memories surrounding the birth.

"I'm only here for two or three weeks, remember?" I said. "And only here at the Midwifery. No more births."

"I know." Abra tugged at her ponytail. "I still want you to have them." She pointed to the new journal. "This could be *your* bible, with your own questions and observations, things you'd do differently."

I laughed. Picking up a pen, I opened the journal to the first clean, blank page.

Things I'd do differently
1. NEVER assist at a birth again.

I closed the journal with a definitive smack. "There," I said. "All done."

Abra pursed her lips. Then they relaxed into a smile. "Diane's coming in today."

Diane Altman. One of my favorite new mothers. She was the coolest. She made me feel like my opinion mattered. And I made her laugh. Her baby was due in May.

"Her next appointment's not for another few weeks," I said.

"She's got some ideas for her birth wish list." Abra shrugged, her eyes shifting to the BOP wall. "There was an opening today."

I narrowed my eyes. Was Abra working an angle? She didn't want me assisting at a birth, but she still wanted me here at the Midwifery. She knew that my seeing Diane would make it harder for me to leave.

"I'd like you to work with her on the music," Abra said, avoiding my gaze.

"But I'm not going to be here later," I said. "Don't you think you should do that?"

"We'll leave it up to Diane," she said. "See what she says."

Tucking both notebooks into my backpack, I returned to my homework.

When Diane walked in two hours later, she got right to the point. "You can't leave me," she said. "I'm counting on you to be a part of this."

"I'll do your music," I said. "I can do that from anywhere."

"Who will talk to me before my appointments?" she said, pulling a chair up to my desk. "And more importantly, who will sing classic rock songs with me?"

I smiled.

"Look," said Diane, her face suddenly serious. "I don't know what happened, but whatever it was, you're being entirely too hard on yourself. It was your first birth, for heaven's sake. And you weren't even prepared."

Abra had told her? That really pissed me off.

"No, Abra didn't tell me," Diane said, reading my mind. "Linda did."

Right. They were friends. I calmed down. A little.

"Well, it's not just that." I couldn't tell her that if I agreed to come back, it was like admitting I'd been an idiot in the first place, and I was tired of feeling like an idiot, tired of Abra being right about me and me not knowing myself well enough to know what was right.

"Well, whatever it is, you need to give yourself time. Meanwhile, don't punish yourself and all of us because you made some mistakes."

I stared at her. "Punish *you*?"

Diane shook her head. "You have no idea what an asset you are around here, do you?"

I snorted.

"All the more reason to stay," she said. "So you can see for yourself."

I rubbed my lips together. It was tempting to say "Okay." To believe her. But something held me back. I wasn't ready to give Abra anything. And I didn't like her calling Diane to try to get me to stay. It was sneaky. "I'm sorry you had to come down here for nothing."

"Nothing?" Diane said as she stood up. "Seeing you and Abra is never nothing."

As if on cue, the door to the Gathering Place—Abra's name for the examination room at the Midwifery—opened and Abra peeked her head out. "Everything okay out here?"

"She'll do my music, but she's not staying."

Abra's smile disappeared, and I felt a stir of satisfaction. She hadn't gotten her way. I'd made sure of that.

"That's too bad," Abra said, smile back in place. "Maybe she'll change her mind."

And then they both were gone, leaving me to wallow alone in my victory.

6

I worked out after I finished at the Midwifery. I thought of it as my "pre-workout," sort of a workout before the workout before the triathlon in July. The Rocky Mountain Women's Triathlon was a sprint tri—short distances for swimming, biking, and running. I was getting in shape so when I started the official tri training in June, I wouldn't make a complete fool of myself.

When I got home, Dad was making dinner and Lucy was watching some teen pop star–wannabe movie. She loved those things, watching them over and over, so she knew all the songs and could belt them out, using the TV clicker, a hot dog, or anything else available for her microphone.

She waved her pencil microphone at my "hi," keeping her eyes on the screen. She was nine, and we got along great in spite of our age difference.

I dropped my backpack and leaned against the island in the center of the kitchen.

"Rough day at the office, Kat?"

I scowled at my dad. I didn't know how much detail Abra

had given him about the whole Linda birth thing or my quitting, and I didn't want to know.

"It was fine," I said, pushing myself away from the counter toward the stove.

"Oh, the word every parent wants to strike from their child's vocabulary—'fine.' "

"Parents aren't supposed to ask yes-or-no questions," I said, lifting the lid to see vegetable soup bubbling deliciously.

"True," he said.

"Where is she?"

He raised his eyebrows at me. "*She* is out in the meditation garden."

I walked to the window over the sink. Abra and I had spent two weeks three summers ago hauling in large rocks for the garden. We'd put in a fountain and a variety of flowers and plants. It was her idea, but I loved it, too. There was a bench, a chair, and a small table for candles or drinks, or whatever else you might want to bring.

Abra was sitting in the chair cross-legged, hands on her knees, eyes closed. She was so still, she looked like a statue. I had to squint to see her chest move in and out as she breathed. I resented her peacefulness, the way she could leave the world and its problems and come back refreshed and renewed. I could rarely do that in my yoga practice. I was doing well if I slowed my heart rate and breathing long enough to get through my next class at school.

I'm sure she didn't think my leaving the Midwifery was a big deal. She probably assumed I'd change my mind and she'd be right and all would be well in the universe. Or she wasn't thinking about me at all.

I sighed and turned my back on the window. "I'll set the table."

After dinner, while Lucy and my dad put away the leftovers, Abra and I did the dishes. We didn't talk; she was far away, inside herself.

"Thinking about your other husband?" my dad teased, putting his arms around her waist from behind.

She smiled faintly and squeezed his wrist. "You're all the husband I need."

"Good thing," he said, "because I'm the only one you've got."

Abra laughed, then sighed. "Just a first-time mother."

"Hard to compete with all those pregnant ladies," Dad said, winking at me. He kissed Abra lightly on the neck. She brushed a hand across his cheek, leaning back into him.

"You should go to bed," Dad said.

"I know," Abra said. "I'm sorry."

"Don't be sorry," he said. "Get some rest." He put his arm around her waist. "You can finish up, can't you, Kat?"

"Sure."

Lucy watched them go. I could tell she had something on her mind.

"What is it?" I asked.

She turned to me. "Emily said she's not my friend anymore."

I stopped wiping and looked at her. "Why? I thought you two were best friends."

"We were," she said. "But we were doing a social studies project together. She was supposed to do the poster and I was doing the report. Then she said maybe I could just do both because I was so good, and when I said no she got all mad and went over to Stacy and Pauline."

I sat down next to her. "She has to be responsible for her work, Luce. You shouldn't be doing it for her. I'm proud of you for standing up for yourself."

"But she's not my friend anymore," Lucy said.

"Would a real friend treat you that way?"

"No," Lucy said. "But she might make Stacy and Pauline not like me, and then I won't have any friends."

I sighed. I remembered fourth-grade politics all too well. "You're a great person, Lucy. The smart people will want to be friends with you."

Lucy smiled up at me. "I hope so."

"I know so." I kissed her cheek. "Hey, how about killing me in a game of dominoes," I said. "That ought to cheer you right up."

"Sure," she said, running to get the box.

After Lucy beat me the third time, she went up to get ready for bed. I headed toward Serenity Space, which was a birthing room at the back of our house. Mothers who weren't able to birth in their own homes for one reason or another could come to Serenity Space. Next to Serenity Space was the Womb, a smaller, separate room that Dad and I had built, my little sanctuary with its own entrance. Dad had named it, actually. "Ah," he'd said when we finished. "A Womb of one's own." It had stuck.

I pushed through the Womb's bead curtain, smiling at the click-clack sound it made, announcing my arrival to the various icons and statues set about the room.

After lighting the candles, I sat on a floor pillow, pulling my legs up so my heels touched my butt, my chin resting on my knees. I loved the sponge painting I'd done on the walls. It had taken hours because I wanted just the right combination of

39

green and blue, and the result was perfect, like an ocean on a calm day.

I brushed my fingers across the wall. It was funny how the only time I didn't feel awkward or invisible was when I was doing something physical like running or biking, or when I was drawing or painting. Probably because both were just for me. Dad often encouraged me to take art in school or join a sports team, but I always refused.

"It's mine," I told him. "I don't want anyone else to see it." I also didn't want anyone else telling me how to do it—art or anything else. I got enough of that in the rest of my life.

I glanced over at the far wall, where I'd painted a mural of a mountain scene—a grove of aspens on one side that met a pine forest, which opened up to a deep pool at the bottom of a waterfall. I'd also painted two women, one arching gracefully in a perfect swan dive, forever frozen above the water. The other stood on shore, watching the diver, trying to get up the courage to climb up and take the plunge herself.

Leaning back, I closed my eyes and breathed deeply, letting the familiar smells of sandalwood, sulfur from the matches, and the slightly musty scent of the futon fill my nostrils. Then I settled in to read Abra's doula and midwife bible.

Observation #2: Being in tune with the mother's feelings and needs should be our primary goal . . . getting to a point where we can almost anticipate her needs.

Abra had listed the ways she would get in tune with the mother, including "asking non-intrusive questions and observing her both during prenatal visits and in her home."

That was so Abra, spending so much time thinking about and practicing getting in touch with the women at the Midwifery while Lucy and I got the leftovers, questions about our day that seemed to be asked out of obligation, not because she really wanted to know. And how could she? She'd spent the last eight to ten hours listening to women talk about their hopes and dreams. She didn't have the time or energy to listen to ours.

I glanced down at her notebook.

Observation #3 (question, really): How in tune do I have to be with my own feelings to be able to be in tune with someone else's?

There was nothing written below it. I flipped the page. It went on to another observation. I frowned. Why hadn't she answered her own question? That would have been helpful to know. I closed the notebook and picked up my journal, reading my one and only entry:

1. NEVER assist at a birth again.

Hmm. It needed something else, like Abra's Observations. But what? What was the statement I was making?

A fact. The facts of my life.

I smiled, squeezing in "Fact of Life #" before the *1*. Somehow that made it more important, authoritative. I'd create a notebook with the facts of my life, about life in general. Kat's wisdom, illustrated.

Well, maybe not a lot of wisdom, but the pictures would keep it interesting. And I'd number the facts randomly, just for fun and, I had to admit, to be different from Abra. Also to confuse anyone who might stumble upon this insightful tome generations from now. They'd scratch their heads, trying to decipher the meaning behind #412 after #29, wondering if they were missing all of those hundreds between 29 and 412, then going forward to see that the next one was #13 or #87. They'd think, *Oh, there must be some complicated mathematical pattern here, and if I can figure it out, I'll solve the mysteries of the universe and find the Holy Grail.* But I'm just using them randomly, so I'll get the last laugh.

I stared at my one and only fact. I underlined "NEVER" twice. I circled it. I drew a thumbs-down next to it. I bit the end of my pen, seeing Diane's face, then Abra's after I said I wasn't coming back to the Midwifery.

> *Fact of Life #59: Revenge is not always sweet.*
> *Sometimes it's so sour your lips pucker.*

I drew a sour face before closing the notebook, my eyes drawn to the mural, jumping from the woman diving in to the one on the shore watching, waiting for her turn to do something special.

7

"And then, man, she was all over me, begging for more."

I glanced up from the water fountain at school. Mitch Lowry was standing a few feet away, head cocked, chest puffed out, bragging about his sexual exploits to his buddies like the male stereotype that he was. They'd probably start in with comparisons next.

"What are you looking at?" Mitch's voice startled me.

"I'm not sure," I said, wiping my mouth.

He glanced at his friends, raising his eyebrows. "She's not sure." He flexed his biceps and winked at me. "How about now?"

"Animal, mineral, or vegetable. Hard to say." I had no idea why I said that. Why I wanted to draw attention to my freak self in front of the Popular People.

The guys laughed and Mitch looked at me for a moment before rolling his eyes. "Whatever," he said, turning to his friends. "Let's get out of here."

Fact of Life #3: Guys who are full of themselves will burst like a balloon one day.

I could see the drawing already: a balloon-like head—think Violet in *Charlie and the Chocolate Factory*—with a giant pin just millimeters away from connecting. I'd have to add that to my journal.

I hustled down the hall to the cafeteria to eat with Christy and her extra appendage—I mean boyfriend—Glen. When I got to the table, Christy was there, Glenless.

"So, where's—"

"Bathroom," she said, smiling up at me through black netting. Wednesday was pillbox hat day. Today's pillbox was probably circa the forties or fifties, black satin with netting covering the entire hat before swooping elegantly down across the bridge of Christy's nose like a spiderweb. The back sported a large black velvet bow, her hair swept up underneath.

"Sit," she said, patting the space beside her on the bench. "Let me look at you."

I dropped down next to her, lunch bag clutched in my hand. "Don't even start." I gave her the evil eye, but she'd already whipped out the familiar red bag with the thick white cross on it—the Buchanan Fashion First Aid Kit. Her "real" makeup kit was in her car because it was the size of a small trunk.

Unzipping the bag, she spilled an array of foundation, mascara, eye shadow, eyeliner, and three lipsticks onto the table. She studied my profile. "No foundation really works in this hideous fluorescent lighting. But I may have something that will pass."

"I'm not wearing makeup." I said the same thing every day. She ignored me every day.

"Check this out." She pushed a bottle in front of my face. I

44

squinted at the label: FLANNEL BEIGE. It sounded like something you'd reupholster a couch with, not use on your face.

"No thanks. I'm eating." To prove it, I took a big bite of my perfect blend of broccoli sprouts, avocado, and sliced free-range turkey sandwich.

"Fine," she said, shoving the bottle back into her bag. "No foundation. How about blush?" She hunted through various plastic cases until she came up with a winner. "Caribbean Casual?"

"Are you coloring your face or picking a vacation outfit?" I pushed the case away.

"You're hopeless, Kat." Christy zipped up her makeup case with finality and stuffed it back into her purse.

"I know." I took another bite of my sandwich as Glen plopped down on the other side of Christy. I got up and moved across the table so we weren't all sitting in a row. Glen was cute in a shy, "don't talk to me or my glasses will fog" kind of way. But when he asked Christy to go to a movie with him in eighth grade, we both knew it was because of her breasts—she had them, the boys noticed them, and they wanted to squeeze them like Koosh balls.

But she went anyway, enacting a no-fly zone over her chest to see what would happen. She said he didn't even try to touch them that night, and not for a long time after they started going out. I guess that's why Christy liked him. He was polite and never pushed and seemed very respectful of her. And he liked her hats, which scored big points.

"Hey, Glen," I said.

Glen nodded. He was a man of few words, which often made me forget he was there. He was like her shadow, and I would start talking about my period or cramps or how I needed a new sports bra because even though I wasn't overly endowed

45

in that arena, I still needed something to control the minor bounce 'n' flounce during a run. Well, his face would turn red, he'd "ahem" or cough, and I'd have to apologize for embarrassing him.

It wasn't easy being part of a triangle, especially an obtuse one.

I pulled out an apple, noticing Glen's eyes slide to Christy's chest. He did this every time he was gone and came back. And periodically throughout their time together.

"They're still there," I said.

Glen blushed and looked away. I guess he didn't know I knew about his little breast check. I'm not sure what he was worried about. That they might pop off her chest on their own and take a stroll somewhere? *Christy, where are your breasts? Oh, they're down the hall in chem lab, doing experiments with Bunsen burners and petri dishes.*

Christy slit her eyes at me and I laughed.

"You guys want to go to the Game Zone Friday night?" Manny often hung out there, and I was ready for another sighting. Friday was better because Christy and Glen usually had their cozy date on Saturday, where Glen would play Find-the-Breast-in-the-Dark. I knew this because I made the mistake of saying yes to going to a movie with the two of them once and he hit my shoulder on the way to her breast.

"Sounds good," Christy said, leaning over to give Glen a kiss. "Okay, sweetie?"

Glen picked at the table, which I guess meant "Okay, sweetie" back.

It was settled.

8

Observation #4: Make as many observations as you can about the mother, noting her likes and dislikes so you can match these during labor and delivery.

—from Abra's doula and midwifery notebook

The Game Zone was packed. Mostly with people trying to pretend they weren't checking each other out. And seeing as how I was going on four years of pathetic Manny lust, it was automatic for me to be one of the checkers. My eyes skimmed the room quickly, like a kid tapping heads in a game of Duck, Duck, Goose. Any dark, wavy-haired, six-foot-two males in the vicinity were then scanned for specific Manny Cruz characteristics—three freckles on bridge of nose, turquoise stud in right ear, thick eyelashes surrounding luscious dark eyes. If Manny was within a fifty-yard radius, he was usually in my crosshairs within ten seconds.

I sucked as a birth assistant but would make a decent sniper. Go figure.

"I wish you'd let me put some blush and mascara on you." Christy was standing with me in the lobby, furrowing her brow. "Just a little. You look all washed-out in this light."

I breathed in quickly, barely listening. There he was, just outside one of the billiard rooms, looking incredibly H-O-T hot in a ratty Black Sabbath T-shirt and jeans. His little basketball team posse surrounded him.

"Manny's here." Christy wasn't looking at him, she was looking at my face, which was obviously announcing his presence to anyone who could read it. She was wearing Friday's hat—a black gambler's hat. People often mistook it for a cowboy hat, but Christy was quick to correct them: "Cowboy hats have a much wider brim, and they're taller on top. Gambler's hats have a more circular brim, with flatter tops." Everything I knew about hats I learned from Christy.

I saw Libby and Mitch join Manny's group. Libby said something that made Manny laugh. Mitch laughed, too, and they were all just one big happy family of laughing people.

"He's kind of out of your league, isn't he?" Glen asked. He glanced quickly at Christy.

I frowned. "I can still look."

"You've liked him forever, right?" Glen was clearly encouraged by the fact that I had replied. "Maybe you should think about moving on?"

"Glen." Christy spoke softly, touching his elbow.

"Sorry," Glen muttered. "But maybe she's wasting her time?" Glen had this annoying habit of talking in questions when he wanted to say something he thought one of us would take the wrong way.

"I didn't know you cared," I said.

"He does." Christy squeezed his arm.

"I do?" Glen said.

"Whatever," I said.

Christy stepped between us. "Now that we've established how much we all care," she said, pulling out her Zone card, "let's go have some fun."

"I'll meet you at the NFL game." I knew that's where Glen would want to go first. He was too small to play football in real life, so he played it virtually. And he was pretty darn good. "I need to go to the bathroom."

Christy poked me. "Don't take too long in the *bathroom*." Then she leaned close to me. "Let me know if you see anything worth reporting."

"Will do," I said, giving her a grateful smile. I made my way to the restroom, securing a place just outside the door, where I had a clear view of Manny and company.

Look over here. I sent my telepathic message without thought to what I might do if Manny actually responded. Maybe I wouldn't have to do anything. Maybe he'd see me and his face would register our connection. He'd walk to me in slo mo, then jog, then run into my arms, where he'd weep over the time lost and the joy at finally finding me.

There appeared to be some interference in the signal or maybe I was in a dead spot, because Manny showed no sign of looking in my direction. In fact, he was deep in conversation with two girls who, according to a Buchanan Field Report, were sophomore cheerleaders.

A few feet away from Manny, a waitress stumbled and dumped the drinks she was carrying on the man in front of her. Libby jumped back, wiping her chest. She snapped at the

49

waitress, then turned and headed toward the front door, Mitch close on her heels. Manny grabbed napkins from a nearby table and gave them to the guy who'd gotten doused.

I was so engrossed in watching Manny be wonderful that I didn't notice Libby until she was just a few feet away, muttering. She walked right past me into the bathroom and I caught a whiff of her perfume, musky but light. So that was Essence of Libby. I sniffed my shoulder. Essence of Kat was a combination of nervous sweat and a touch of citrus—the eco-detergent we used. A good smell, but certainly not thick with boy-attracting scents.

I turned my attention to Manny. Some guy was mopping up, and the waitress was talking to Manny as if there wasn't a table somewhere with three people wondering where their drinks were, not knowing that two people and the floor were wearing them.

"Can you believe her?"

Startled, I turned. Libby was standing next to me. She wasn't looking at me—she was looking out toward Manny and the waitress—but it seemed like she was talking to me. I checked around. There was no one else. My invisibility shield must be down.

"This is angora," she said. "It might be ruined."

"It looks fine to me," I said, irritated that my voice sounded high, nervous.

She glanced over at the waitress. "I know it was an accident, but she didn't even say anything to me." Her eyes narrowed. "And flirting with Cruz. God, she's like five years older than him. Gross."

"Gross," I said. Who would have thought I'd be standing near the girls' bathroom at the Game Zone agreeing with Libby Giles about the grossness of a waitress?

"You okay?" Mitch Lowry was between us, his arm around her shoulders. My shield must have reengaged: he almost stepped on my foot.

Libby pushed out her chest. "How does it look? Can you see anything?"

"I can see plenty," Mitch said with a sly smile. I rolled my eyes. Being invisible meant I had to put up with stuff like this. It's a wonder I'm not doing the Flynn Field Report.

Libby smacked him. "A stain," she said. "Can you see any sign of a stain?"

Mitch shook his head. "But I may need to examine things more closely." He reached his hand out, stopping about an inch from her breast. He continued to live up to his Neanderthal image. What did Libby see in this guy? She was smart. Sure, he was hot, but that could only get you so far. There had to be something I was missing.

"Easy there, mister," Libby said. "Let's go rescue Manny from Mrs. Robinson."

"Who?" Mitch asked as Libby grabbed his arm, dragging him across the room.

"Mrs. Robinson," I whispered as they walked away. *The Graduate*." I was impressed that Libby Giles knew about the classic 1967 movie. How the main character is seduced by an older woman. In any case, Libby was a year older than Manny and had seduced him last spring, so she knew about these things. I wondered if Libby's seduction made her Mrs. Robinson, Jr.

Manny had dated Libby for three weeks, give or take a few days and some hours, depending on which version of the breakup you believed. Personally, I went with the Buchanan Field Report, which said three weeks, five days, and ten hours, with Manny breaking up with Libby and Libby saying she was "going to dump his ass anyway." I think she was just trying to save face. But now they were friends. Good friends.

According to Christy, early spring was when the older girls started trolling the younger classes looking for new blood, either to piss off the boys who had dissed them for younger girls, or just because they were bored. Libby had asked Manny out on Tuesday, April 10. I knew this because I happened to be around the corner from the gym locker rooms, invisible (surprise) as I lowered myself into the Downward-Facing Dog yoga pose to stretch my back and legs and get the blood flowing to my brain, since I had a test next period.

I relaxed my head, focusing on my breathing and posture.

"Hey, Manny."

Libby's words penetrated my dogness.

"Lib."

Now, I was supposed to be deep inside myself, centered, in touch with my own Inner Voice. But Manny's voice was stronger, louder, and a bit more sexy than the Voice Within. So I shifted my attention, though I stayed in my yoga position, pushing into the heels of my hands to press my hips back and up, feeling the pull in my calves.

"I think we should go out," Libby said. Just like that. *I think we should go out.* What if I said that to a boy? *Hey, Johnny, I think we should go out.* He'd probably say, *Yeah? Well, I think you should stick your head in the toilet and flush.*

"Really," Manny said in this cool, "I'm not sure I care what you think" voice. But I had a feeling she'd wear him down. She was gorgeous, and known for her abundant extracurricular activities with boys. Manny, for all his coolness, probably wouldn't be able to pass that up.

I lowered myself into Table pose, then dropped into Child Pose, rounding my spine and rocking slightly. Then I rose slowly to my feet.

"Are you autistic or something?" A girl was standing a few feet away, staring at me.

"I'm doing yoga."

She wrinkled her nose and scurried away.

I leaned forward, venturing a peek around the wall. Libby stood close to Manny, her right breast touching his arm. Manny's eyes dropped. I pulled back against the wall, adjusting my bra over my barely-B's.

"I guess we could go out," he said, sounding a bit strangled. "Once."

"Just once?" Libby teased.

So they went out for a few weeks, went to the Junior-Senior Prom, and then boom—they broke up. No one really knew why. My own theory was that there was a little seed inside him, the seed of realization, telling him he was really looking for tall, toned, and kinky-haired instead of petite, round (in all the right places), and gorgeous.

Unfortunately, that seed was taking a long time to sprout.

"Okay, enough Manny-gazing." Christy tugged at my sleeve.

"Huh?" I blinked, my vision returning to the Game Zone.

"Your eyeballs are going to be imprinted permanently with images of Manny Cruz," Christy said. "Let's go play."

"That wouldn't be all bad, you know," I said, following her through the throngs. "I could live with seeing only him all day, every day."

"And not ever see me in my hats? I'm crushed."

I smiled. "I'll leave a little part of my left eye for you."

She laughed. "Gee, thanks."

After we ran out of cash, Christy and I stood in the lobby waiting for Glen, who had had one too many Cokes during the course of me beating him soundly in a variety of video games.

"So tell me about this triathlon," Christy said. "Is it some Ironman gig? Are you going to run over mountains and ford streams?"

"Ford streams?" I laughed. "My little triathlon is nothing like the Ironman." I thought about some of the women who'd competed and won Ironman competitions. They were my idols. "That's like a two-and-a-half-mile swim—in an ocean—a hundred-and-twelve-mile bike ride, and a full marathon—about twenty-six-point-two miles." I shook my head. "Mine's a lot shorter—about a half-mile swim in the reservoir, a twelve-and-a-half-mile bike ride, and a three-mile run." It sounded so wimpy compared to the Ironman distances, but jeez, I wasn't a pro. I had to start small.

"So more like Teflon or Aluminum Man," Christy joked.

"That's Teflon Woman to you."

Christy chuckled, then suddenly shoved me, putting a finger to her lips. I looked over my shoulder. Manny would have to pass me to get to either the bathroom or the front door. Oh, man. Oh, Manny.

As Manny started walking toward us, my heart just about flipped out of my chest.

Christy nudged me and smiled, which meant *Smile at him. Nod hello,* which of course I wouldn't do because I'd rather eat a live cockroach than smile at Manny Cruz and have him pretend he didn't see me, that I didn't exist. Or worse, scowl at me with a look that said, *What the hell are you doing smiling at me?*

I would be content just to have him walk nearby so I could absorb his aura.

Christy elbowed me. This meant *He's almost within smiling range.* I ignored her and checked my cell phone again. Christy tugged at my purse. I winced as the strap dug into my shoulder. My fingers tingled, which is probably why, when Christy pinched me—which meant *He's in range, do it now*—

I did. Smile, that is. Wide. Stupidly.

And Manny Cruz, Mr. Unattainable, the man who made my heart do backflips inside my chest . . .

. . . smiled back.

9

I knew Melanie Robertson was trouble the second she walked through the door of Abra's Midwifery last March. She had worn spiked red high heels, bright lipstick, and a 'do that really didn't. Before she even introduced herself, she announced, "I will birth standing up, wearing these shoes, and will bring my child into the world to the soothing sounds of the Beatles."

Pregnant women come in all shapes and sizes, but the ones who come to see a midwife and want a home birth are usually a little more in touch with their Earth Mother side and subscribe to *Mothering* magazine rather than *Cosmo*. Not Melanie Robertson. She brought her own copy of *Cosmo* (since Abra didn't carry it in the Midwifery) and apparently was having a home birth because one of her friends dared her to.

"That's probably not the best reason to give birth naturally," Abra had told Melanie. "Part of the process is being in tune with your body, being able to give in to the pain so it will help you, not hinder you."

But Melanie kept saying she wanted to do it and she knew

she could, blah, blah, blah. Abra seemed oblivious to Melanie's anti-midwiferyness, so I pulled her aside.

"Do you see what's going on here?" I whispered. "She acts like childbirth is a contest so she can prove something to her friends."

"I know it seems that way," Abra admitted. "But I sense she really wants to do this. Perhaps in the process she'll discover other reasons to give birth naturally at home."

"And if she doesn't?" I had visions of Abra being sued for "pain and suffering" because she hadn't warned Melanie sufficiently.

"It will be fine," Abra said, patting my arm like I was a child who'd dropped her sucker in the dirt.

"She also thinks I'm too young and stupid to be working with a midwife," I said, hoping this slam on her own daughter might change Abra's mind.

"Did she actually call you stupid?"

"Well, no. I believe her exact words were 'I hope you're not involved in any of the important aspects of my pregnancy.'"

"She's just nervous," Abra had said. "She'll warm up to you."

I knew we'd never get to thaw.

Melanie was scowling when she came through the door on Thursday afternoon. Tuesday was supposed to have been my last day, but Diane kept thinking of things to keep me around, so here I was. When I'd told Christy I'd quit, she had smacked my arm.

"What were you thinking? You love that job!"

"I know, but . . ." I shrugged. "Abra just . . ." I wasn't even sure how to explain it.

Christy had started to say something, then stopped. Finally she said, "Well, I hope you know what you're doing."

"Don't I always?" I asked. And we both laughed.

"I've lost my figure," Melanie said, bringing me back to the Midwifery. She was now seven months pregnant, her round belly tight under her maternity shirt.

I flicked my eyes at her—*Hello? You're pregnant*—then went back to reviewing appointments on the computer. She sat down in the chair opposite my desk. "I heard what happened with you and that other mother."

I cringed. Why did bad news always have a way of leaking out?

Melanie wasn't looking at me, so I pretended I hadn't heard. She shook her head as she pulled the latest issue of *Cosmo* out of her bag. "Poor thing. What a memory to carry with you."

"It was an accident," I said before I could stop myself. "All of it."

"Kids should not be allowed at a birth," Melanie said, as if I hadn't spoken.

"I'm sixteen," I said, narrowing my eyes. "And she sent me a thank-you card." I pulled it out of the desk drawer and held it up. "She said I made it very memorable. In a good way."

Melanie did not look up from her magazine. "Obviously suffering from some post-birth delirium." She tsk-tsked as she flipped the page.

I'll show you some post-birth delirium. I felt like leaping over the desk and pouncing on her, sinking my three thousand dollars' worth of orthodontia into her shoulder. Instead, I gritted my teeth and breathed in deeply through my nose. I would not let her get to me. I was not attached to this place anymore. When my jaw relaxed, I pulled my journal out of my backpack, flipping to a clean page.

Fact of Life #13: People really love it when other people screw up.

I drew a giant screw digging into someone's back, with another person screwing it in tight, laughing like crazy.

People couldn't care less if you do something really great. It's the mistakes they love. Abra says it's only insecure people who feel that way. It makes them feel better about themselves. Superior. I guess that means 99% of the population is insecure.

And why would Melanie need to feel superior to me?

Melanie stood and walked over to the bookcase. She picked up the wooden rake in the miniature Zen garden we kept on top, brushed it once across the sand, then dropped it.

"I don't get that at all," she muttered, returning to her seat.

I peeked at her through my hair. Melanie didn't seem to be warming to the idea of a home birth. And not because she wasn't into the Zen garden. She just didn't seem relaxed and interested overall, or committed to the idea, which didn't make things very pleasant. And I couldn't understand why Abra didn't see it.

"Melanie!" Abra opened the door to the Gathering Place, smiling widely.

Melanie smiled back, though it looked more like a grimace.

She dropped the *Cosmo* into her bag and pushed herself up using the arms of the chair. "I've lost my figure."

Abra laughed. "You have the beautiful figure of a pregnant woman. Most pregnant women would envy the way your maternity clothes flatter you completely."

"You're just saying that," Melanie said, but she smiled for real this time.

"No, she's not," I said. Because she wasn't. Abra actually believed what she said. That's how she saw Melanie. Pregnant and beautiful, kind and wonderful, ready to embrace natural childbirth for all the right reasons, any day now.

Abra never saw people as they really were.

Observation #5: No two women are alike. Take each one as a unique individual, using her rhythms as your guide.

—from Abra's doula and
midwifery notebook

I snorted as I closed the notebook, wondering why Abra wasn't applying these gems to her own daughters. I didn't think she saw me as an individual at all; she was too busy making sure I was following her instructions.

After the last appointment of the day, I helped Abra straighten up the Gathering Place, running the carpet sweeper while she organized her paperwork.

"Did I see you writing in your journal earlier?" she asked.

I shrugged. Didn't want her to think I was into it or anything. I folded the blanket on the exam table, then crossed the room to check the plants on the table next to the sofa.

"Great," she said. "Keep it up. It will really help clarify things for you." She put her hands on her hips and looked around. "Well, I think we're all set here." She crossed to the exam table and unfolded the blanket I'd just folded. "Boom, boom, boom," she said, refolding it in three easy strokes. "Now it will roll out easily for the next person."

Another lesson. *Thanks, Professor.* I couldn't tell if she knew I had just folded it or not. My way had been perfectly fine.

"By the way, your dad and I are meeting some friends for dinner tonight," Abra said. "Can you hang out with Lucinda?"

My social life for this evening consisted of homework, e-mail, and a shower. Not exactly the party night of the century.

"Sure." I turned to the bookcase and slid an herbal remedy book into its spot.

"Great," Abra said. She patted me on the shoulder. "It's too bad you're quitting, because I really think you could do so much more."

But not assist. It was clear that particular door was closed to me forever. And even if I wanted to do it, I could never do it with Abra, because she didn't believe in me. I moved a book on breast-feeding to the After Baby section in the bookcase.

"I think you'd like to stay at the Midwifery but you're feeling like you need to stick with what you said earlier."

I think you need to not tell me how I feel. Especially when you're right. Er.

She sighed. "Well, I've put the word out. I'm starting to accept resumes."

I nodded. "I'll file them for you—by experience." I stepped out of the Gathering Place and closed the door.

10

Lucy and I played dominoes at the kitchen table that night. We were on our fifth game. I'd won one game, she'd won three.

"Read it and weep," she said, placing her last tile on one of the trains.

"Where in the world did you hear that expression?" I asked.

Lucy shrugged. "TV."

"Dang," I said, frowning at my remaining tiles. "I've got a lot of points left." I tallied the score sheet as Lucy gathered up the tiles for another game.

"It's bedtime for Domino Dominators," I said.

"One more game?" she said. "Please?"

I glanced at the clock. "Abra will kill me if I let you stay up. You still have to take a shower and read. Besides, I have to recover from my embarrassing loss."

Lucy smiled. "Okay. Rematch tomorrow?"

"Maybe," I said. "If my ego isn't too bruised."

Lucy stacked the tiles in the metal box. "Why do you call Mom Abra?"

I paused at the unexpected question. "That's her name."

"But she's your mom." She placed the lid on the box, pushing it down tightly.

I furrowed my brow. "I don't know. I always have."

"You call Dad Dad."

I shrugged. "He's Dad and she's Abra." I'd never really thought about it before. Dad called her Abra so I called her Abra, and no one had ever corrected me. *Mom. Mom.* When I pictured Abra in my head and called her Mom, it didn't work.

After I'd dried Lucy's hair, we snuggled into her bed and alternated reading chapters of her book. She ran through the words easily, adding her own inflections, like Dad did when he read to her.

"You're very good," I said. "I remember back when you were in kindergarten, sounding out the words. Do you remember saying you'd never be able to read 'big kid' books?"

She shook her head, smiling.

I picked up her clothes from the floor and folded them on the end of the bed. As I folded the white cami she wore under her shirts, I paused. Wow. Pretty soon she'd need a bra.

"Has Abra had The Talk with you yet?"

"You mean about periods and stuff?" Lucy said. "The facts of life?"

The facts of life. Did they still call it that? I smiled, thinking of my journal.

Lucy shook her head. "We have a class in school next year."

"But Abra will want you to hear it from her first," I said, sitting back down on her bed.

Lucy bit her lip. "I want to hear it from you."

"Me?" I said. "Why?"

She shifted her eyes, picking at her comforter. "I don't know," she said. "I just do." She glanced at me. "Do you think Mom would be mad if you told me?"

"Not mad," I said. "But disappointed. She likes to do that kind of stuff."

"I know," Lucy said. "That's why I want you. You'll talk to me like I'm a person." She glanced at me, then away. "Do you know what I mean?"

"Yeah," I said. "I do."

Fact of Life #8: Sometimes being a big sister means being more than a sister.

I drew a happy face with Lucy's curls on top.

I wish Abra was more involved in Lucy's life. She helps her with her homework and asks about school and shares stuff about when she was younger, but I can see Lucy doing the same thing I do—not bringing up certain things to talk about because it will become a lecture or a lesson, not a conversation. Sometimes we just want someone to hear us, to tell us what we're feeling is okay, that we're okay. Why can Abra do that for her women but not for us?

Lucy looks at me like I matter. Like maybe I make a difference in her life. I know she makes a difference in mine.

I took out a fresh sheet of art paper and sketched Lucy in a dance pose, her mouth open in song, a microphone close to her lips. Her eyes were shut, her other arm outstretched. I wrote *Lucy ROX!* beneath it and set the picture next to her clock so it would be the first thing she saw when she woke up.

When Abra got home that night, she knocked softly on my bedroom door. I turned down my iPod. "Come in," I said.

She took two steps in and stopped, as if she were afraid a trapdoor might open up and drop her into a dungeon. "Everything go okay?"

"Just fine." I wondered if I should tell her about Lucy and The Talk but decided they would work it out. And if Lucy really wanted me to tell her, she'd ask again.

"Good," Abra said. She glanced around the room, nodding her head. "So how are things going with you? School, relationships, things like that."

I furrowed my brow. Abra hadn't asked about my personal life in months. What was she up to? Maybe she was on some sort of calendar every six to nine months, check in with oldest daughter on all those teen things like boys, zits, and if she was still using eco-friendly tampons.

"Fine." Like I would tell her if they weren't.

"And no significant other in your life?"

Significant other. Abra would never assume "boyfriend" like a lot of parents, even though she knew I was straight.

"What if we assumed one over the other and you got the wrong message?" she had asked once. "You might suppress it because you were afraid it might send your dad and me off the deep end."

Of course, this meant questions were kept general and

vague. "So do you like anyone?" she would ask. If either of my parents made an observation about people my age, it was always balanced. "He's cute, isn't he? Oh, but look at her. She's got a nice butt"; "Do you like long hair or short hair? That girl has long, and so does that boy."

Hearing Abra comment on the shape of a girl's butt in the interest of PC parenting got to be a little much at times. But there wasn't a lot I could do. Finally I told them that I was pretty sure I liked boys.

"Does this mean we can stop the whole he/she, whosit whatsit thing?" my dad said.

Indeed they could. My journey through Crushland began with David Bentley in fifth grade (who, ironically, turned out to be gay) and continued with a succession of cute and awkward boys right up to the present infatuation, Manny Cruz, aka Mr. Unattainable.

My Wish-He-Was-My-Significant-Other, who had smiled at me at the Game Zone. And had asked to borrow a pen in Spanish. It occurred to me now that he'd never given the pen back.

I looked at Abra standing near my door. A part of me wanted to tell her about Manny. How I was still crazy about him, how he hardly looked at me except to ask about Spanish homework. How I was still insane over him, and had she ever felt like that? Maybe she'd look at me like she did some of the women she worked with, grasping both of my hands in hers, looking in my eyes, and saying exactly the right thing to make me know it would be all right.

But we didn't have conversations like that. And if I told her, she'd probably go into some big lecture on male-female attraction and how it would fade eventually and that it wasn't love, which was "far more complex and messy than infatuation," as she'd said to me once.

"Boyfriend," I said. "That's the word I believe you want. And no, I don't have one. Significant or otherwise."

"These things come in time. And you certainly don't need a man to complete you."

Maybe not, but I'd like to see if he could add a little something.

She smiled. "At least you don't have a crush on that boy you liked in middle school anymore. Marcus? Matty?"

"Manny," I said automatically, immediately regretting it.

"Right." She brushed a hair off her cheek. "Some girls pine after the same guy for years. It's sad. And such a waste." She stepped back into the hall. "But you're not like that."

Why? Because you're not?

"I didn't raise my girls to be piners."

Yes, you did. Well, at least one of them.

11

On Friday morning I got to school just as the first bell went off. The halls were crowded. I watched for a break in the action, resisting the urge to put my hands up and roll them back in a circle as if I was trying to jump into double Dutch jump ropes.

There was no break. I just had to go for it. Shutting my eyes, I took a deep, cleansing breath, ducked my head, stepped into the stream—

—and felt something soft give way beneath my shoe.

"Ow! God."

I opened my eyes, finding myself face to face with Libby Giles. Actually, it was more like chin to hair follicles, since I was six inches taller than her.

"You stepped on my foot." She frowned up at me. There wasn't even a flicker of recognition after our angora sweater–gross waitress bonding convo at the Game Zone.

"I'm sorry," I said. "Are you okay?"

"I think so," she said, wincing as she stretched her foot. "Why are you walking around with your eyes closed?"

"I'm really sorry," I said again.

She leaned over and squeezed the top of her sneaker, no doubt checking for broken bones or maybe a nick in a perfectly manicured toenail. I glanced down at her head and saw something interesting. I wondered if this would be a good time to share it. Probably not, but something came over me and I did it anyway.

"Um, Libby?"

She glanced up, looking puzzled. "Do I know you?"

"Well, no," I said. "Not really." I didn't remind her about the Game Zone. It sounded too groupie-like—*You probably don't remember, but I met you backstage at Red Rocks in '06*. I licked my lips. "But I think you should know something."

She was still squishing her shoe, checking her foot. I wasn't sure she'd heard me, but I decided to keep going. I leaned down so no one else could hear.

"Your roots are showing," I whispered. "It's about time to, you know." That was one bonus to being tall. From my vantage point, I could provide a lot of important personal hygiene tips for anyone who needed them. Dandruff, bad parts, and in Libby's case, the need for a touch-up with her hair-coloring expert of choice.

She furrowed her brow as she straightened up. "Whatever. I'm late for class."

"Just trying to help," I called after her. It was kind of like when your fly was open or you had something between your teeth. You wanted people to tell you, right? Sure, it was embarrassing at that moment, but it saved a lot of embarrassment going forward.

Fact of Life #91: Trying to help popular people only leads to ingratitude.

I glanced down the hall, where I could see Libby whispering to one of her friends. "I was just trying to help," I muttered. But I was already feeling stupid. Why had I said that? Was I insane? Did I think commenting on her hair-coloring needs was going to make her like me any better? And why did I want her to like me, anyway?

"What are you looking at?"

Mitch stood a few feet away, holding a book against his leg.

"Your girlfriend," I said. "Her roots are showing."

Mitch snorted. "I hope you didn't tell her that. She's really sensitive about her hair."

"Now you tell me." I opened my locker.

"Whatever," he said. Then he was gone.

The following Thursday afternoon was quiet at the Midwifery. I had finished my homework, dusted, reorganized the magazine rack, and cleaned the toys in the toy box. Now I was plotting out my pretraining schedule. I knew the hardest transition in the tri would be from the bike to the run, because the bike is practically all quads and the run uses the hamstrings more. I'd talked to women who said their legs felt like lead when they got off their bikes and they could hardly move their feet. That was not going to happen to me.

"Any mail?" Abra asked as she stepped into the reception area.

"A few more resumes." I held out several sheets of paper. "Or have you found my replacement already?"

Abra took the resumes from me without looking at them. "Have you changed your mind about staying?"

"You didn't answer my question."

Abra stared at me. "What if I said yes? What if your

replacement is starting next week and you need to stay a little longer to train him?"

"Him?" The fact that she had replaced me barely registered. I smacked the desk with my hand and stood up. "You're replacing me with a *guy*? When did this happen? Why didn't you tell me? How exactly is this going to work?"

"That's a lot of questions, Katima."

"I need some answers." I glanced around. Some strange guy was going to be dusting the Babies on Parade wall? What if he forgot? You can't have dust on a newborn's sweet little face. And would he remember to keep the books in the Gathering Place in order, first by topic and then alphabetically by author? I knew no men who were that detail-oriented. And there was no way the women would want a man in there with them during a prenatal visit, even if he could regurgitate classic rock lyrics.

I squeezed the back of the office chair I'd picked out myself. Abra was going to let some strange dude with possible jock itch plant his butt in my chair, scratching his unmentionables when no one was looking? (I had no problem using correct terminology for female genitalia, but it was a whole different story for the guys' equipment, which drove Abra crazy.)

"You're insane," I said. "You can't have a man in here. Look, I'm all for equal opportunity, but you've created this amazing space for women, by women. You can't bring testosterone in here. It will ruin everything."

Abra laughed. It was a strange sound. Abra did a lot of smiling, but not much laughing. "What about the husbands?"

"They're different."

She shook her head. "I said—" She couldn't finish. She was still laughing.

"Yeah?"

"I said—" She sniffled. Wiped her eyes. "I said, 'What if?' "

"What if."

She nodded, taking a deep breath. "I said, *what if* I said yes? *What if* he started next week?" She smiled. "I didn't say I'd hired him."

"Unbelievable." I flopped down in my chair, exhausted.

"You're the one who jumped to conclusions." She hung up her jacket, grinning. "That was nice, what you said about what I've created here. Now, can't you just admit you want to stay and do it?"

"I admit nothing," I said, crossing my arms.

The door opened, and Diane was standing in the doorway. "Oh. I'm not interrupting, am I?"

"No," Abra and I said in unison.

"We were just discussing Kat staying on," Abra said. I stared at her.

Diane's eyes lit up. "Oh, Kat, are you? That's fantastic."

While she hung up her coat, I glared at Abra behind Diane's back. "Just through your pregnancy," I said through clenched teeth.

"Great," Diane said, turning around. "I'm glad that's settled." She looked from Abra to me and must have seen something in our faces, because she turned abruptly and headed for the Gathering Place. "Meet you inside."

"How could you?" I hissed after the door closed.

"What?" Abra said. "You want to stay. You just needed a little nudge."

"Quit telling me what I want." I turned away from her to stare at the computer screen.

"Oh, Katima." She reached toward me, but I brushed her

hand away. "I don't mean to. It just seems like you—well, what do I know?" She sighed and squeezed her hands together.

Nothing. You know nothing. And don't put on that "poor me, my daughter never talks to me" face.

"Well, I'm glad you're staying," she said, stepping toward the Gathering Place door.

"Only until Diane has her baby."

"Only until Diane has her baby," she repeated. "I know." But I could tell she didn't, that she thought I'd be here forever or as long as she wanted me to be here, whichever came last.

12

"My cousin Eric is coming from Pennsylvania," Christy said. It was the first Tuesday of October and I'd just gotten off work. "He's shadowing Dad at the radio station on Saturday to see if he'd like to go into broadcasting." Tuesday was French beret day, and Christy was wearing a black one tilted slightly to one side. We stood in line at our usual Starbucks reading the menu, which was kind of stupid because we each got the same thing every time. Christy ordered Sumatra—"Intense, earthy, and aromatic." That was my coffee of choice until I decided that switching coffees might help in the Manny arena, so I now drank decaf Shade Grown Mexico—"Light-to-medium-bodied with a refreshing finish"—in honor of my of-Mexican-descent hunk. Glen always ordered the House Blend—yawn—but he liked it, and I never argue with that.

We sat down at our usual table, with the two of them snuggled together on one side, almost like a single person, and me on the other side, legs stretched out.

I took a sip of my coffee. "And you're telling me about your cousin because . . . ?" But I knew why. I was sixteen, a junior in high school, and had been on exactly four dates, three of them set up by Christy—who, though she supported my Manny fantasy, also tried to get me to move into reality occasionally.

I didn't wait for her to answer. "Manny talked to me in Spanish today," I said. He'd just asked about a test, but still. I'd had the smile incident at the Game Zone, the pen request, and a previous homework question. Who needed a cousin from Pennsylvania? At this rate, Manny and I would be married by Christmas.

"Great," she said. "I thought the four of us could go out Friday night. He's a senior."

"Is that supposed to impress me?" I asked, stirring more sugar into my coffee.

"No," Christy said. "I'm just trying to paint a picture."

"Do you *have* a picture?" I took another sip.

Christy shook her head. "But he's related to me," she said. "He's got to be hot." She laughed and Glen smiled, nuzzling her neck.

"Right," I said, but I felt a ripple of excitement. Even though my heart belonged to Manny, I could still look around. Maybe the Cousin would be the one to wipe all memory of Manny Cruz from my cells. Maybe there was life beyond Manny Cruz. "Okay," I said. "I'll go."

Observation #6: Be open to new possibilities as you tune in to the mothers. Gather as much information as you can and avoid making assumptions.

—from Abra's doula and midwifery notebook

On Friday afternoon, I drove over to Christy's to check out the Cousin when he arrived from the airport with Christy's parents. They arrived about half an hour later, while Christy and I were in her room.

"Christy, Eric is here!" Her mom's voice was singsong, indicating to me that Eric might have some horrible disfigurement she was trying to cover up. We stepped out into the hall. At the top of the stairs, I paused and took a deep, cleansing breath. I put my hands in prayer position, closed my eyes, and took a few more breaths.

"What are you doing?" Christy whispered.

"Trying to get centered," I said. "I'll be less likely to react from my ego, think it's all about me, if I can speak and act from my center." This centering business was tough. I could get myself centered, but when someone started talking, I almost always went forward, backward, or sideways, leaving my center in the dust.

When Christy's parents introduced me to Eric, I gave him a polite smile and a "hi." He gave me a look of disbelief and said, "You're, like, a freaking Amazon."

Be still, my beating heart.

He was barely five foot five, maybe five foot six if you counted the tallest point in his spiked hair. I wanted to say he was a freaking shrimp, but I bit my tongue. What would a centered person do?

"Yes," I said. "I'm tall. Thank you for noticing."

The Buchanans beamed. The Cousin appeared not to have heard. I looked at Christy. She looked at me.

"We'll let you get settled in," Christy said. "We'll leave in about an hour." We turned and ran upstairs to her room.

"He used to be so cute," Christy said as she closed the door behind us.

"Are you saying that you, of the Buchanan Field Report, didn't know what he looked like?"

"I tried," Christy said. "Honest. He wasn't on MySpace or Facebook or anywhere, and our families aren't superclose. He's like my third cousin or something."

"So the last time you saw him was . . ."

"I think he was ten," Christy said miserably.

"Ten? Ten years old? That totally doesn't count!" I shook my head as I paced in front of her. "That's before puberty, Christy. Before hair sprouts and boys get gangly and stupid and smelly."

"I'm sorry, Kat," Christy said, wringing her hands. "But you saw how excited my parents are about it. It would be fun to double-date."

"It's never been fun to double-date," I said. "You always set me up, and the night turns into a complete disaster."

"I wouldn't call the Nate date a complete disaster."

"Christy, he was passed out in the backseat the entire night."

"What better way to avoid inane conversation?"

"How about no conversation," I said, "while Glen was trying to feel you up in the front seat and nearly drove us off the road."

"All right, all right. The Nate night was a disaster." Christy slipped her legs under her and sat cross-legged on her bed, her head bent. Then she looked up. "But it isn't all about looks, is it? Especially for centered people."

That was *so* unfair.

Seconds ticked by.

"Oh, for God's sake," I said finally. "Fine. Just wipe the pout off, okay?"

13

An hour later, the four of us stopped at Chili's to grab a bite to eat before heading to a party Christy knew about.

> Buchanan Field Report: J. Noonan Party
> - Status: Senior, athlete, Key Club (popular, but not Libby level)
> - Booze: Keg, no mixed drinks
> - Tunes: Stereo throughout house
> - Drug availability: unknown

I'm not particularly fond of high school parties because I rarely drink, due to my strict workout regimen. If you've ever experienced a party as a completely sober person, it can make you wish you were part of a different subclass of mammal. The flirting, the tossing off of clothes, the swearing and slurring of words, the bad breath, the confessions, the upchucking. It was like being in a horror movie without a director there to yell "Cut!" But parties were a good way to find out which girls were currently on Manny's radar and adjust my competition chart accordingly. So sometimes I went.

After we were settled at a table, I glanced around for our server. And that's when I almost peed my pants.

"Oh my God," I stage-whispered across the table at Christy. "It's Manny. Why didn't you tell me he worked here?"

"I didn't know," she whispered back, the brim of her gambler's hat low over her eyes. "Last I heard, he only had the computer store job."

A Buchanan Field Report breakdown? Impossible. "Don't look," I said. "I don't want him to see us." Especially me with Eric. "Let's go somewhere else."

Christy and Glen reached for their jackets, but it was too late.

"Name's Manny. I'll be your culinary tour guide tonight." He looked at me, furrowing his brow, and I could tell his mind was click-clacking away behind those beautiful brown eyes: *I know this girl. I stole a pen from her. Is she here with dorkface?*

My cheeks burned.

Manny smiled. *"Hola. ¿Como estás?"*

"Así así," I said.

Manny glanced at Eric, then back at me. I rolled my eyes to indicate *Set up, not my choice.* He smirked. Yes. Message transmitted successfully.

"Katima." He said my name like Señora García-Smith did, with this perfect accent and the emphasis in just the right place. Normally I didn't like people calling me by my full name, but when Manny said it, well, he could keep saying it all night long and I wouldn't mind.

I nodded. "Or Kat."

"What can I get you to drink, Kat?" Manny asked.

"Aren't you too young to be working the tables?"

"I usually bus tables," he said. "But my uncle's the manager and he's in a pinch. He saw you were all 'young people,' as he says, so he figured it was okay."

"Not all of us are 'young people,' " Eric said, puffing out his measly chest.

Manny raised an eyebrow.

"I was hoping to get a recommendation for a good beer."

Christy and I exchanged pained looks. It was bad enough that I had to be with him, but now he was going to make a fool of himself in front of the Cruzable.

I took a deep, cleansing breath, closing my eyes. If I was Abra, I would probably smile and try to help Eric out of his dilemma, try to smooth things over to lessen his embarrassment.

But I wasn't Abra. So I decided to let this thing run its course.

"I'll have to get someone of age to bring it over," Manny said. "Can I see some ID?"

I hid a smile. And Glen wondered why I loved Manny and would wait forever? He was totally onto Eric. It was beautiful.

Eric made a production of patting all his pockets. "I must have left my wallet back at the house. But I'm a junior at Penn State." He pulled out what looked like a student ID card and handed it to Manny.

"This isn't you," Manny said.

"Yes, it is."

"This guy weighs over two hundred pounds and has black hair." He looked Eric up and down. "You might tip the scale at what? One fifty? And your hair is blond." Manny was probably a cool one eighty or something. Yum.

"Puh-*leeze*," said Eric, but I could tell he was getting uncomfortable. Probably because he was closer to one forty-five. Eric rubbed a hand over his head. "It's a dye job."

"Besides," said Manny, ignoring the comment and handing back the ID, "this doesn't have a DOB on it. You could be a child prodigy for all I know, going to college at twelve."

Eric looked confused.

"Date of birth," I said. Working at a midwifery came in handy sometimes.

Eric took the ID back. "I'll have a Coke," he said miserably.

"Strawberry lemonade for me," I said.

After Christy and Glen ordered and Manny left, Eric shook his head. "It works back east. These guys are just lame out here."

"He's not lame," I said. "He's just doing his job."

"Well, there'd better be some brew at this party later or I'm busting out on my own."

Bust away, I wanted to say. *Do us all a favor.* I glanced at Christy. I could tell she felt bad. I sighed. One more chance for her. I was about to ask Eric a question when a bunch of people walked by our table on their way out. One girl stopped.

"Don't I know you?" she said to Eric.

"I'm from Philadelphia," he said, sitting up straighter.

"No, no," she said. "You look like that little kid on those re-runs." She turned to the guy standing next to her. "What's his name?"

"No idea," the guy said. "Let's go."

They took off, the girl cycling through a list of child actor names.

"I get that all the time," Eric said, sliding his silverware to the side. "Girls think I look like some TV or movie star. It's like I'm a magnet or something."

I raised my eyebrows. "Yeah, I noticed all those paper clips attached to your back when we came in."

Eric frowned. Christy snorted, then caught my eye. I puffed out my cheeks in reply.

"I had this one girl who was IM'ing me, like, ten times a day," Eric said as we picked up our menus. "I finally had to just tell her to stop. It was getting crazy."

"You know, Eric," I said, "talking about other girls when you're out with a girl is considered bad form. If you're trying to impress me, it's not working."

"Why would I try to impress you?" Eric said.

Well, he had me there.

I scooted as far over to the edge of the bench as I could without falling onto the floor.

"This is fun," I said. "Why don't we all go bash our heads on the gumball machine next?"

"What about your center?" Christy asked.

"It just left," I said. "I need to catch up to it."

Eric gave Glen a baffled look. Glen shrugged.

I shoved myself out of the booth and stood up. "I'm getting one of my raging migraines. I think I'd better go." I turned to Eric. "I'm really sorry. I had several hot Rocky Mountain babes I was going to introduce you to."

"Really?" His eyes lit up.

Hello? Did he think I was serious?

"No, you doofus. You're supposed to be out on a date with *me*. Why would I be taking you to meet other girls?" I tossed a twenty at Christy. "I can't do it. Money-back guarantee."

As I walked through the restaurant, I heard Eric whine, "You paid her to go out with me? Twenty bucks? I'm only worth twenty bucks? You should have been paying *me* to go out with *her.* She's like some overgrown bamboo shoot with two knobs on top."

Knobs? My breasts had just been described as *knobs?* Excuse me? Like, I know they're nothing to write Penthouse Forum about, but come on. Give them a little credit for at least having some shape. I resisted the urge to go back and comment on what may or may not have been curled up in his pants like a measly little earthworm and stalked toward the front door.

Stopping in the foyer, I assumed my yoga breathing position. I couldn't leave feeling like my insides were in a gymnastics meet. Three breaths later, I felt much better. I wasn't centered, but at least I was in the same vicinity.

"Leaving so soon?"

I opened one eye. Manny stood in front of me, balancing our drinks on a tray. He held out a plastic to-go cup. "I had a feeling it wasn't a match made in heaven."

"It was hell," I admitted, taking the cup from him as I dropped a few dollars on the tray. I couldn't believe I'd said that, so calm and cool.

Manny laughed. His eyes met mine and a tingle went through my body. He kept looking at me, his eyes roaming my face like he was seeing me for the first time. And I guess he kind of was.

I shifted, uncomfortable under his gaze. "So," I said, "I haven't gotten a ransom note."

"What?"

"You've still got my pen from Spanish class. You're obviously holding it hostage."

Manny chuckled. "Right. How much are you willing to pay for it?"

"You're the pen-napper," I said. "That's for you to say."

"Fair enough," he said. "I'll come up with a reasonable demand. What's your e-mail?" He pulled out a napkin and pen and I wrote my address, heart racing. Manny Cruz had my e-mail. Pinch, pinch.

His eyes flicked back to the restaurant. "I should probably get back to work," he said. But he didn't seem to be in any hurry to deliver the drinks to the table. "There's a party at Jenna Noonan's tonight," he said. "Supposed to be a good one."

"That's where we were going next." I jerked my head in the direction of our booth. "But home's looking much better right now."

"He a friend of Hat Girl's?" Of course Manny knew Christy. She was the Crazy Hat Girl, but she was also "cute, with a great personality"—so said every other signature in her yearbook.

"Cousin."

Manny shivered. "Hard to believe they're related. They don't look alike at all."

As if on cue, Christy showed up.

"Maybe I should just serve all your drinks right here at the front door," Manny said.

Christy smiled. "Sorry, Manny. We just have a situation here." She turned to me. "I'm sorry this turned into another disaster," she said. "Are you really leaving?"

"I can't stay," I said. "I already made my big exit."

She frowned. "I guess not. But does that mean you're not going to the party?"

"No way. I can't be within a hundred yards of that guy. Call me when he's at Penn State."

84

Christy sighed and held out my twenty-dollar bill. "Here's your money back. He was not happy about that little theatric."

Manny laughed.

Christy raised an eyebrow slightly, her gaze moving from Manny to me, then back to Manny. I could almost hear her mind clicking away: *What's going on here? Do I need to be filing a field report?*

"Nothing." I didn't realize I'd answered her aloud until they both looked at me.

"What's nothing?" Christy asked.

"Nothing is nothing. I'm just thinking out loud."

"So you were sharing the contents of your brain with us." Christy flipped her hair over her shoulder.

"Very funny."

"I'm sorry you're not coming." She hugged me. "I'll call you later."

Manny followed her back to the booth with the drinks, looking over his shoulder at me before disappearing around the corner.

I stepped out into the cool October night, pulling my jacket closer around me. Thankfully, I'd worn my sneakers and not the flat-heeled boots Christy had suggested. I guess maybe I knew all along I'd be taking a walk.

14

The smell of Italian sausage frying in oil and garlic hit me as I walked through the door. It could only mean one thing.

"Abra has a delivery." A statement, not a question. Abra was an avowed vegetarian. When she was gone, all bets—and bean curd—were off.

"Yep." Dad slid dry spaghetti into one of the pots with one hand while turning a sausage expertly with the other. "Date over already?"

"Yep." I peered around him to gauge how long before dinner.

"I think that's a new record," he said, glancing at the clock. "Disaster?"

"Beyond," I said. "He called me a 'freaking Amazon' when we first met. It was pretty much downhill from there."

"Short guy, eh?" My dad nodded. "Some men are very sensitive about their height."

"Tell me about it." Abra had given me the heads-up when I complained one night, just after I'd started high school, that some of the guys were calling me "giraffe" and other endearing names.

"It's been ingrained in us that men should be taller than women," she had told me. "Height and size equal strength. Women aren't supposed to be strong. You intimidate them."

Great. I could use this intimidation factor if I decided to interrogate criminals or work for a loan shark collecting debts. It obviously wasn't helping me win friends and influence people.

Lucy came over to stand by us. "Mom's going to be mad you're making meat."

"Man shall not live by tofu alone," Dad said as he turned the sausage down to Low. "Though apparently Woman can."

"Not all women," I said, lifting the lid off the fry pan. "I'll have one of those. Looks like you've got enough."

Dad cut me a look. I knew what he was thinking. I'd rarely eaten any pork or beef for the last two years, knowing it was healthier and, if I was honest with myself, wanting to make Abra happy. And I'd just said yes to a huge pink link.

Dad opened his arms with a flourish. "For you, there's always enough."

I pecked him on the cheek. "Great. Just don't say anything to Abra."

"My links are sealed." I rolled my eyes at his bad pun. He ignored me and stepped to the island, where he sliced a loaf of French bread. "Carbs be damned," he said. "At least I'm using whole wheat pasta." He'd always been the primary cook, since his own law practice left him able to have flexible hours. He'd learned to make all kinds of vegetarian dishes to please Abra, and most of them we'd all grown to like.

"So what's the latest with the triathlon?" he asked. "Have you picked one to do?"

"I think so." I told him about the Rocky Mountain Women's

Triathlon in July. "It's going to be great, Dad. I'll get to see all these amazing athletes and find out what I'm really capable of."

My dad grinned. "It's great to see you so excited about this, Kat. And boy, am I impressed with your dedication. I was a slug in high school. You couldn't get me out of bed at five in the morning for anything."

I chopped the remaining tomatoes. "If you want something bad enough . . ."

He nodded. "And on another topic, Lucy showed me the drawing you did of her. It was great." He lowered his voice. "She wants to buy a frame for it so she can hang it over her bed." He patted my shoulder. "She thinks you're the greatest."

I glanced over at Lucy, who was now busy coloring something for school. "You didn't set her straight?"

My dad smiled. "The girl deserves a few fantasies."

I smacked him.

After dinner I was feeling the heaviness of the sausage. "I'm going for a bike ride," I announced.

"Helmet, reflectors, take your cell," my dad said. He was camped out in front of the TV watching the Avs slam the ice.

I headed for the garage, turning on my cell. I sent Christy a quick text about Manny:

Wat's he doin?

The familiar jingle told me she was quick with a reply.

Hangin' w his posse From: HatGirl Cell, 11:02 pm
Gs?

88

A few but WHO CARES—he asked about u! From: HatGirl
    Cell, 11:03 pm
WAT???
omg E is making out w a girl RITE NOW! From:
    HatGirl Cell, 11:05 pm

The Cousin scored? Unbelievable. I guess it's true what they said about there being someone for everyone, especially if one of them was drunk and it was dark.

The shrimp scores? no way—but wat did M say abt me?

I stared at the screen, waiting for the text jingle. My phone was annoyingly quiet.

*Fact of Life #299: Best friends who leave
you hanging should be tossed into a vat of
Jell-O.*

I sighed as I strapped on my helmet, wrapping reflective bands around my calves and biceps. She was probably blowing it way out of proportion. Manny had probably said "How's Kat?" and she interpreted this to mean "I want to marry Kat and have her babies." Wouldn't that be nice—both parts.

My phone chimed again.

M said expect email—go along or pen gets it—wassup?
    From: HatGirl Cell, 11:10 pm

I grinned. Manny had a sense of humor.

```
Tell u later goin 4 ride Cu
No fair! call me 18r  From: HatGirl Cell, 11:11 pm
k–keep I on my guy
(Salute)  From: HatGirl Cell, 11:12 pm
```

When I got home, Abra was still gone. I tiptoed into Lucy's room and saw the picture I'd drawn taped above her bed. On my own bed, I found a drawing from her. It was a picture of me wearing a crown with the words BEST SISTER across my shirt.

I smiled, leaning my picture against the lamp on the night-stand. I guess we'd need two frames. After showering and putting on my sleep T-shirt and shorts, I hopped online. My heart flipped when I saw a message from Manny:

From: DaMan@yahoo.com
To: KatBrat@msn.com
Subject: Ransom Demand
School prk lot Mon, 7:50am—Special Dark bar. B there or the pen gets it.

Shaking my head, I realized I actually owed the Cousin a thank-you. If I hadn't gone out with him, I never would have talked to Manny, he wouldn't have asked for my e-mail, and I wouldn't be having a ransom rendezvous.

I sent a text to Christy, who called me seconds later to hear about the pen-napping.

"This is good," she said. "This is very good." Then she sighed. "Sometimes I miss the fun of the chase, you know? The anticipation, the wondering, the planning to accidentally on purpose run into them."

I laughed. "And I'd kill for the solid, secure relationship you have with Glen."

Christy chuckled. "I just remember all those crushes I had before Glen. They were kind of fun."

"Fun?" I said. "You were miserable. Most of our seventh-grade year was made up of you whining over one guy or another—'Did he look at me?' 'What do you think that look meant?' 'Do you think he likes me?' " I rolled my eyes. "You have a very short memory, my friend."

Christy laughed. "I guess you're right. And speaking of Glen, he's calling through. Guess he didn't get enough of me tonight."

"He never does," I said. "Say hey for me."

After we'd hung up, I read Manny's e-mail again. *DaMan*. Loved that screen name. I got a little tingle looking at it. I read it two more times before I finally climbed into bed and fell asleep.

I pulled into the school parking lot on Monday at 7:48. As I passed Mitch's truck on my way to the sidewalk, I noticed the windows were fogged. Libby and Mitch were already going at it.

"Katima."

I glanced over my shoulder to see Manny about five feet behind me. I slowed down.

"Hey, Manny."

"You come alone?"

I glanced around. The parking lot was full of people laughing, talking, smoking. "Yeah," I said. "I'm alone."

Manny nodded, all serious. "You got the goods?"

I pulled a Special Dark—the big one—out of my backpack. "You got my pen?"

Manny pulled out my Pilot. He grabbed the chocolate bar and I grabbed the pen. "You drive a hard bargain," I said.

Manny laughed. "See you in Spanish," he said, hustling to meet some friends.

I wanted to leap up, fists pumping the air: *Yes, yes, YES!* But I just waved. "See you."

Christy was waiting for me at my locker. "So how did it go? Was the pen traumatized?"

"Very," I said. "I'm afraid it will need therapy."

She laughed. "So you've made contact outside of Spanish class. Now what?"

"Now nothing," I said, tugging at my books. "I'll go with the flow."

Christy leaned closer. "You should flow into asking him out."

Now it was my turn to laugh. "Yeah, right," I said, shaking my head. "I'm not asking Manny Cruz out."

Christy raised an eyebrow. "This from the offspring of Abra With No Last Name."

I sighed. Abra always said it was outdated nonsense to wait for the guy to ask—she had proposed to my dad, who claimed he said, "I thought you'd never ask"—and not fair to always put him in a position of possibly getting rejected, and I agreed in theory. But Christy knew Manny and I were separated by social galaxies. My rocket didn't have enough fuel to get over there.

"Chicken," Christy said, giving me a shove before heading to her own locker.

"Bawk, bawk."

After school, I went for a ten-mile bike ride. I rode hard, feeling good, and slowed down with a half mile to go as I turned in to my neighborhood. I imagined the tri finish line: the throngs of people cheering me, my dad snapping pictures, Christy and Lucy jumping up and down, maybe Manny raising a victory fist while Abra clapped, wearing an expression that said, *That's my daughter.*

I wondered what that would look like. But did it matter? No. What mattered was finishing. Knowing I'd accomplished this big thing *I'd* decided to do. I smiled as I saw that finish line, felt the heat of the sun on my face, the sweat drenching my body.

It was going to be sweet.

Nearing my own street, I saw a girl jogging. Libby. It was weird to see her outside of school. She seemed different, smaller, without her friends and Mitch hanging all over her. Her face was tight, her arms jerky by her sides, her stride short—she must be pissed at something or someone. As she stepped out to cross the street, a car turned the corner. She didn't even flinch.

I flipped my bike around.

"Hey!" I called as I rode up. "You should check out the street. Drivers can be crazy around here."

She didn't make a move to acknowledge me. Then I noticed the thin cords snaking down from her ears, disappearing into her jacket. I pulled up alongside her. The movement caught her attention. Pulling out one of her earbuds, she stopped.

"Hi," I said. "I just wanted to tell you to be careful. A car was coming when you crossed the street. I don't think you saw it."

She glanced nervously over her shoulder.

"Huh. Thanks." She put her earbud back in and took off.

When I wheeled my bike into the garage, I couldn't help smiling. Maybe we'd turned a corner in our relationship. Then I caught my reflection in the mirror Dad had hung up in the garage. With my helmet and racing sunglasses, there was no way she would have recognized me. Sighing, I stepped inside the house.

"Frames," my dad said when he saw me. Lucy and I followed him upstairs. I helped Lucy put her picture in hers; then we did mine. We both hung them over our beds.

"Perfect," I said. "Now I can see it every night before I go to sleep."

Lucy grinned, and I could tell she was really proud. "It matches," she said, pointing to the light blue frame and the dark blue of the wall.

"Just like us," I said, putting my arm around her and giving her a squeeze.

"That was so great that you drew each other pictures," Abra said later when I came downstairs to get some water. "Yours really captures Lucinda's essence."

I always felt weird when Abra praised my art. She had raved about the mural, but it was like she was excited about what I'd done, not about *me*. Maybe it was stupid to feel like there was a difference, but the way she said it, that's how it felt.

"Thanks," I mumbled, snatching my water glass and hurrying back upstairs.

On a Tuesday afternoon in late October, I plopped down in my chair at Abra's Midwifery and looked around. I loved it here. I was an idiot to be leaving. But I just couldn't give Abra the satisfaction.

"Hi," I said to the Fate Goddess as I made a fresh pot of decaf coffee. Just as it started to drip, Diane stepped in. She looked right at me, grinning like crazy.

"What?"

She strode over, reaching out to squeeze my arms. "Sit."

I sat in one of the comfy chairs. Diane sat next to me.

"Okay, now don't answer right away. Don't start protesting or making excuses or anything like that. Just listen."

I gave her a look. "Okaaay."

"So here's the thing," she said, taking my hand. "Jeff and I want you to assist at our birth."

My mouth dropped open. "Diane—"

"I told you not to say anything right away. Just *think* about it."

"Have *you* thought about it?"

Diane laughed. "Of course, silly. Jeff and I have talked about it off and on for a couple of weeks. We just wanted to make sure you had gotten over your first experience and were ready to try again."

For a moment, I let myself imagine it: how alert I'd be, how attentive, watching for cords and plastic covering the floor. I'd know exactly what to do and do it. I would make it a birth experience beyond all birth experiences, and women would flock from all over to have me assist.

And maybe pigs would fly and I'd be crowned prom queen in the spring.

I sighed. Abra would watch my every move, judging it, not wanting me there. No thanks.

"Look, Kat," Diane said. "The point is that Jeff and I really like you. We're comfortable with you. Abra recommended some doulas and midwives she works with, but we want you."

I stared at her. "Why?"

"Because you're you."

"That's not a reason." I crossed my arms over my chest, looking at her. Was this some charity thing? She felt sorry for me and wanted to help me along my way to self-confidence? I scowled. I didn't need that. I checked her face. No trace of pity. She seemed like she really meant it.

Diane squeezed my arm. "Think about it, Kat. That's all I'm asking. I won't take that as your final answer."

I sighed. "Fine," I said. "I'll think about it."

Fact of Life #87: People often believe what they want to believe.

Diane believes I can assist at a birth without causing grave bodily harm to anyone in the room.

Abra believes I shouldn't assist, though she hasn't said it out loud. She wants me in the Midwifery, helping it run smoothly, but she wants me to leave the real stuff, the stuff that matters, to her.

I'd like to believe I could assist. And if I was actually going to assist at another birth (which I'm not), Diane's would be the one. I love her. I love Jeff. It would be amazing to be part of their birth experience.

I'd like to believe I could do it. But I can't quite believe it. And the fact that Abra really doesn't want me to means that I won't.

15

I discovered that hanging out in your car in the school parking lot has spy-like qualities, and if your invisibility shield is up, you see and hear things you probably shouldn't see or hear.

It was the first Monday of November, and I had stayed after school to lift weights. Now I was in my car, having decided it was past time to clean it, so I sat in the parking lot wiping the dash, which had a nice layer of dust across it. I was parked three spaces away from Mitch's truck, with an ancient slug bug between us. Manny's Range Rover was a few cars away from Mitch's truck. I looked across the parking lot. Libby's sweet little red Ford Escape crouched in another row, like a cat waiting to pounce.

When Libby and Mitch came out of the school, I stopped dusting and slumped down in my seat. Not that I was trying to hide or anything, but I really didn't want anyone to see me. So I guess I was trying to hide.

I peeked over the edge of my door through the window as they climbed into the backseat of Libby's Escape. They got right down to business, didn't they? And that was the car to do business in. It had a moon roof, privacy glass (of course), and, according to the BFR, an awesome stereo system with speakers everywhere. I glanced at my dashboard with the hairline crack running across it, the broken heat vent, the ripped upholstery.

Libby was totally spoiled.

A few minutes later, Manny came out, talking with some guys before they headed to their cars. He opened the hatch of his Rover and tossed in his duffle just as a door slammed.

Mitch was stalking away from Libby's car, his face twisted in an expression I couldn't decipher. He climbed into his truck and slammed the door, revving his engine. Glancing down the row, I saw Libby back her car out of its spot. She drove forward. Then stopped. She started creeping slowly back toward Mitch's truck.

Manny shut the hatch and walked over to Mitch's truck. He knocked on the window and Mitch turned off his engine, getting out to glare at Libby.

I slunk down in my seat again, feeling a little guilty for listening. Then I pressed the window button and felt a whoosh of cold air as the window lowered all the way. If I was going to listen, I might as well get it all.

"What's up, bro?" Manny's voice.

"Who knows?" Mitch said. "One minute we're"—he stopped—"and the next minute she's kicking me out of the car."

I risked a peek. Libby's car was idling about ten yards away.

"Dumping my ass," Mitch muttered, "then hanging around to watch it swing in the breeze." He started toward her. "Bitch!" he yelled. "Get the hell out of here!"

Libby honked and drove in a big circle around him before flipping him off and driving away. Mitch flipped her off.

"Come on, bro." Manny tugged at his arm. "You need to cool down. Let's go to Flipflops." Flipflops was a twenty-four-hour breakfast place where a lot of people hung out.

Mitch just stared at the spot where Libby had been.

"Come on, man," Manny said. "You don't need her."

Mitch looked away, sniffing hard. He hacked and spit. "Yeah. Right." His voice dropped. "I can't believe it's over." He turned to Manny's car, but not before I saw his face—not Mitch-tough at all.

"This is huge," Christy said when I called her that night. "HUGE." She paused, and I knew she was writing in her notebook. "I can't believe you got this, Kat. Tell me again."

I repeated the story, Christy interrupting me every so often to write something down.

I heard pages flipping. "Here," she said, "listen to this from last year. Buchanan Field Report: LG & Men Part 2. Libby likes her men. Libby likes her men only once. Result: Once broken up, always broken up."

This seemed to go back to the try-on-clothing theory. If you try something on and it doesn't fit, why would you try it on again? It sounded like she approached her relationships in a very systematic and logical way. We could all learn from this. Except for the breakup methods. Seems like you can just place that jacket back on the rack if it doesn't fit. No need to stomp on it, mangle it, and smack it against the wall first.

"So you don't think they'll get back together?" I leaned back and closed my eyes, the phone pressed against my ear.

"Nope," Christy said. "It goes against her code."

"But she's been with him longer than anyone else. Maybe this is different." I didn't know why it mattered to me. Libby and Mitch lived in another galaxy. Why did I care about their love life? And why couldn't I get Mitch's face out of my mind?

"Libby Giles is nothing if not predictable, Kat," Christy said with a knowing air. "They're over. Finished. *Fini*."

We talked for a few more minutes, and then Christy's mom needed the phone. "I'll call you back on my cell," she said.

"I need to chill out," I said. "Let's talk tomorrow."

"I'll meet you at your locker," she said. "You can tell me everything."

I laughed. "I already told you everything." Almost. I hadn't told her the way Mitch had looked before he'd gotten into Manny's car. I felt like I'd violated his privacy, peeked into his soul for a second, and it didn't seem right to talk about it.

We hung up and I headed for the Womb, where I cued up some Celtic music and lit a few candles, sinking back against the pillows. I felt sad and angry and frustrated, and I couldn't figure out why. I really didn't care what happened between Libby and Mitch. I should be happy they wouldn't be making out in front of me anymore.

So why did I feel sad? And why was I regretting telling Christy, who had been faithfully filing Manny Cruz reports for me for the last four years?

It must be the guilt of seeing something I shouldn't have seen. Manny taking care of Mitch. Mitch's face when he let him. Like he might cry but didn't want to. Like he didn't know where he was or what he was doing. Scared and lost.

Like he was human. Like me.

16

Apparently Mitch had left his humanness in the school parking lot, because when I got to school the next day, his face was hard—no sign at all of the sad, lost eyes I'd glimpsed less than twenty-four hours before.

Maybe I'd imagined them. Maybe I'd imagined the whole thing and he and Libby hadn't even broken up. Then I happened to be near the jock lock, an area of lockers that was supposed to help maintain that team cohesion feeling among the athletes but really just made them think they were even cooler than they already thought they were. Volleyball-playing Libby was huddled in a large group off to one side, her friends surrounding her. Every so often one of them would glare Mitch's way, but he was the Ice Man.

And why were they glaring at *him*? He was the dumpee. I'd have to ask Christy. She knew more about this relationship stuff than I did.

"You did the right thing," one girl said, nodding in that knowing way people did when they wanted to be a part of the group. Please. I couldn't see Libby, so I had no idea if she was agreeing. But I could see Mitch. He strode over to the girl, who shrank a little under his gaze.

"She doesn't know *what* she did," he said. "Mind your own damn business."

"She's my friend." The girl stood up straighter, but her voice quavered. "It is my business."

Mitch rolled his eyes. "Bitch."

He walked away, heading in my direction. I averted my eyes, staring at a poster on the wall about the dangers of drinking and driving.

"What are you looking at?" I felt Mitch's breath on my neck.

"A poster," I said, pointing at the obvious without turning around. "You?"

"The back of your ugly head."

"Here's the front of my ugly head," I said, turning to face him. "Now your day is complete."

"You are really weird."

"So I've heard."

It might have been a trick of light, but I could have sworn the right side of his mouth twitched slightly, like he might smile.

"Whatever," he said, and was gone.

At 7:53 a.m. on Wednesday, Libby stepped out of her car and lit up. I knew this because I was sitting in my car, combing my still-damp hair after a swim at the rec center. I'd had a late start and hadn't had time to blow-dry. I hated coming to school with wet hair. It made me feel like people were looking at me, knowing I'd just taken a shower and might be trying to picture my skinny butt naked. Ugh.

A minute later, Mitch's truck rolled in next to Libby's Escape.

Interesting parking choice. A sophomore cheerleader stepped out of the passenger side. Huh. Mitch didn't strike me as the revenge type. People were full of surprises. Especially when you really didn't know them and were going strictly on surface observation and stereotypes.

Libby blew smoke in the cheerleader's direction, staring her down. The girl coughed but stayed where she was, so Mitch had to come to the other side, in front of Libby, to put his arm around her shoulder. He didn't lay it easily across the width of the girl's shoulders like he did with Libby. His hand cupped her shoulder, his elbow bent far down behind her back. His arm didn't look completely comfortable where it was. He glanced at Libby, but I couldn't read his expression. Then he clicked his remote to lock the truck and led the cheerleader toward school.

Libby just stood there, smoking calmly, as if seeing her ex with another girl was no big deal. And I guess it wasn't. After all, she'd been the one to break up with Mitch. She didn't care about him anymore. I couldn't imagine what that would be like, to be that calm and cool. Even if you broke up with someone, I had to believe there was just a teeny-tiny bit of feeling for that person tucked away somewhere in a small crevice of your heart.

Maybe Libby had no crevices.

But then she turned her head and I could see she was watching Mitch. She inhaled slowly, holding the smoke for a few seconds before exhaling just as slowly. She dropped the cigarette on the asphalt and ground it out with the toe of her shoe. Then she lit another.

One of her friends came up, and they started talking. Libby waved the cigarette-laden hand in the direction Mitch and the cheerleader had taken. Her friend followed her gesture, shaking her head. Then she said something to Libby, thumbing over her shoulder.

I looked.

Manny was walking between the cars, talking to some friends. I scrambled for my backpack, snagging the strap on the stick shift. Fumbling to release it, I scraped my hand. "Damn."

When I finally got myself and the backpack out of the car, Manny was standing in front of Libby. She was talking quickly, her cigarette hand waving around.

The first bell rang. Manny leaned close to Libby's ear. My heart flipped, seeing his lips so close to her earlobe. At first she nodded, like she agreed with him; then she was shaking her head, as if what he'd told her was completely impossible. She shoved him away and stalked off, flipping her hair over her shoulder.

I hitched my backpack up and started to wind my way through the cars toward school.

"Hey," Manny said when he saw me.

"Hey." I glanced toward the building, where Libby was just disappearing inside. "Trouble in popularity paradise?"

"Libby is so stubborn sometimes." He shook his head. "Smart, but stupid. You know."

"Sure," I said, even though I had no idea what he was talking about.

"Cruz, check out this download." One of Manny's pals had bumped into him.

"Cool." Manny strode ahead, leaving me and our brief moment behind.

Second Trimester

During this exciting second phase, you'll find yourself a bit scatterbrained and you'll start to "show." You'll probably have sleeping problems and feel a few Braxton Hicks contractions—a tightening of your abdomen.

During the second trimester, your baby will grow hair and her senses will begin to develop. Talk to her! She already knows your voice!

17

There was a special running route on the High Line Canal that took me on a tour of upgraded housing, beginning with modest one-story homes and ending with mammoth houses surrounded by rolling green lawns and perfect landscaping. In between, fields stretched out, waving grassy fingers in a cool fall breeze. Sometimes I got lucky and caught sight of a fox, or a hawk flying above in search of the elusive field mouse or squirrel.

Saturday was a cool but not cold November day, and I smelled dirt and grass mingled with the sweet, faintly rotting scent of fallen leaves. I was just at the curve in the trail when I heard footsteps. My heart skipped a beat, even though I knew it had to be just another jogger. I'd seen many of them on my runs.

Except today. Today the trail had been empty.

Visions of a stalker, ready to kidnap me at knifepoint, flashed through my mind. I sped up, pretending to check the cross path for bikers or other runners to see if I could glimpse whoever was behind me. But they were just outside my field of vision. I sped up and headed for a playground behind the church where I knew a few parents and their kids often hung out.

"Short or long distance?"

Fact of Life #648: When the crush of your life shows up on your running trail, try not to FREAK OUT.

"What are you doing on my trail?" I pulled the tail of my shirt up and wiped the sweat off my face.

Manny laughed behind me. "*Your* trail?"

I nodded. Omigod, omigod, omigod. Manny was on my trail.

He matched my stride. Of course. Manny was a Runner with a capital R. He entered half-marathons, maybe even full marathons. He was, like, a running *god*. I was a running peon.

"How far do you go?" he asked as we rounded a bend.

"Five miles today. Usually four."

"You in training for something? I saw you biking the other day."

He saw me and I didn't see him? Who's filing *that* report?

"Pretraining," I said, telling him about the Rocky Mountain Women's Tri. I was trying to ignore the fact that our arms were inches apart. Our arm hairs could almost touch. "I want to be in shape for the real training in June."

"My sister did that tri a few years ago. It's a good one," he said. "You're smart to do one of those official training sessions. My sister said it really helped."

I took a deep breath. I'm just having a normal conversation with the Cruzable. No need to get flustered. "How'd she do?"

"Better than she thought," he said. "Her goal was to do it all in two hours, and she did it in an hour fifty."

"Wow." The trail sloped gradually upward, and my breath came quicker now.

"Can I ask you a question?"

Omigod. Was he going to ask me out? Wait. How could I even think that? Why would Manny Cruz ask me out in the middle of a running trail? Or anywhere else, for that matter. I probably had some strange growth coming out of my neck that I hadn't noticed before and he was going to be nice enough to point it out to me.

"Sure."

He glanced at me. "Will you help me study for the Spanish final?"

I let out a breath—of relief or disappointment, I wasn't sure. I furrowed my brow.

"And yes, I see the irony of someone with a name like Manuel Cruz asking a gringa for help in Spanish."

I laughed. "I don't think you can afford me."

"Really. What's your rate? A dozen pens? Ten pounds of Special Dark?"

How about ten thousand kisses? Ugh. That sounds so girly-sick. But oh so good, too.

"Worse," I said, sucking in a breath as the trail leveled out again. "Starbucks decaf Shade Grown Mexico and one dozen Krispy Kreme cinnamon apple donuts, payable in advance."

Manny laughed. "Is this some special training diet?"

"You bet."

We ran for a while in silence. I was acutely aware of how our shoes hit the dirt path at the same time, sending small poufs of dust up around our ankles. I stole a glance at Manny. He didn't seem to mind that he was running with someone who wasn't on the social ladder, not even the bottom rung. And I was amazed at how comfortable I felt, as if we did this all the time. Christy would freak out if I told her.

Huh. *If* I told her, not *when*. But I didn't want to make a big deal out of it. We'd run into each other—literally, almost—and he wanted some help with Spanish. End of story.

"Hey," Manny said, bringing me out of my thoughts. "Race me to the bridge?"

When I caught up with him, he was standing next to the fence. "This is my favorite trail," he said. He turned to look past me, through the trees. "Though I usually don't do this stretch."

That explained why we had never seen each other before today. I kept sneaking peeks at his profile. He was so beautiful, with his dark, wavy hair, his stubbled chin jutting out slightly as he looked out across the greenbelt that stretched between two neighborhoods. Having him this close to me made my skin buzz. I felt light-headed and crazy, my emotions going wild. I had a sudden urge to attack him right there on the dusty trail, in front of squirrels and joggers and everyone.

Since cowards don't follow their urges, I sucked in my breath and we headed back at a slower pace. He glanced at me and I looked away, embarrassed to be caught staring.

"Mind if I give you a little tip?"

"A fashion tip?"

He laughed. "A running tip."

"Oh, one of those. Sure."

"Keep your arms closer to your body," Manny said, demonstrating. "It's more efficient."

I nodded and tried it, sprinting ahead of him. After a few minutes, he grabbed my arm.

"Look." He pointed to the sky. A hawk circled above the trees.

"It's beautiful," I murmured, aware of the little electrical impulses Manny's touch was sending through my arm.

"I love hawks," Manny said. "They're just cool, you know?"

I nodded. I did know. How my own body longed to soar, to feel that sense of freedom. But not just that. I also loved the power of a hawk, a predatory bird that swooped down on its prey and had no real natural enemies.

Manny told me how he'd seen a hawk on his thirteenth birthday. (May 16. I made a note of that—we were practically twins, with my birthday on May 9.) He was going to ESPN Zone with some friends later, but his mother had insisted they have some "quality family time" that morning, so she'd packed everyone up in the family Suburban and they'd headed for the mountains.

"I was so pissed off," Manny said. "I mean, shouldn't I get to decide what to do for the whole day, since it's *my* birthday?"

"Absolutely." I'd give him his whole thirteenth year. I'd bear his children. Heck, I'd deliver them, too. As we jogged back toward the rec center, he told me how he had stomped off.

"I just needed to chill, you know? The trail started to go up, and then it opened up. That's where I saw the hawk. It glided into this clearing and landed on a branch about ten yards away from me. I couldn't believe it."

His voice got quiet, his eyes distant, and I knew he was back there on the mountain, seeing his hawk.

"It was like it was there just for me, you know?" He blushed. "Stupid, huh?"

"No, I know exactly what you mean," I said. "I felt the same way when I saw a bighorn sheep up on a cliff once. I remember thinking, if only I was that surefooted, that confident, maybe I'd try things more often." I shrugged. "And somehow, seeing it made me feel like I was, or at least could try to be." I looked away, embarrassed that I'd revealed so much. "I guess that sounds stupid, too."

He shook his head. "I have no idea why I told you that story. I've never told anyone."

"Me either," I said.

We continued jogging, the silence between us like an old friend.

18

Fact of Life #47: Spanish ROCKS.

I drew little Mexican flags in my journal Monday morning.

Manny smiled at me when I turned around, our eyes locking briefly. But we didn't say a word to each other. It was so mysterious. I loved it.

And last night we had IM'd:

DaMan: How are yr legs?
KatBrat: Could lie & say gr8.
DaMan: & if u don't lie?
KatBrat: Could hardly walk yesterday. Shouldn't have tried 2 keep up w/ u.
DaMan: I was keeping up w/ u.
KatBrat: Liar.
DaMan: :-D
KatBrat: Truth.
DaMan: So—tutoring. Wed, 7?

I had paused, fingers poised over the keyboard. Christy and I had a stretch-and-tone workshop on Wednesday night.

KatBrat: No prob.

"You're the one who wanted to go to this stretch-and-tone workshop," Christy said when I told her I couldn't go. "They don't offer it again until spring."

"I know," I said. "But Abra really needs me."

I couldn't believe I'd just lied to my best friend. Wouldn't a normal person be screaming about having a study date with the guy she'd been in love with forever? Wouldn't she want to shout it out to the world?

But I wasn't normal, I guess. I didn't want Christy to make it out to be more than it was, to keep asking about it and wondering about it and make me ask and wonder. I just wanted to have this thing be all my own without interference from anyone else.

That afternoon I was at the Midwifery on the Internet, checking out some tri tips, when Diane came in. I had told her I didn't think I was ready to assist at the birth, and she had told me there was still time, so I should keep thinking about it. So I was.

"What about some classic rock to start?" Diane asked as she took off her coat.

I grinned as I opened the Birth Wish List notebook I'd set up and flipped to Diane and Jeff's page. Diane flopped down in the chair next to my desk. "How classic?" I asked. "Like ancient classic? The Stones, The Who, Grand Funk Railroad—"

"Grand Funk Railroad!" Diane grabbed my arm. "Do you

have that? Weren't they the ones who sang that song about a captain?"

I nodded. " '*I'm getting closer to my home.*' " I attempted to sing, but it came out more like a squawk. "I can't sing worth a baby's first poop," I said, echoing Abra.

"I recognized it anyway," Diane said, laughing. "Put that on the list."

Abra stepped out from the Gathering Place, peering over my shoulder. "Ah, the famous music list for the birth?"

"Yeah," Diane said. Then she shook her head. "Jeff wants some kind of a sports theme, but I told him he can't catch the baby with a catcher's mitt. It's unsanitary."

Abra smiled. "I've known a few fathers to bring them as a joke," she said. "But there's nothing like skin on skin to get dad and baby bonding immediately." She leaned over my shoulder. "You should divide the page into sections based on the phases, giving yourself plenty of leeway in terms of the number of songs, since we never know Baby's plan."

I scowled. I knew exactly how I wanted to do this. I'd already done it with Linda. For me, it was about flow. One set of songs flowing into another. I didn't need to divide up the page. This wasn't a comparison chart.

"You can keep track of things a little easier." Abra flipped the notebook to a clean page and drew lines, dividing it into sections. "See?"

I didn't reply.

"Great," she said, straightening up. "Well, Diane, I'm ready when you are." She motioned to the Gathering Place. "Katima, I'm sure Diane would love for you to chat with us during the exam."

I didn't want to be in the same room with Abra right now. I might start dividing *her* up into sections. Arrgh. I should have quit when I said I would.

Diane glanced at me, then back at Abra. "Actually, I've got some things I want to discuss that I think would bore Kat to tears." She looked at me. "Do you mind?"

"No," I said, relieved. She, at least, could feel the tension. "I've got a test to study for, anyway."

When the door closed, I picked up the Birth Wish List notebook and went out into the hall. I ripped out Abra's divided page in one swift move. Balling it up, I hurried down the hall to the bathroom and tossed it in the trash.

When I got back, I could have kicked myself. Why had I snuck out to the hall to rip it out? Why did I care if she heard? Or found it wadded up in the trash?

I dropped into my seat and pulled out my calculus, hoping a little mental aerobics would take my mind off of the fact that I was afraid to say what I really wanted to say to Abra.

The next afternoon, I was crouching outside the gym, lacing up my running shoes. I couldn't believe I was actually going to be with Manny Cruz tonight—our first tutoring session.

"What are you looking at?"

I glanced over my shoulder. Mitch stood a few feet away from me, arms crossed as he stared down the hall. Clearly, he was talking to me but didn't want to look like he was.

I sighed an exaggerated sigh. "Is that all you ever have to say to me? Our relationship is so predictable."

Mitch smiled. "Yeah, well—"

"—whatever," I finished for him. "I know."

I watched him walk away, wondering what strange brain cells were misfiring so that he felt an urge to say something when he was around me. But he had smiled. I felt victorious.

Manny and I met at the Starbucks near the computer store where he worked, camping out at a table near the back.

"One decaf Shade Grown Mexico and one dozen Krispy Kreme cinnamon apple donuts," Manny said as I sat down. He slid the box over to my side of the table.

"Thank you, sir," I said, setting the box down on the chair next to me. "I like your sense of responsibility." I took a sip of coffee and pulled out a sheet of paper I'd prepared the night before. "Here's my game plan," I said, sliding the paper over so he could see. "Tonight we should start with paragraph translation, then move forward through Q and A and vocabulary."

Manny picked up the sheet, shaking his head. "You are one organized person."

I shrugged. "It's important to have a plan. Then we can track your progress." That sounded familiar. Gee, should I divide the page into sections?

"Sometimes I think I need to go back to Spanish I." Manny sighed. "I wish my parents had kept it up. But *their* parents said 'English only,' so it got lost once it got to me." He shrugged. "Everyone regrets it, but there's not much we can do except this." He pointed to the textbook.

"Práctica, práctica," I said.

We ate donuts, conjugated stem-changing verbs, and laughed at each other's accents when we read from a Spanish collection of short stories. At eight-thirty we packed up.

"Muchas gracias, amiga," Manny said as we headed out the door.

"¿Pastel?" I asked, holding out the donut box.

"Uno solamente." He took one and bit into it. I grabbed one, too, as we walked across the parking lot. *"¿Donde está tu coche?"*

"Allí." I pointed to my Honda hybrid, parked directly under a light in the middle of a row. *"Tu español—es muy excelente."*

"Tengo una buena maestra." He grinned at me, and I blushed. *I have a good teacher.*

We reached my car and I unlocked it. I turned, seeing his face more clearly under the glow of the light. "You've got—" Would he be mad like Libby was when I told her about her dye job? Oh, to heck with it. I wiggled my fingers toward his face. "You know."

"En español, Katima."

I smiled. *"¿Como se dice* 'donut dust mustache' *en español?"*

He wiggled his mouth. "Hey, I want it there." Squinting at me under the lights, he smiled. "You've got one, too."

"I *don't* want it there," I said, reaching up.

But he was faster. He brushed his fingers across my upper lip. "There. All gone."

My lip was electrified.

"Muchas gracias," I whispered.

"De nada."

I stood there, staring at him. Could he be any hotter, with that donut dust mustache? Look at those lips, perfect for kissing, with a little donut dust to sweeten the deal. Oh, if only—

"Uh, do you want to get in?" Manny said. "I need to help get the sibs to bed."

"Right. Sorry." Could I have been more obvious? Oh, he touched me, I'm melting. Gag, gag, triple vomit. He must think I'm still in middle school. "Just distracted." *Because you're, like, a foot away from me*. He nodded as I opened the door and tossed my backpack on the passenger seat. "Thanks for walking me to my car."

"De nada."

"In English, please."

Manny laughed. "Have a good one, Kat."

Oh, believe me, Manuel León Cruz, I will.

19

"Oh, it's a disaster. Just a disaster," Melanie wailed into my ear the next afternoon. "We have mold in our house. We've had to move out. I can't have the birth I want. I had everything set up—the curtains, the music, the strobe light—"

"The strobe light?" I had started to zone out until she said that.

"For effect," Melanie said. "And now we're with my in-laws."

I wasn't sure what effect she was going for, and I was not going to ask.

"Do they have a nice room for birthing?" I asked, like an idiot. This was Abra's problem. And I had been having warm thoughts about Manny—could he be even more perfect, walking me to my car, going home to help put his little siblings to bed?

"Oh, God, no." Melanie's voice rose. "My mother-in-law believes I'm putting my life and the life of my baby in danger. She'd never be a party to that." Melanie sighed, and I almost felt sorry for her. "It's just a disaster," she said again.

She was right. It was a disaster. For *us*. Because if she didn't have the baby at her house or this mother-in-law's, then she'd probably have it at ours, in Serenity Space. Egads.

Christy was waiting for me at my locker when I got to school on Friday morning. And she got right to the point.

"Is there something going on between you and Manny?"

I coughed. "What?"

She stared at me. "I'm getting these—vibes." She waved her hands in front of her, as if they were divining rods that could detect a Kat-and-Manny connection.

"Nothing's going on," I said, closing my locker door. "And if you pull out your notebook or start making assumptions or predictions, I'll tell Glen you snort-snore and talk in your sleep about movie stars."

Christy's eyes grew wide. "So I'm right. It's a something that's nothing, which is probably really something but—" She stopped when I gave her a look. "Okay. It's nothing. So no notebook or anything else. Scout's honor."

"You were never a Scout," I said. "You can't use their honor."

She pulled her gambler's hat off her head. Now it was my turn for wide eyes. Christy never took her hats off in school. Ever. Even when she wore the wide-brims, she just sat in the back so others could see the board.

"I swear on my vintage hat collection, I will abide by your conditions."

"Wow," I said. "Okay. Because this is no big deal, and if you try to make it into one—"

She put her hat back on. "I know, I know. Snort-snore and movie stars."

121

I took a breath. "I tutored Manny in Spanish on Wednesday night. That's why I missed our stretch-and-tone class."

Christy blinked rapidly. She worked her mouth. I knew she wanted desperately to say something—to ask questions, analyze words, seating arrangements, food and beverage orders. Her fingers flitted around the front of her backpack, where the Field Report notebook stuck out of a pocket. She swallowed hard, then took a breath, placing her hat calmly back on her head. Smoothing her hair over her shoulders, she smiled. "Well, he should ace his final."

I smiled.

Then she turned, thrust her arms in the air, and crowed. "Yeeehawww!"

I grabbed her arm and spun her around. "Christy! You promised you wouldn't make a big deal out of it." But I grinned like mad. I felt like letting out a yeehaw myself.

"I can't help it," Christy said. "I'm so psyched for you."

"But it's just tutoring," I said, "and just the one time." Christy's enthusiasm could take me places I would never go in real life, and I couldn't let that happen. I looked over her shoulder. "Here comes Glen."

"I've still got it." She waved her hands again. "The vibes. I knew there was a connection of some kind."

I smiled. "Yes, you've still got it."

She smiled as Glen wrapped his arms around her from behind and kissed her neck. "Well, we're off to class. See you later."

I watched them walk away, my smile fading. They were such a cute couple. He was three inches taller, his arm fitting neatly around her back, hers comfortably around his. That might be how Manny and I would look if— *Stop it. It's not going to happen. And I wouldn't want it on display like that anyway.*

• • •

On Monday, after school, I headed for the gym. I'd left my favorite sports bra in a locker and I wanted it for my run. As I was coming out of the gym locker room, I saw Mitch standing next to Libby at her locker. Libby brushed her hair back over her shoulder, and I was struck again by how beautiful she was. That perfect nose with just a few freckles across it, her lips brushed with a soft pink, her skin smooth across her cheeks.

"Come on, Lib," he said. "Just coffee. Nothing else."

"Will your little cheerleader friend be coming along?"

"That was—stupid," Mitch said. "It would be just us." Mitch leaned in closer to her, but I could still hear him. "What do you say?"

"I say no." Libby slammed her locker, startling Mitch. As she stalked away, he stood there, watching her go.

Then he turned and his eye caught mine. "What—"

"You," I said. "I'm looking at you, okay? That's what I'm looking at."

"Well, stop. It's creeping me out." His eyes shifted back down the hall, where Libby was barely visible. "Why are you always around?"

"*I'm* always around? No, *you're* always around. And it's creeping me out."

Mitch turned to look at me. "*I'm* creeping *you* out?"

"Yeah," I said, holding his gaze. "And you don't have to say it like that. Jerk."

His left cheek twitched. Then he laughed.

"You are one kooky chick." He cocked his head at me. "What's your name?"

"Kat," I said. "Kat Flynn."

He nodded.

123

"And you are?" I said.

"You know who I am."

"An arrogant prick?"

He laughed again, then held out his hand. "Mitch," he said. "Mitch Lowry."

I shook it. "Yeah," I said. "I know."

"Smart-ass."

We both laughed.

"See ya around, Kat Flynn." He turned and strode down the hall.

"I hope not," I called after him. "You creep me out."

He waved a hand, but kept walking. Maybe I could see a little bit of what Libby had seen in him. If I squinted and crossed my eyes just right.

20

"Is that your *Spanish* homework?" Christy stood next to me at my locker on the Wednesday before Thanksgiving, sporting a white pillbox.

"Don't even try to go there, Chris."

"I wasn't going anywhere."

"But you want to."

"Can you blame me?" she asked. "You're tutoring the crush of your life and I'm not allowed to talk about it under penalty of extreme humiliation."

"I'm sorry," I said, pulling out my books and shutting the locker door. "I know it sounds stupid, but I feel like if I talk about it too much, I'll jinx it. Not that there's anything to jinx, but I like being friends with him and I don't want to make it out to be more than it is. I just want it to be what it is." We started down the hall toward our first class. "Does that make sense?"

"Coming from you? Yes." She sighed. "Any other girl would be wondering what it meant if he sat across from her, rather than next to her." She raised an eyebrow.

"Across from me," I said, to answer her unasked question. "See, that's what I mean. I don't want to wonder about everything. If he touched my hand, was it an accident or on purpose? And, omigod, what did that look mean?"

"You're taking all the fun out of it." Christy fake-pouted and adjusted her hat.

"I'm making sure I'm not setting myself up for disappointment," I said, staring straight ahead. "It's enough that we're friends."

I felt her eyes on me. "Really?" she said softly.

I nodded. "Really."

"Hey, teach," Manny said when he saw me that night. We were meeting at a different Starbucks this time, one closer to the rec center.

"Hey, stude." I almost said "stud," which would have been really embarrassing.

After we'd finished our Spanish review, we talked about running and the trail, and then got into hobbies. Somehow we segued into workouts and how guys watch themselves in the weight room mirror far more than girls do.

"So," he said, "want to go for a bike ride this weekend?"

I sucked in my breath. Bike riding was not a date, but it was also not studying for Spanish.

"Sure," I said, keeping my voice calm. "I've even got a cool place to show you."

Observation #7: Trust your instincts. Use your intuition to detect subtle shifts through body language and voice inflection.

—from Abra's doula and midwifery notebook

126

On Saturday morning we met near a tunnel under the highway. It was part of the High Line Canal trail that ran for miles north and south. It was a cool-weird kind of place. Under the traffic, but still in sight of the outside world.

We pulled our bikes inside. I tilted my head, listening to the traffic overhead.

"So," Manny said, "do you have a job? You always disappear after fourth period Tuesdays and Thursdays."

Manny was watching me disappear? Whoa.

"I'm a spy," I said. "You know, high school undercover. I'm really twenty-five."

"Yeah, me, too," he said. "CIA?"

"MI5," I said. "Can't you detect my British accent?"

"I wondered why your Spanish was so bad."

I smacked him and he cringed in mock pain. Then he straightened up.

"So you've got a pager," he said. "You work for a doctor or something?"

"Or something." I straddled the bike, ready to push off.

But Manny wasn't in a hurry. He leaned back against the wall, crossing his arms, his bike propped up next to him. His jacket hung open, his T-shirt tight against his chest. He looked, well, gorgeous. "Why all the mystery?"

"I work for a home birth midwife, okay? She delivers babies in people's bedrooms." I waited for the buzzer to go off announcing FREAK, lights flashing on the cement walls.

"That's cool. Why didn't you just say that?"

I stared at him for a second, then shrugged. "Some people think it's weird. Like she's some hokey throwback to medieval times."

"My aunt's a labor and delivery nurse," Manny said. "She sees some midwives come into the hospital to deliver. She says they're great."

"Abra isn't a certified nurse-midwife, so she can't deliver at a hospital," I said. "And she wouldn't want to. But if one of her mothers needs to go to the hospital, she fully supports it." I sounded like an advertisement for Abra the Great. And now it was like she'd intruded, ready to judge or correct me.

"Let's go," I said.

We rode the next five miles in silence. For some reason I didn't have an urge to talk, to fill up the quiet with the sound of my own voice. I felt strangely calm around Manny. Able to just be. Myself.

When we got back to our starting point, I wiped the sweat from my brow. "Thanks for pushing me. I'm going to be hurting tomorrow."

"You're in great shape," he said. He stared at me until my cheeks warmed and I had to look away. He nudged his bike against mine and I looked back as he leaned toward me. "I feel like there's something between us," he said in mock seriousness.

"Bikes," I said, pointing to the obvious.

"Ah, yes."

Omigod. He was going to kiss me. Manny Cruz was going to kiss me. My heart pounded crazily in my chest.

But then he looked down the trail. Of course he wasn't going to kiss me. This was exactly what I was talking to Christy about. *It's enough that we're friends,* I'd told her. With a straight face, no less.

"We should do this again sometime," Manny said, still looking down the trail. I followed his gaze, wondering what could be so interesting.

"Sure," I said. "Whenever."

He looked back at me and smiled. "See you in school."

"See you."

I watched him walk his bike off the trail and into the parking lot before pushing my bike toward my car. I was glad Christy wasn't here to analyze the scene. She would have told me I should have kissed him first, and I would have known she was right and that I'd chickened out. Except what if she was wrong and I'd done it and he'd wiped his mouth and rode away like I had some horrible disease? So really, I'd barely escaped an incredibly humiliating moment by not taking advice that Christy hadn't given me.

I loaded my bike on the bike rack, feeling relief, mixed with a little disappointment.

21

*Fact of Life #564: Being friends with the man of
your dreams is better than nothing.*

Right?

Sunday afternoon I was curled up on the futon in the Womb,
candles flickering around me. I wasn't a relationship expert, but
there are some things you just know, like when your period is
about to say hello, and when your show is about to come back
from commercial if you're still stuck without a DVR.

So even though I'm not a relationship guru, I knew Manny
wanted to kiss me. This sent shivers across my skin, with the occasional blip of disbelief because, really, why would he?

Breathing deeply, I closed my eyes. Whatever was going
to happen with Manny was going to happen. I had to just go
with it. I practiced several yoga poses to center myself, then
went to find Lucy. She and Abra were finishing up a game of
dominoes.

"Did she thoroughly trounce you?" I asked Abra.

Abra nodded. "What else? She's got the magic touch."

Lucy grinned, and I felt a little twinge of jealousy. It had been a long time since Abra and I had done anything like that together.

"Want to go for a walk with me, Luce?"

The sky was slipping from blue to gray as dusk came on, the air brisk and fresh. We had walked several blocks when we reached another neighborhood intersection.

"Which way?" I asked.

"That way." Lucy pointed to the left. Libby's street.

We walked another block, Lucy chattering on about school and Emily.

"So you're friends again?"

"We were friends the next day."

"I'm glad you worked it out." Actually, I wasn't sure I was, because Emily seemed to be a little fourth-grade manipulator, but Lucy was so happy about it, I didn't want to ruin it for her. She slipped her hand in mine and I squeezed. I was glad she didn't feel too old to hold hands. It felt nice.

"Do you know that girl?"

I looked up. Libby was stepping out the front door of her house.

"She goes to my school."

"She's really pretty." Lucy sped up, as if she wanted a closer look. I released her hand and she stopped, looking back at me. "What?"

"Nothing," I said. "I just don't want to go as fast as you." What I really wanted to do was turn around and go the other way. It felt strange to be walking by Libby's house, almost like we were trespassing, even though we were on the sidewalk.

"Elizabeth!" A woman was standing in the doorway, her arms wrapped around herself. Her hair was up in a towel turban, her face pale. "Where do you think you're going?"

"Out." Libby was at her car, unlocking the door. "And don't call me that."

"But Jack's coming to take us out to dinner," Mrs. Giles said. "You aren't ready."

"I'm not going."

"You *are* going." Mrs. Giles pushed open the door and placed a tentative bare foot on the front porch, then pulled it back quickly. "Get back in this house."

Libby answered by slamming the car door and starting the engine. She backed out of the driveway, tires squealing. We stood frozen in place as she roared past. Lucy was gripping my hand so hard my fingers tingled.

I snuck a peek at Mrs. Giles. She glared at me as if I was the one who'd sent Libby away.

"Dammit," she said, slamming the front door so hard the windows on either side rattled.

I squeezed Lucy's hand in both of mine. "Let's go home," I said.

On Tuesday after my last class, Manny was talking to someone near my locker. My heart bounced all over, especially when the girl left and he stayed.

"Here's that thing you asked about," he said, holding out a slip of paper.

I stared stupidly for a second. "Oh, right. Thanks." I slid it into my back pocket, as if Manny Cruz handed me notes every day.

He touched me lightly on the arm. "See you."

I wanted to say, *When? Where?* But I just said "See you" back and watched him walk away, wondering how just a few words, the proximity of our bodies, could send me shooting into elated orbit.

I was dying to read the note. As I reached back, I saw Libby out of the corner of my eye, two friends flanking her, giggling and talking. And even though they weren't looking at me and had no idea what had just happened, I suddenly felt like Loser Girl in a teen movie, the one the popular boy flirted with either because someone dared him or just because he could. My heart said Manny wasn't like that, but with Queen Libby over there, it felt pretty middle school to get all excited over a little arm touch and a note.

I sighed. I knew the note was just a piece of paper with something written on it. It was probably Nothing with a capital N—probably stuff about Spanish. I could take it out right now in the middle of the hallway and read it, no big deal.

I could, but I didn't, because a voice inside was saying: *What if the note isn't Nothing? What if it's really Something with a capital S? As long as you don't open it, it can be anything you want it to be.*

Exactly. I slid my fingers in my pocket until they touched paper, then pulled them out quickly, a thrill running through me. I wouldn't read it right now. I'd wait until I was at the Midwifery, where I'd have some peace and quiet and could savor the moment without any distractions. Who cared if that was middle school? It was what I wanted to do.

It felt a little like Christmas, looking forward to what Santa had left me under the tree. I grinned and hugged my books to my chest, butterflies dancing in my belly.

• • •

I had to wait a while to find out what Santa Manny had left me in my back pocket. When I got to the Midwifery that afternoon, Abra didn't have a lot of appointments, so she hovered around the reception area, directing me to clean this cabinet or dust that shelf. I breathed a sigh of relief when Diane walked through the door—they'd go into the Gathering Place and I could finally read Manny's note.

"So Jeff and I have this great idea for our theme," Diane said, sitting down in the chair next to my desk.

Or not. Sighing, I tried to look interested.

Abra smiled and patted Diane's shoulder.

"Well, it was really my idea and he's going along with it," Diane continued. "But I don't want to tell you, because I want it to be a surprise."

I furrowed my brow. "Saying you have an idea and then not saying what it is—that's a mild form of torture." Of course, it didn't compare to the torture of having a note from Manny Cruz burning a hole in my butt cheek. Why didn't I just read it at school like a normal person?

Go have your appointment already!

Diane laughed. "It'll be worth it, I promise."

Abra's face clouded briefly; then she smiled. "Whenever you're ready, Di," she said before slipping into the Gathering Place. Who knew what that look meant. Who cared? *Just let me read this note!*

"Want to hang out with me today?" Diane asked.

Any other day I would have said yes, since I no longer felt like dividing Abra up into sections. But any other day I didn't have a note from Manny.

"I'd love to," I said, "but I've got a major test."

"Say no more," Diane said, standing up. "Next time."

134

"Definitely," I said. When the door to the GP closed behind her, I waited until I heard soft music and their low voices on the other side of the wall.

Finally.

Licking my lips, I tugged the note out and set it on the desk, letting my fingers rest on top. What if, after all this drama and buildup, it was nothing?

Just open it.

Butterflies flipping, I unfolded the note and smoothed it out, seeing Manny's now-familiar scribbling.

There's something between us. Th4-HLC-2m.

My heart skipped a beat. This note was not Nothing. Manny Cruz felt *Something* between us. And maybe not just bikes. *Th4-HLC-2m*. It took me a minute to figure it out, but when I did, I couldn't help grinning.

I left the Midwifery early on Thursday, so I was at the two-mile marker on the High Line Canal trail at four o'clock. I'd worn my running clothes, warmed up, and jogged slowly to the marker. No sense wasting a good trail. I stood near the bench, one leg up, stretching my hamstring. Manny showed up about a minute later.

"I knew you'd know." He took a step toward me. He was breathing a little heavily, and sweat glistened on his forehead. He'd run to the mile marker, too.

I smiled. "Good code."

"This was where we first ran into each other, no pun intended."

My, aren't we romantic.

"I thought it would be a good place to start."

I looked at him. "Start what?"

But he didn't answer. He just kissed me.

135

22

Fact of Life #78: When a fantasy becomes reality, it doesn't feel real. Why is that?

There was no way I was drawing stupid hearts and cupids on the page. I drew a dragon with wings, soaring over a castle.

What do you do when the fantasy you've been having for the last four years actually happens? Do you go out dancing in the streets? Do you run and call your best friend, who has supported this fantasy since the beginning? Or do you stand in the spot where he left you, unable to move, convinced it was all a dream in spite of the welts rising on your arms from pinching yourself over and over?

Manny Cruz kissed me. Me, Kat Flynn. Yoga Girl. Frizzy-haired freak. After we had kissed, he had looked at me, then looked away, laughing nervously.

"Well," I had said. "That was unexpected."

He laughed again, this time for real. "That's your reaction?"

"Shock can do that to a person." My brain tried to process the fact that my face was inches from his; my lips had just recently been connected to his, with a bit of tongue action going on. Delicious. No doubt about it.

Manny stepped back, taking a deep breath. I couldn't read his face. Did he regret it? Was he worried someone had seen? Did I suck as a kisser? The fact that he wasn't looking at me anymore made me nervous. He'd crossed his arms and was flexing and unflexing his fingers.

"I didn't know I was going to do that until I did it," he said. "I was just going to talk."

"Oh." I waited, but he didn't say anything else. "Okay," I said, my voice a little shaky. "So is this the part where we say it didn't mean anything, that it was all a mistake and it will never happen again?"

He stopped flexing. "Was it a mistake?"

"Hey, that's your call. You started it."

"You helped finish it."

I crossed my arms as a breeze sifted through my jacket. "Look, Manny, I'm not going to lie and say I wouldn't want to do it again. But if you want an out, you've got it. I'm a go-with-the-flow kind of person."

Manny shook his head. "You're pretty amazing. You know that?"

I shrugged. "Things happen. Sometimes you mean for them to, sometimes you don't."

"Okay," he said. "What about this: Can we just see how things go? How we feel? Or is that lame?" He ran his fingers through his hair, making it stand up on top of his head. Adorable. "I came off two pretty intense relationships last spring and summer and hadn't really planned on getting into anything for a while."

I frowned. According to the Buchanan Field Report, he'd had a summer fling, nothing serious. She must have gotten bad information. In the spring he was going out with Libby. How intense was it?

"Exactly what I said. Unexpected—for both of us."

"Yeah." He nodded. "I guess it is."

"So we'll see what happens," I said. "In the meantime, I'm freezing my butt off. Let's run." I took off down the path, and he joined me. When we got to the road, Manny grabbed my arm.

"Wait," he said. I stopped, my breath coming fast, my heart pounding—from excitement or exertion, I didn't know. He put his arms around me and we kissed again. It was a long, warm, sweet kiss that sent me tumbling down to a place I'd never been before. When we finally pulled apart, I kept my arms around his neck. They felt comfortable there, like they belonged.

We just looked into each other's eyes, our breath puffing white between us. "So," I said huskily, "how are things going so far?"

Manny grinned. "Unbelievable." And he kissed me again.

When we came up for air a second time, he hugged me tight, one arm around my waist, his other arm higher up, across my back. Then he let go and took off running.

I followed. Wherever he wanted to lead.

23

That night I must have picked up the phone to dial Christy's number ten times before hanging up. I wasn't sure what was stopping me, except maybe the fact that I wasn't sure what was going on. I'd never had a boyfriend before. Was it normal for a guy to say he wanted to see how things went and then make out two more times right after that?

I grinned. He'd kissed me. Manny Cruz had kissed me three times without being dared or paid money to do it. I lay on my bed, my fingers fluttering over my lips. *Go with the flow.* Who was I kidding? Yeah, I'd go with the flow, as long as it was all about Manny Cruz.

> *Fact of Life #5: Kissing is completely underrated.*
> *And whoever said that you should never go out with*
> *someone you're crushing on because it will never*
> *be as good as you imagined and you'll only be*
> *disappointed has never crushed on and kissed MC.*
> *And they'd better not.*

I admit to drawing kissy lips on this page.

The next day he smiled at me when we passed in the hall. It was a small, almost secret smile, and I smiled back. I tingled all over. I was a kissed woman. I had made out with Manny Cruz and neither of us was drunk.

I turned the corner, catching sight of Libby with a football player. She was leaning back against the wall, laughing up at him, and he was smiling down at her, his hand on the wall next to her, like he was doing a one-armed push-up.

I felt a twinge and glanced around. Mitch was way down at the end of the hall. I couldn't tell if he saw her. Then I shook my head. Why would I care if he did? Mitch and Libby were not my business. What was my business was the fact that Manny Cruz had kissed me.

In Spanish, Manny asked to borrow a pen.

"Sure," I said. "Just make sure you return it this time." My voice was completely normal, as if I was talking to anyone in the class, not Manny Cruz, the guy who'd kissed me three times the day before. But it had to be. For all I knew, he had decided overnight that it had all been a big mistake. Or he had looked at me in this horrendous classroom lighting and been appalled that he'd actually kissed these lips willingly, been that close to this face.

"No problem," he said, his fingers briefly brushing mine as he took the pen.

Electric.

We met that night for an impromptu study date—"I really need help with future tense," Manny had said with a sly smile. It felt like a date because we hadn't opened our books or even gotten out of the car. We were just sitting in the back of his Range Rover, our coffees sending up little steam streams from the rear cup holders. I shifted in my seat and told him about Abra.

"So your boss is also your mom?"

"Yeah, I guess."

"You *guess*?"

I laughed, embarrassed. "Well, it's just—weird. She's very businesslike and acts like my teacher or mentor most of the time, not my mother—or at least not what I think mothers are supposed to act like. I wouldn't know, since all I have is Abra." I looked away. It was the first time I'd identified what was different about my relationship with her, why it felt better calling her Abra than Mom.

I just didn't get how she could be so in tune with all of the women who came to see her but with me it was all "Here's your labia, your vagina is inside your body; try to see the essence of a person, not just their exterior; brush your teeth and let me show you how to floss." Instructions or corrections of my behavior; nothing, really, about my life. Sometimes I wanted to be able to talk to her about things—like Manny—but most of the time I didn't want to hear her theories on dating or relationships or whatever else she might tell me. Instead of being a shared experience between us, it would become a teacher-student moment—a time for me to learn and grow from her experience and wisdom.

No thanks.

"Parents are just weird sometimes," Manny said as we each took a sip of our coffee. "My dad used to want me to become a doctor. I told him I faint at the sight of blood—well, not anymore, but I really did when I was a kid. He told me I wasn't tough enough and somehow got me to shadow some ER doc.

He thought I'd get all the gunshot victims and stabbings and it would help me along." Manny chuckled. "There was one broken arm—guy flew over the handlebars of his bike—and one concussion. I told my dad the bone was sticking out and there was blood everywhere and the concussion was a guy whose head was split wide open."

I laughed. "He must have been very pleased."

Manny nodded. "He was. Then I told him I thought maybe he ought to come next time. He turned kind of green and said, 'How far was the bone sticking out?' When I said, 'this far' "—Manny put his hand about six inches above his arm—"he nearly hit the floor." Manny tapped his hands on the back of the seat in front of him. "He hasn't mentioned it since. He did say he thought some of those corporate lawyers were pretty cool." He shrugged. "So I'm guessing that will be his next thing."

We sat in silence for a moment. I was aware of the cocoon feel of the car, how sounds were muted or blocked out completely. The windows were fogged from our breath, and I tugged at my jacket.

"Cold?" Manny scooted over and put his arm around me. I sank into his side, sliding down so I could rest my head on his shoulder.

"So what do you really want to do?" I asked.

Manny rubbed his cheek on top of my head. "I'm not sure. I kind of want to teach in a high school, coach basketball. I think that would be cool. Or maybe work for the Forest Service, checking on the wild animals and stuff. The hawks, bighorn sheep." I could feel him smiling on top of my head, my hair shifting to make room.

"That would be cool," I said.

"I have no idea what that takes. Do you?"

"Nope. But I bet it's easy to find out." I sighed a deep, contented sigh. "Manny Cruz, wild animal protector."

"That's me." He squeezed me tight. "You're my first charge."

"Ha." I smacked him. We settled back, content to be in each other's arms.

On Monday, I saw Manny chatting with a few girls outside the front door. What would it be like to walk up to him and have him put his arms around me in front of them? To see their expressions when he kissed me?

But I didn't. I couldn't. We'd had our completely-together-two-nights last week, with polite-but-distant electrically charged days at school. Neither of us had ever said anything about it; we had just done it that way. Not consciously, but automatically, as if our subconscious knew that what we had was special, not to be tainted by outside elements, and directed us accordingly.

As I got closer, he caught my eye and held my gaze for a moment, sending every kind of feeling my way. My face grew warm, almost as if I'd been kissed.

I looked away, smiling.

I didn't really want those looks, the attention. I just wanted him.

And I had him, whether anyone else knew it or not.

I smacked the wall happily as I stepped inside. I *had* him. I had Manny Cruz.

And it was time to file a field report.

24

I picked up Christy about an hour after I'd gotten home from school and we grabbed some coffee before driving to a nearby park. Since it was the beginning of December, the park was deserted, except for a few geese pecking at the hard ground around a frosted pond.

"What's this all about?" she asked as we sat in the car, sipping.

"I have some bad news," I said. "And I thought this would be a good place to share it."

She looked stricken, so I said quickly, "No, not bad bad. Just funny bad."

"Oh." She still didn't looked convinced. "What is it?"

"I think your vibe detector is broken."

She looked confused, then narrowed her eyes, suspicious. "What are you saying, Kat?"

I grinned. "Put your coffee cup down."

She did, her face expectant.

I told her everything. The first kiss on the trail. The talking.

The two nights in a row of "Spanish" lessons. The e-mails and IM'ing.

She screamed and threw her hands in the air, drumming her feet on the floor. Rolling down her window, she shouted, "Kat Flynn is going out with Manny Cruz! Wahooooo!" She turned to me, trying for an awkward hug between the bucket seats. "This is amazing! I can't believe it!" Then she rolled up her window. "And I can't believe how cold it is! Why in the world did you bring me *here* to tell me your great news?"

I laughed. "Are you saying you don't know why I brought you, Christy Scream-and-Jump-Up-and-Down Buchanan, to an empty park to tell you I think I'm going out with Manny and we don't want everyone to know?"

She laughed, too. "Got it." Then she shoved me playfully. "Are you freaking out or what?" She started bouncing in her seat. "Omigod, omigod. You and Manny Cruz. You, Kat Flynn. And Manny Cruz. Finally." She squealed and smacked her hands on the dashboard. "So let's figure out where this is going and how serious he really is." She took a sip of her coffee. "I may need a completely separate notebook for this." I could see her mind clicking away with questions and possibilities, analysis and predictions.

I sighed deeply as I backed the car out and headed for the road. Christy Buchanan was my best friend. She knew I liked sleeping on my side with my hands tucked under my cheek. She knew I could run a seven-minute mile and that my body fat percentage was 19 percent. She knew that when Eddie Bowen chased me on the playground in fourth grade it was not because he liked me but because I'd seen him putting a note with candy hearts in Bonnie Sebring's desk and he wanted to kill me so I wouldn't tell anyone it was him.

But she didn't know some things. Like that I cared what Libby Giles thought of me. Like even though most times I didn't mind being tall, sometimes I hated it. And like why hashing over every detail about Manny would ruin it, make it less special, take it away from being something that belonged to us to something that belonged to everyone else.

I wished my best friend would just know that already, without me having to tell her.

I stopped at the entrance to the park, then pulled into traffic. "Can we not dissect it, Chris? It's—well, it's only been a few days. And I want it to be something special between us, you know? Not analyze every little thing." I glanced at her. "Okay?"

"That's very Kat Flynn," Christy said, smiling. "I can respect that." Leaning back, she crossed her arms. "I love the idea of a secret relationship. It's so romantic." She let out another Christy-squeal, then raised her hands and wiggled her butt.

"Do you have to go to the bathroom?"

She pretended to pout. "Don't you recognize a victory dance when you see it?"

"Is that what that is?"

She smacked me. "Manny likes Kat. Kat likes Manny. Yeah!"

I laughed. She might not understand why I didn't want to talk about Manny nonstop, but Christy Buchanan did know how to celebrate good news.

At the next stoplight, I joined her with a butt wiggle of my own.

Wednesday night, instead of tutoring, Manny and I went to a movie. We drove fifteen miles to a dollar theater and didn't see any of the movie because we were all over each other. By day an invisible freak, by night (or darkened movie theater), Make-Out Queen.

"Didn't you love the part when—" Manny said when we came out.

"Yeah," I said. "But my favorite part was—" And I kissed him. Me. Kat Flynn. Making the first move with Manny Cruz after only a week of being *together* together. It was astonishing.

But I felt different. Alive. Brave. Confident. The world seemed happier, friendlier; the colors more vibrant. Manny Cruz liked me and wanted to be with me. It was a miracle to end all miracles. I felt transformed.

The next night I sat in the Womb, gazing at the mural. It felt like it needed something else, but I wasn't sure what. Was it the women? Was it the water or the mountains? I placed drop cloths in front of it, lined up my paints and brushes neatly on top—and sat back, closing my eyes.

"What are you doing?"

Lucy stood in the doorway, peering at me through the door beads. She was wearing a T-shirt we had tie-dyed together last summer. It was too big for her, hanging down to her knees.

"Just going to add some things to my mural."

"Can I watch?"

I nodded. "But I don't know if I'll do anything today. Right now I'm just waiting."

"For what?" She sat down next to me, crossing her legs.

"For new things to come to me."

"Oh." We sat quietly, side by side, our shifting and the occasional sigh the only sounds for a while. I looked at the woman standing on the side in the mural, then at the one caught in mid-dive. I picked up a brush, then put it down again.

"Nothing coming?"

I shook my head. "Nothing."

She was quiet for a moment. Then: "Jimmy Wannamaker tried to pull my pants down today, but I was wearing a belt."

"That was lucky."

"Everyone laughed anyway."

"I'm sorry, Luce." I put my arm around her and drew her close. "What happened next?"

"I told him he was a dork."

I laughed. "And what did he say?"

"He said, 'You're a dork,' and I said, 'Dork,' and then he said, 'Dork,' and then I said, 'Double dork,' and then he said I was a triple dork, and then the playground lady told us to stop the name-calling."

"I bet you feel pretty dorky."

Lucy tried to scowl but ended up laughing. "You always make me feel better, Kat."

I dropped my cheek on top of her head. "You make me feel better, too."

25

"Oh, God." Moan. Groan. "Oh my GOD!"

I could hear them—in spite of the series of walls and floors and doors that separated their room from mine—through the earbuds rolling the latest Nickelback tune over my eardrums. It was the second Friday of December and I was lying in bed, not sleeping for obvious reasons.

It would be one thing if I was listening to two people having wild, passionate, eyes-rolled-back-inside-their-heads sex. That would be interesting, something I'd definitely take off my headphones for. *Oh, God. Yes, yes, YES!*

But what I heard now was "No, no, NO!" Melanie was screaming and cussing like a madwoman, and Mr. Robertson was shouting along with her. They were in Serenity Space, just as I had predicted, and they were not even close to serene.

Fact of Life #312: Melanie Robertson + Karaoke + Strobe Lights + Spike High Heels = Chaotic

They had turned on the karaoke machine around six, just as my dad, Lucy, and I had sat down to pizza in the kitchen.

"What the hell is that?" Dad had said through a mouthful of cheese and crust.

"You shouldn't swear, Dad," Lucy said.

"I'm sorry," he said, swallowing the last of his pizza. "You're right."

"It's karaoke," I said, by way of explanation. "With strobe lights for effect."

My dad cringed. "Well, got to run."

"You can't abandon us to this," I said.

Melanie and her husband were singing oldie duets like "I Got You Babe" by Sonny and Cher and "You're the One That I Want" from the *Grease* sound track.

"I'm sorry, honey," my dad said. "If these guys I'm taking to the game weren't my clients, I'd stay."

"Liar."

He kissed us both on the head. "Maybe you should go help." He tilted his head in the direction of Serenity Space. "It sounds like they could use you."

"According to Melanie, I'm incompetent," I said. "Besides, I wasn't invited." No one was. She didn't want anyone besides Abra and her husband.

"You'll survive," he said. "I promise." And then he was gone.

Lucy and I had cringed at the table as Melanie went solo, belting out Janis Joplin's "Piece of My Heart," but replacing the word "heart" with "uterus," which didn't really work since it had three syllables and "heart" only had one. She kept emphasizing the line "But I'm gonna show you, baby, that a woman can be tough," and I could picture her, naked in her red spikes

150

with that large belly, pointing at her husband as she screeched. Yikes.

I pulled my covers over my head and adjusted the volume on my iPod to Deaf.

Bang, bang, bang. "KAT!" Bang. "Kat, Kat, KAT!"

"Come in!" I shouted, tossing the covers off.

The door clicked open. Lucy stood in rumpled pajamas, her dark hair matted above her ear where she'd been lying on it. Her eyes looked sunken.

"Can't sleep?" I motioned her to my bed.

"Mrs. Robertson sounds like she's going to die," Lucy said as she shuffled toward me.

"It hurts to have a baby." I clicked through my playlist, trying to find a song that might block out the screams better.

"Other women don't scream this loud," Lucy said.

"Other women go with the pain, not against it," I said. I didn't say what I was thinking—that some women just weren't the giving-birth-naturally type.

Lucy frowned and climbed up next to me, resting her head against my arm. "I'm not going to have any babies."

I smiled, then leaned across the bed, pulling a pair of large padded ear protectors from the night stand, the kind construction workers wear when they're using a jackhammer and air traffic controllers use on the tarmac. "Here, put these on. Then lay down and I'll rub your back."

"Where'd you get those?"

"Dad gave them to me after the first birth in Serenity Space kept me up."

Lucy put them on, stretching out on my bed. "I can't hear anything!" she shouted.

I lifted the edge of one of the protectors. "You don't have to shout," I said. "I can hear you just fine."

"Sorry," she murmured. She closed her eyes and I stroked her back. She looked so cute in the ear protectors, like she might begin waving in planes at any moment. After she fell asleep, I stretched out on the window seat, leaning my head against the cool glass.

The wailing woke me up. It was 12:14 a.m.

"Another piece of my uterus, baby!"

Karaoke again. But Melanie's voice sounded different. Strained. And not just from singing. Couldn't Abra hear that? Couldn't she hear the tears beneath the words?

I stood outside the door to Serenity Space, my hand raised to knock. But I couldn't. It was a sacred space, no matter how noisy. And even if I walked in, what would I do once I got inside? Ask Abra if she'd heard what I'd heard? Tell everyone to shut up and get Melanie to the hospital? What if I was wrong?

I turned away, pacing back and forth in the hall. Just when I had decided to go back to my room, the door to Serenity Space flew open and I looked into the red, sweaty face of Mr. Robertson. If I didn't know better, I'd think he was the one in labor.

"I—I—" He looked like he'd been caught stealing money or something. Wiping his face with his shirt, he took a breath and let it out.

"You look like you could use some air," I said.

He nodded gratefully.

I guided him down the hallway to the door leading to the backyard. We stepped outside, both gasping as the sharp winter air filled our mouths. Mr. Robertson sighed deeply and looked out across the yard.

"It's hard to watch someone you love in pain," I said softly, "even if you know the pain is getting your baby out."

"Abra's tried everything, but Melanie—" Mr. Robertson sighed heavily. "I don't know if I can go back in there."

I took a deep, cleansing breath. "Look," I said, "I know I'm only sixteen and your wife doesn't think I know anything, and she's pretty much right. But I do know that she doesn't have to prove anything to anyone and you should all have the birth experience that works for you and your baby. That's all that matters. You two and your baby."

Mr. Robertson seemed to snap out of it. "What are you saying?"

"I think she'd rather be in the hospital," I said quietly, "with you right next to her."

Mr. Robertson shook his head. "She keeps saying she can do it this way. That she wants to do it this way."

I crossed my arms against the cold, my eyes on the meditation garden, where a few dried tulip stalks poked out of crusted snow. "Maybe she just needs someone to tell her it's okay if she doesn't."

After Melanie and Mr. Robertson had driven off to the hospital, with Abra following in her car, I retreated to my room, where Lucy was snoring softly. I couldn't sleep, so I pulled out a pencil and drawing paper. I drew a picture of the Red Spikes family, complete with tiny red high heels on the baby's feet. I started to put a baby bottle in Melanie's hand, but something stopped me.

I erased her shirt and drew her breast, the baby's head turned, the mouth reaching for the nipple. I was surprised at how right it looked. I'd always imagined Melanie would use a bottle, couldn't be bothered with breast-feeding her baby.

But there she was on my page, happy and serene, no bottle in sight.

I got a thrill when I saw Manny's green Range Rover coming into the rec center parking lot late Sunday afternoon after my workout. Manny Cruz was picking me up. It was remarkable.

"Hey," he said as I climbed in. He leaned over and we kissed deeply, his hand squeezing my thigh. My body tingled, and I wrapped both my arms around his neck. When we pulled away, I sighed.

"These bucket seats suck," I said.

"I know," Manny said. "That's why we have a backseat."

I laughed.

"So how's it going with Spikes and Spikes Junior?" I had told him about Melanie's birth experience on the phone earlier and that they were staying in Serenity Space for a few days until they got the all clear to go back to their house. I hadn't told him how I'd talked to Mr. Robertson. I wasn't sure why. I guess I just wanted it to be their thing.

"Fine," I said. "She's been giving us orders, but she also turned out to be a nice person." And I had to admit that Spikes Junior—Ann Louise—was adorable.

"I'm sure the drugs helped."

I laughed. "Yeah. I heard she calmed right down and was laughing and joking and kept kissing her husband at the hospital. And the Beatles were playing when the baby was born." So she'd gotten that, at least.

He smiled. "How's your mom?" Manny never called her Abra, even though that's the only way I referred to her. He always said "your mom," like he was trying to impose a new identity on her.

I shrugged, remembering the brief conversation Abra and I had had in the kitchen after she had gotten back from the hospital.

"Well," Abra had said as she dropped her bag against the wall. "That was interesting."

I'd busied myself filling up my glass with ice. I had finished the birth drawing and still couldn't sleep, so I'd come downstairs. It was 4:00 a.m.

"Mr. Robertson had gone out to get some air, and when he came back, he was like a new person," Abra said, getting her own glass from the cupboard. "He told Mel she was a wonderful, amazing woman and what mattered was her and the baby and who cares what anyone else thought—if a hospital was where she wanted to be, that's where she should be."

"Uh-huh," I said, shifting my glass from the ice dispenser to the waterspout in the door of the fridge.

"It was almost like someone had convinced him." She stopped, and I could feel her eyes on me.

I stepped back as she filled her own glass, moving to the other side of the island so we had it between us. "Well, I'm glad everyone is okay."

"Yes," Abra said. "Everyone is doing very well." She took a sip of water. "I just wish we'd talked about the hospital again when she went into labor. I brought it up once, and she seemed so determined—I just didn't see it." Her voice trailed off and she drank more water. "Well, all's well that ends well, as they say." She put her glass on the counter and turned around. "I'm going

155

to bed, and you should do the same." She paused. "Why are you up, anyway?"

I shrugged. "The karaoke woke me up and I couldn't go back to sleep."

She'd nodded. "I guess we let that go on a little too long."

"A little," I'd said.

"Kat?" Manny's voice cut through the memory. "I asked how your mom was."

"Sorry," I said, looking out the car window. "Abra's good. Tired but good. You know, happy, healthy parents and baby and all that." But I knew she was disappointed, too. Not about Melanie going to the hospital, but about not seeing that was what Melanie really wanted. It was so weird that she hadn't seen that. And I had.

"Well, it's a good thing her husband talked to her about the hospital," Manny said. "It sounds like that was the right way to go." He smiled as he reached over and squeezed my hand.

When we got to our secluded park spot, we started with small coffee-laced kisses, gentle and exploring. We moved to the backseat as the kisses became more urgent, our mouths wider, our tongues probing deeper, our breath faster. I felt like I'd been shot into outer space, orbiting around the farthest planet, so far from Earth I didn't think I'd ever come back.

But then I did. Because Manny's hand slid out from behind my neck and rested on the outside of my shirt, pressing gently into my stomach. I held my breath. *Not my barely-B's. Please, no. That will ruin everything.*

He moved around to my back, his fingers slipping under my shirt to stroke my skin. As his hand moved again to my stomach, I flinched. He pulled away slowly.

"I wasn't going anywhere, I promise," he said. "I just wanted to touch your stomach."

"Okay." I was grateful he hadn't just headed on up, hoping to scale mountains and finding only foothills.

"We won't do anything you don't want to do."

I nodded. He brought his hand out from under my shirt, tucking the ends tenderly into my jeans, like he was taking care of a child.

"I want you to," I said, "but . . ."

"But what?"

I dropped my eyes. "They're so small." My cheeks flamed.

Manny smiled, brushing my hair away from my face. "May I?"

I bit my lip. Then I nodded, still not looking at him. As his hand moved gently beneath my shirt, unhooking my bra with one hand (why was he so good at that? I didn't want to think about it), I closed my eyes. My shoulders tensed as his hand found its way to one of my breasts. He cupped it gently and leaned forward, his mouth by my ear.

"It's a perfect fit," he whispered.

I smiled, fighting the tears that had suddenly sprung to my eyes. Maybe he was just saying that, maybe it was a way to get me to keep going. I don't know. But he seemed to mean it, and it did seem as if my breast was made just for his hand. It felt warm and safe there, and when his thumb brushed over my nipple, I felt it all the way down to my toes. We kissed, and after a few minutes I felt brave enough to tug his shirt up, rubbing my hand over his bare chest. I felt the smoothness between his nipples, the softness of the few hairs lying against his skin. I pressed my palm over his heart, feeling the steady beat. He wrapped his arms around me and pulled me close. I kept my hand where it was, laying my head over my hand to hear his heart beat. We stayed that way for a long time, not noticing the cold, the dark, or the time passing outside the window.

26

Fact of Life #528: One touch can be electrifying and connecting at the same time.

I can't even write about it. Too amazing. And no way am I drawing a picture.

At school on Monday, nothing had changed.

Except me.

I could still feel Manny's heartbeat under my palm, my breast cupped in his hand. I could feel us sitting there together, the only people on the planet, comfortable in each other's company, not feeling compelled to say anything to fill the silence. Happy to just be. Together.

I remember feeling that I wanted to somehow climb inside of him or have him climb inside of me because we were so close to being one person. I could see now why people had sex. Why they wanted to.

I was still feeling great when I headed down the hall to AP English, barely aware of people running into me and throwing me off balance. I passed Manny in the hall, and he grinned wide. I smiled back as he was swept away in the mass of people hurrying to class.

In Spanish he didn't say anything, but I could feel him behind me, the air between us shivering with energy. When I turned to pass his quiz back to him, our fingers touched and my heart skipped. We both smiled and turned away, knowing everything in that brief moment. After class, I sent Christy a text:

```
omg I'm so in luv Help!
WAT HAPPENED??? From: HatGirl Cell, 10:55 am
Just—he's AMAZING
r u going 2 . . . From: HatGirl Cell, 10:56 am
NO! But—
But??? From: HatGirl Cell, 10:56 am
I no it would b amazing
(Squeal!) Just b careful HatGirl Cell, 10:57 am
No worries I will
Luv u From: HatGirl Cell, 10:56 am
Luv u 2
```

After school, I literally ran into Mitch Lowry. The first December snow had melted, and I was about to go out the door to the school track for a run when I remembered I'd left my water bottle in my locker. I turned just before pushing open the door and ran smack into Mitch.

"Shoot! I'm sorry."

"No big," he said. He shrugged on his jacket and looked at me. His eyes roamed over my body, and I could suddenly see what he saw—kinky hair pulled hastily back in a band; my barely-B's pushing out feebly under my sports bra, which he could see because I hadn't zipped my jacket. He continued down to my thin but rock-hard legs in running pants, my feet tucked snugly into my RYKÄs.

"What are you looking at?"

He smiled. "You," he said. "Kat Flynn."

"Whatever."

He laughed. It was a warm, amused laugh. I couldn't help smiling.

He nodded. "Yeah," he said, almost to himself, "I can see it."

I furrowed my brow. "See what?" I said, imagining something hideous. "Is there something stuck in my teeth?" I rubbed my nose to check for stray boogers. "You can tell me. I want to know." Unlike Libby.

He laughed again. "No. You're fine. It's nothing."

But he'd seen something. He'd said he had.

"You like Spanish?"

I was confused. "You mean the class?"

He nodded.

"It's okay. Señora García-Smith is cool." Maybe he wanted to take it next semester. No, that would be stupid. He was a senior. One semester wouldn't do anything for him in college.

"So you like the teacher in that class, huh?"

I got a funny feeling in my stomach.

"Hey, Lowry!" One of the basketball players was standing at the end of the hall. "You coming or what?"

Mitch waved back. "Yeah. But I think I dropped my stopwatch on the track."

I breathed out, grateful for the change in topic. "I can look for it," I said. "I'm going out there anyway."

"Really?" Mitch said. "That would be great. If you find it, find me. My locker's 348." He raised his eyebrows. "But you probably knew that already."

"Arrogant prick."

He smiled. "Smart-ass."

He headed down the hall, toward his friend. As I watched, Mitch's hand came up behind his back, forming a perfect thumbs-up. I wondered what it meant. Was it a "yeah, I know your secret" thumbs-up or a "thank you for looking for my stopwatch" thumbs-up?

I had no idea. And at that moment I didn't care, because it occurred to me that he knew I'd watch him walk away and would see the thumbs-up.

I smiled. Arrogant prick.

I found Mitch's stopwatch about a quarter of the way around the track, half hidden in the brown grass in the middle. Besides having a few dirt traces, it looked like it was in good shape. I cleaned it up and tucked it into my pocket.

As I turned down the jock-lock hall the next day, the noise rose. Mitch was leaning against his locker, spinning a basketball on his finger. I could see Manny, laughing and slapping someone on the back. I shifted my eyes to Mitch and pulled the stopwatch out of my pocket. "Here," I said. "I cleaned it up a little. It works fine." I felt curious eyes on me but didn't look up.

"Thanks," Mitch said, slipping the stopwatch into his pocket.

"Hi," I said to Manny.

"Hey," he said.

It was enough to carry me back to my own galaxy.

• • •

Diane sat on the couch in the Gathering Place that afternoon while I straightened the bookcase. She leaned back and crossed her arms over her chest, resting them over her slightly swelling belly. She glanced out the window. "Sometimes I get scared."

I stopped rearranging the books and looked up. "Of labor?" I asked. "Being a mother? Losing your freedom?"

"All three." She cocked her head at me. "See? This is why we want you at our birth."

I shrugged. "I learned from the best."

"Abra sure is great," she said, leaning back.

"Why, thank you." Abra smiled as she stepped inside. She leaned down to give Diane a hug. "You look amazing."

Abra walked over to the counter to check Diane's chart. I noticed that Diane's ankles were a little swollen. Grabbing the ottoman that was pushed against the wall, I set it in front of her and helped her put her legs up.

"Thanks, Kat." She adjusted herself. Then she sat back, sighing. "I'm starving," she said. "I'm always starving."

"At least your morning sickness is gone," I said, handing her a nutrition bar.

She smiled, ripping off the wrapper. "This is just what I needed."

I poured her a glass of water and set it on the table beside her.

"If you keep treating me like this," Diane said, "I might never leave."

"Stay as long as you want," I said. "We've got chocolate."

Diane laughed.

As I stepped into the reception area, I heard her say, "Kat's quite the assistant."

163

"She's finding her way," Abra said.

I bristled. Finding my way? What the heck did that mean? I responded to Diane's needs without being asked. I was even folding the blanket Abra's way—boom, boom, boom. And what about getting Melanie to the hospital, where she belonged? Of course, Abra didn't know it was me, but still.

Fact of Life #129: Some people put you where they want you to be, not where you actually are.

I pulled out my books and started my homework.

27

The next morning, I was sitting in my car in the school parking lot, taking a few quiet moments before facing the hordes.

Tap, tap, tap.

Mitch Lowry's face was only inches from my own, with the thin pane of glass that was my car window separating us. He made a circling motion with his hand.

I rolled down my window. "What's up?"

"Not here," he said. "Meet me over there." He pointed to a stand of pine trees next to the parking lot. The administration had threatened to cut them down because kids would go there to make out or, if they were fast and brave enough, do even more. But environment-minded parents and students put a stop to the chop, so the school added some strategically placed boulders, making it difficult to get comfortable or hidden enough for any sort of extracurricular activity.

Okay. Mitch Lowry wanted to meet me in the grove. Cue the *Twilight Zone* theme music. I opened my door, curiosity getting the better of me.

"Why all the secrecy?" I asked when I joined him in the trees.

"I don't want her to see me." He shuffled his feet, peering out between the branches at the cars.

This was weird. I glanced at my watch. "Bell rings in five minutes."

He nodded. "Libby is pissing me off, but I still want her."

I waited for more. It didn't come. "And you're telling me this because . . ."

Mitch shrugged. "I don't know. I need to talk to someone, and Cruz is sick of hearing about it."

"But why me?"

He laughed. "You give it right back to me. You're different from other girls." Then he looked at me. "And you're *friends* with Cruz, so that counts for something."

The way he said *"friends"* made me think he knew we were more than that.

"You guys want to keep it private, that's your business," Mitch said, peering through the branches. "The thing is, I don't have a lot of friends who are girls. I need, like, the female perspective."

You could have knocked me over with a pacifier. First because Mitch Lowry knew about Manny and me and didn't seem to think it was a big deal, and second because he actually thought I had a female perspective on relationships.

He turned around and leaned against one of the boulders, crossing his arms over his chest. "You ever like someone and have them dump you and not be able to get over them because you knew it was right, and they were freaking out for some reason they won't talk about but you know they'll eventually come around to see they made a mistake?"

I furrowed my brow, trying to follow everything he'd said. "Not exactly."

"Cruz says I should move on, but I can't." He turned back to the parking lot. "There's just something about her."

I peered out through the branches. Yeah, a couple of somethings. But I didn't say it out loud. Libby was next to her car, talking to two girls, who puffed away on cigarettes. Libby held an unlit cigarette between her fingers, waving it around as she talked. Too busy yapping it up to even light the darn thing. Laughing, she put one foot up on the bumper and placed an elbow on her knee. She ran her fingers through her hair, then tossed it over her shoulder. Mitch sighed beside me.

"You may not have noticed this," I said. "But I'm not exactly a relationship expert."

"I know."

That stung a bit. "So you're not looking for advice?"

"Not really," he said. "More just some clue as to what the fuck is going on in her head. I mean, one minute we're all into each other; the next minute she's kicking me out of her car and out of her life."

"Girls can be . . . moody," I said. That was pretty safe.

"No shit." Mitch shook his head. "I just don't understand why."

"Did you ask her?"

"I tried. She just kept telling me to get out. At the end, she was practically yelling it. Now she just ignores me." He pushed his hair out of his eyes, squinting at Libby. "I don't get it. All I did was—" He stopped. "Never mind."

We both looked back toward Libby, who was still laughing with her friends. I wished I could say something brilliant and insightful. Abra would say something brilliant and insightful. She'd know just the right thing to make Mitch feel warm and loved and on his way to being a well-adjusted male in our society.

"I'm sorry," I said. "I have no idea what's going on in Libby's mind. I don't think anyone does, including Libby."

Got a smile out of him with that. But his eyes were still on Libby.

The bell rang. He didn't move. Neither did I. I wasn't sure why not. I didn't like to be late and wasn't ever late. But it didn't feel right to just leave if he wasn't.

"Maybe her mom finally won." Mitch spoke in a low voice, as if he were talking to himself. "Get rid of the guy, he'll hold you back." He scowled and glanced at me. "I wasn't part of the Rosemary Giles Perfect Plan for Her Daughter. Got to get rid of everything that isn't part of the Perfect Plan." He blinked and looked through the branches. Libby was heading in with her friends. "But I can't believe she'd go along with it."

I glanced at him, then back at Libby. Did the Queen actually have an Empress above her, calling the shots? It didn't seem possible. Libby was so confident, always doing what she wanted, getting everything and everyone she wanted. I found it hard to believe Mrs. Giles didn't give her everything she wanted, too.

"She's never gone back to a guy after they've broken up," Mitch said. "Did you know that?"

I thought of Christy's field report. How she was so sure about Libby and Mitch's breakup. "They're over. Finished. *Fini,*" she'd said.

"People can change." I avoided his eyes, keeping mine on Libby.

He squinted out at Libby. "I'm counting on it."

28

That Saturday I came out of the rec center, crunching over crusty snow. Manny was sitting in his car right out front, the engine running. Right on time.

"Where are we going?" I asked, tossing my duffle into the backseat.

"You'll see." He grinned mischievously as we pulled out of the parking lot. "So what's the latest with the tri?"

"Not much right now," I said. "Just trying to stay in shape. July seems so far away."

"It'll be here like that," Manny said, snapping his fingers. "And you'll do great."

After we'd pulled into the parking lot at the Botanic Gardens several minutes later, Manny lifted a cooler out of the trunk. He'd brought lunch, too. Very cool. Well, I had a surprise or two of my own. And I couldn't wait to show him.

We walked toward the entrance and I wrapped my jacket tighter around me. "Are they even open?"

"They're open all year round," Manny said. "My mom loves this place. She comes, like, twice a month."

"Isn't everything dead?"

"Sleeping," he said.

After we entered the main gate, we headed through the Children's Secret Path, stopping halfway down to kiss. Then Manny grabbed my hand and we walked through some bushes onto the main path. We crossed over a small stream and entered the Romantic Gardens.

"Wow," I said. I'd never been there in the winter before. It was beautiful.

Manny pulled me into one of the white gazebos and we kissed again. Then he squeezed my breast through my jacket and made a honking noise. I cracked up. How amazing to be so comfortable with his touch. And I never thought that stuff could be funny. But with Manny, everything was fun.

"This is so cool," I said, looking around the Gardens. "How did you find out about it?"

"My sisters used to drag me here when they were meeting their boyfriends and had to babysit me. They'd make me go over by the pond while they got busy in here." He smiled. "I'd watch the tadpoles and fish and pretend I was catching them with my little fishing pole." He kissed me again. "Little did I know they were cluing me in on a great date spot."

"So you bring all of your dates here."

Manny laughed and wrapped his arms around me. "Only the best ones."

I wanted to ask him how many bests he'd had, but I didn't want to ruin the moment. I leaned back against him. "So what do you have in that cooler? I'm starved."

"That's another thing I like about you," he said, leaning over to flip open the cooler lid. "You eat."

I snorted.

"You know how girls can be," Manny said. "Libby eats, like, three pieces of lettuce and some fruit." He held out a sandwich. "Chicken salad."

"Thanks." I took it from him, trying to ignore the fact that he was so familiar with Libby's eating habits. "Mitch is still totally in love with her," I said to change the subject.

Manny rolled his eyes. "I just wish she'd talk to him. She tells me all this stuff when she should be telling him. Girls."

He nudged me and I smiled before pulling a large envelope and a small box out of my backpack. "I have something for you."

"What's this?" He opened the envelope and pulled out a packet of information on what he'd need to study in college to become a ranger.

"Whoa," he said. "This is awesome. Where did you get it all?"

"I just did some research online," I said. "Some of it I sent away for."

He flipped through the pages. "Wow. I can't wait to go through it."

"You can do that later," I said. "Open the box."

He lifted the lid and pulled out a tiny ranger's hat. "Cool." He put it on top of his head. "How do I look?"

"Like you're ready to care for wild animals."

He growled at me and I growled back, and soon we were wrestling on the cold cement. Then my arms were around him and his were around me and we were kissing hard and deep and everything around us disappeared.

The Monday before winter break, I sat with Christy and Glen as usual. I'd just bitten into my sandwich when Mitch walked by. He stopped, rapped his knuckles on the table, and without looking at me said, "Kat Flynn. New Year's Eve party, 878

Fairway Lane, nine o'clock or whenever." He waved his hand at Christy and Glen, who were staring at Mitch like he was a rock star or something, which I guess, in the world of high school social structure, he kind of was. "They can come, too." His eyes remained fixed on something or someone across the cafeteria.

"What are you not looking at, Lowry?" I asked.

Mitch's eyes flicked briefly in my direction, a smile playing at the corner of his lips. "You," he said. "I'm not looking at you."

"Arrogant prick."

"Smart-ass."

Then he was gone. I took another bite of my sandwich, chewing slowly. Christy and Glen turned their heads at the same time and stared at me.

"Did Mitch Lowry just invite us to his New Year's Eve party?" Christy asked, tugging at her fedora.

"Yep." I took a swig of water.

"This rocks," Glen said.

"Why?" Christy asked me. "And what was all that stuff about not looking and the prick/smart-ass thing?"

I shrugged. "Just a joke."

Christy pulled out her field notebook, flipping to a clean page. "Since when do you have inside jokes with Mitch Lowry?"

"It's just the one," I said. "And it's about run its course."

Christy scribbled, then closed her notebook. "What are we going to wear?"

I shrugged again. "Plenty of time to decide."

"This so rocks," Glen said.

I looked at him. His face was pink, his eyes bright. He couldn't seem to stop moving his hands around his lunch tray.

I'd never seen him so excited. In fact, he was so excited, he hadn't checked on Christy's breasts. Not once.

I wasn't sure how I felt. Could I go through a whole night with Manny just across the room and act like I didn't want to jump his bones, watching other girls flirt with him and not being able to do it myself?

"It'll be fun," Christy said, as if reading my mind. Her foot nudged mine under the table.

I nodded. *Just go with the flow, Flynn. That's what you do best.*

29

The next afternoon I was at the Midwifery, catching up on some filing. Abra had just finished with her last appointment and dropped the file on my desk.

"Let's talk about Diane's invitation to assist at her birth," she said, picking up some stray toys and placing them back in the box. Translation: Abra would talk and I would listen.

She sat down with a doll in her lap, fixing its hair. "I thought you said no, but Diane seems to think you're still thinking about it."

I *was* still thinking about it, but suddenly I wanted to say yes, just because.

Abra gave the doll a final pat and placed her in the toy box. "I have to be honest, Katima. I'm not sure I can provide the best birth experience with you there."

I knew she wanted me to ask why, but I didn't say anything, just looked at her.

She took a deep breath and let it out. "You've got some good instincts, but you don't have any experience."

I didn't point out that Diane was giving me a chance to get some.

"I think if we take some time to review my books, and maybe see if we can get you into a workshop, then we could start thinking about you assisting at some of the births."

It occurred to me that I hadn't read Abra's doula and midwifery notebook for a while. I didn't even know where it was. When did that happen?

Abra stood up, smoothing her pants with her hands. "How does that sound?" She smiled the smile she used on the women who came to see her, the one that always seemed to reassure them.

I didn't feel reassured at all.

"I don't want to make you uncomfortable," I said.

"It's not about me, Katima," she said. "It's about making sure we can provide the best birth experience possible."

"We" who? She'd just pushed me out of the equation. It *was* about her. Diane and Jeff really wanted me there, but she didn't. So that was that.

"Fine," I said, standing up and crossing in front of her to grab my coat. I needed to get out of there. I needed to see Manny, even if I was just *seeing* him and not actually being with him. "I've got things to do."

"Okay," she said, smiling again as if everything was fine and she hadn't just dissed me. "Will you call her and tell her, or shall I?"

"I will," I said through clenched teeth, before heading out the door to the school.

I pulled into the school parking lot at 4:30. The team still had another half hour of basketball practice. I leaned against the seat, breathing in, then out, slowly calming myself. Then I sat up and looked around. Libby's car was a few rows away. I wondered idly what she was doing here after school. Maybe Mitch had worn her down and she was watching him at practice.

I flipped down the visor and checked my face in the mirror. Pretty clean. I brushed my fingers through my hair, fluffing my bangs. Teeth? Not bad. Breath? I reached for my Altoids.

5:01. They were probably showering now. I took some breaths and called Diane. She wasn't there, so I did the chicken thing and left her a voice-mail about not assisting. I knew we'd talk about it later.

5:15. Manny walked out of the building with Libby and a few other players. Manny and Libby were talking to each other, breaking off from the group. Had Libby come to watch *Manny* practice? They stopped when they reached her Escape and continued their conversation. Libby was facing the school, Manny the rest of the parking lot, leaning slightly against her car door. Every few seconds, she would punctuate something she said with a poke in Manny's chest or a squeeze to his arm. My stomach flipped, and I took a deep breath. *Easy, Kat. He can talk to anyone he wants. He can accept jabs to his awesome chest from one of the most beautiful girls in the school. You don't own him.*

And it really wasn't her fault. As far as she knew, Manny Cruz was unattached and available. Biting my lip, I glanced toward the school. Mitch stepped out, dribbling his basketball as he talked to another player. He glanced up, caught sight of Libby, and stopped walking. But he kept dribbling the ball, slowly and deliberately—smack, smack, smack.

Manny turned and waved at Mitch.

Libby tugged at Manny's sleeve and giggled. Mitch's dribbling sped up. She peeked around Manny to look at Mitch. Then she pulled herself up and kissed Manny on the lips. He immediately pushed her away, saying something that looked like "Hey."

Wham. Mitch slammed the basketball into the pavement. It bounced up, flying past his outstretched hand and careening into the parking lot. It hit a rock and bounced crazily across the blacktop, heading straight for my car.

Without thinking, I opened my door and snatched the ball in mid-bounce. All eyes turned to look at me. Manny's face flashed surprise; then he looked away.

Silence. Except for the occasional car driving by. We all stayed in our places, frozen, waiting for someone to do something so we could do something.

Mitch took a few steps toward me. I sent him a perfect bounce pass. He caught it and nodded. Without looking at anyone, he started dribbling again. The bounces were sharp, snapping up to meet his hand with a definitive smack. He dribbled toward his truck, walking right past Libby and Manny as if they weren't there. Manny leaned forward to say something to Mitch, then stopped, his shoulders slumping.

Mitch got into his truck, revved the engine, and drove away. This seemed to be the signal for everyone else to move. And we did. Quickly. Each of us going in a different direction. I pulled out of the parking lot as fast as I could, ignoring the jingle that told me I had gotten a text message on my cell. The image of Libby kissing Manny made me want to scream.

When I stopped at a light, I picked up my phone and checked the text message:

`1 way k From: DaMan Cell, 5:24 pm`

I knew the kiss was a one-way. I'd seen how he'd reacted. But maybe he still liked it. Maybe he was remembering when they'd been together and was wishing he had kissed her back.

I stared at the message, my feelings going up and down and back and forth like Mitch's basketball. On the one hand, I was jealous of Libby for kissing Manny. On the other hand, I knew Manny hadn't kissed her back.

On the one foot, I knew Libby was just trying to make Mitch jealous, but on the other foot, did she have to do it with Manny?

A car behind me honked. I looked up and saw the light was green. Waving at the driver, I pulled through the intersection toward home. At the next light, I flipped my cell open.

U there?
Wassup? From: HatGirl Cell, 5:25 pm
LG is using MC to make ML jealous! She KISSED MC!
  He pushed her away but it's killing me
omg—talk to him From: HatGirl Cell, 5:26 pm
wat do I say?
tell him how u feel—then call me l8r! Gotta go Luv
  u From: HatGirl Cell, 5:26 pm
Luv u 2

The next night, Wednesday, Manny and I went out to celebrate the end of tutoring since our final exam had been that morning. He brought up what had happened in the parking lot right away.

"So you're cool with the un-kiss?" he asked. His face was open, ready to accept whatever I had to say. I started to tell him it nearly killed me, that seeing him with Libby or any other girl

178

was like a skewer in my gut. But I couldn't. It sounded too whiny, jealous girlfriend, and I didn't want that to be me.

"I'm cool," I said. How could I not be, snuggled next to him in the back of the Rover while Libby was who knows where?

After a long make-out session, I told him about the whole Abra/Diane birth thing.

"Why don't you just say you want to do it?"

"Because it's about Diane and Jeff," I said. "If Abra doesn't want me there and I'm there, it will affect their experience, and I want it to go well for them."

"You're too nice," Manny said, nuzzling my neck.

Yeah, maybe I am, I thought. *About a lot of things.*

Christy was not happy that I didn't tell Manny how I felt. We were heading down the hall before first period the next morning, two days away from winter break.

"I couldn't," I said. "You should have seen his face. He felt horrible, even though he hadn't done anything. I didn't want to be one of those annoying jealous girlfriends."

"It's not annoying to tell someone how you feel," Christy said.

"It's all good," I said. "He's good."

"Okay," Christy said as the bell rang. "It's your gig."

"I just want you to know," Diane said as she hung up her jacket that afternoon, "that Jeff and I are planning on more kids. So maybe next time you'll be ready."

"Absolutely," I said, wondering if Abra would let me by then. If I'd even be here. "So how are you feeling?"

"I've got lots of energy," she said. "It's great."

"Good," I said. "How's the baby's room coming along?"

179

"We've got all the furniture, but our artist broke her wrist ski-ing," Diane said. "I don't suppose you know anyone who does wall murals?"

I started. "Well, I—"

"Katima paints," Abra said.

I hadn't noticed her standing in the doorway of the Gathering Place. Hadn't even heard the door open.

"She did that one." Abra pointed to the BOP wall, the parade of animals and floats carrying the baby photos.

"Wow," Diane said, and I heard the admiration in her voice. "I didn't know that."

"I also did a mural in our meditation room at home."

"It's beautiful," Abra said. "You should come over and see it."

"I'd love to," Diane said. She looked from the BOP wall back to me. "Would you be interested in doing the baby's room? I can show you our design and the quote the artist gave us."

"You mean you'd pay me?"

Diane laughed. "Of course we'd pay you, Kat. Anna had quoted us a thousand dollars."

A thousand dollars? Did she say a thousand dollars? What the heck was I doing working at Abra's Midwifery for a few bucks over minimum wage when I could be getting big bucks for doing something like painting? Sure, I loved the Midwifery and I'd probably miss it, but *a thousand dollars?*

I took a breath. "Maybe you should see the other mural before you decide."

Diane smiled. "Spoken like a true professional." She pulled out her Palm Pilot. "What about tomorrow afternoon? What time do you get home from school?"

"I work out until about five." I was hoping to go out with

Manny later, but I didn't say that. What would Abra say if she knew I had not only tutored Marcus, Matty, Manny but was making out with him afterward? The thought made me smile.

"How about five-thirty?" Diane said. "Is that too soon after your workout?"

"Nope, that's fine."

It felt a little strange having an outsider in the Womb. It was my private space—no one but family and Christy had ever been inside—but it was nice, too. Because I knew Diane appreciated it.

I tried to see the mural through Diane's eyes—the waterfall, the woman diving, the woman onshore—I wondered how quickly she had identified the women as Abra and me.

"This is amazing," Diane said, shaking her head. She turned to me and held out her hand. "You're hired. One way or another, you'll be involved with this baby."

30

I never thought I would be the one dragging someone to the mall. But then again, I never thought I'd be buying a Christmas present for Manny Cruz. It was December 22 and I was frantic to find the perfect gift.

"Why did we get out of school so late this year?" I asked Christy as we started at one end of the mall.

"Why didn't you start shopping earlier?"

"I wasn't sure," I said. "About anything."

"And now you are?"

"No," I admitted, "but I want to get him something anyway."

"What about a shirt or a CD?" Christy said as we passed the throng of kids waiting to sit on Santa's lap under the big Christmas tree.

I rolled my eyes. Boring.

"Boxers?" she asked.

I wrinkled my nose. "I'm not buying him underwear."

"What about a poster? Software? A new iPod?"

"No, no, and no."

Christy pouted. "Why did you bring me if you weren't going to listen to my suggestions?"

"I'm waiting for an inspired suggestion," I said. "What did you get Glen?"

Christy blushed. "A shirt. But it was from Urban Outfitters. He loves that place."

"You're going to marry Glen. You can afford to get him something boring."

She stuck out her tongue at me.

I walked down the center of the mall, my eyes skimming the kiosks as we passed. Sunglasses, stuffed animals, stupid electronic gadgets. Then something caught my eye. Feathers.

"Hold on," I said, stopping in front of a small kiosk. Dreamcatchers dangled from the sides of one wall. I fingered one, letting my eyes drop to the shelf below. I sucked in my breath. Sitting back behind a series of leather dolls was a large pewter hawk. It clung to a pewter cliff, wings outstretched, about to take flight.

"You like the *halcón?*" I hadn't even noticed the woman sitting on a stool. She had wavy dark hair and skin like Manny's. She stepped around to my side.

"It's beautiful," I said.

She pulled it out from its hiding place and handed it to me. It was lighter than I'd imagined. I turned it over and checked the price. Way too much. My face must have given away my disappointment, because the woman smiled.

"It is for a gift, no?"

I nodded.

"¿Su novio?"

I blushed. *Dare I call Manny my boyfriend?* I nodded.

183

"I have just the thing." She went around to the other side and came back with a necklace. Dangling from the chain was a silver hawk in full flight.

"He can wear this all the time, no?" she said, holding it out to me. "And think of you. Not like a bird he might put on a shelf and not notice anymore."

I took the necklace and brought it close. The detail was exquisite, the chain heavy and masculine. I wanted to throw my arms around her and hug her.

"I'll take it," I said, reaching inside my purse.

"You didn't even check the price," Christy whispered as the woman rang up my purchase.

"I don't care how much it is," I said. "It's perfect."

Christmas Eve was perfect, too. Manny and I met at the rec center after we both dealt with a bunch of family festivities. We each had a coffee, so we carried those plus our packages on crusted snow to the bench at the start of the running trail.

"This is also to say thanks for helping me with Spanish," he said. "I never thought I'd get a B on the final."

"You're welcome," I said. "It was fun."

"Yeah," he said, raising his eyebrows mischievously. "It was." Then he pulled out a silver-wrapped box. "You first."

I shook the box, pretending to try to identify its contents. "An elliptical machine?" I asked. "You shouldn't have."

He laughed. "Yeah. You blow it up."

I tugged off the ribbon. Inside the box were two gifts. I picked up the one I knew was a book. I tore the paper off to reveal a triathlete book. Flipping through the pages, I grinned. "Wow, Manny. This is great." I loved that he knew how much the race meant to me.

He smiled. "Next one," he said, pointing.

The second one was narrow and heavy. Inside was a gold-plated ballpoint pen. It was sleek and shiny, and when I picked it up, its weight felt good and solid between my fingers.

"You didn't strike me as the jewelry/perfume type."

"I'm not," I said, loving that he knew that about me, too, without having to ask.

"Turn it over," he said.

He'd had it engraved: *KF: Take no prisoners.*

I laughed out loud. "Does this mean it's safe from abduction?"

"Absolutely."

"I love it," I said.

He wrapped his arm around me and gave me a frosty kiss.

"Now you." I jiggled my legs in the cold, watching as he tore the paper, my heart beating in anticipation. Would he love it as much as I thought he would? Maybe, like me, he wasn't the jewelry/cologne type, except for his earring. I bit my lip as he raised the lid.

"Wow." Manny lifted the chain out carefully, taking the hawk between his thumb and forefinger. "This is the coolest thing anyone has ever given me." He examined it in detail, running his finger over the smooth curves of the wings.

"It's *halcón* in Spanish," I whispered, leaning against his shoulder.

"Halcón," he repeated, holding it out. "Put it on?"

I pulled the chain around his neck, my cold fingers fumbling with the clasp. Finally I got it. I adjusted the hawk in front, where it sat cradled in the hollow of his neck.

Manny touched the hawk again. "Thank you. I'll never take it off."

"Good," I said. I would have said more, but his lips covered mine and I was gone.

Fact of Life #96: Writing too many facts of life about special experiences might jinx them.

The only thing I wrote in my journal was *M gave me a very special pen—engraving said "KF: Take no prisoners." LOVED the hawk necklace*. I still couldn't bring myself to write out his name, even though I knew no one would probably read my collection of facts.

I looked at the words. The pen had rolled smoothly over the paper, the ink line fine and clear. He knew I liked to draw and paint, but he didn't know about the journal. And yet maybe he did know, or had guessed. The idea made me love him all the more.

I kept rolling the pen over to read the engraving and smiling, loving that we had this fun thing—the pen-napping—that we shared. It was the perfect pen, and I sent Manny an e-mail about its perfectness.

I'm so glad you like it, he'd written back. *The hawk rox.*

Christmas and the day after were a letdown after the frenzy and excitement of Christmas Eve with Manny. Manny worked and had to help watch his sibs, so I thought I wasn't going to see him until Mitch's New Year's party. But then he sent a text as I was leaving Diane and Jeff's after working on the baby's mural, which had taken on a life of its own. The original artist had sketched an elaborate ocean scene, with lots of big sea creatures and plants. I'd chosen to do something a little more subtle, hiding creatures behind plants and coral so there would be surprises. I'd prepped the wall and had sketched out part of it in pencil, and was surprised at how excited I felt about doing it. And my excitement had nothing to do with the money I'd get at the end of the project. Just thinking about how much they would enjoy it, how their baby, when he or she was older, would find the hidden creatures—it just made me smile. And Manny's text made me smile, too.

> want 2 do somethin Fri? From: DaMan Cell, 7:25 pm
> Sure wat do u want 2 do?
> u name it From: DaMan Cell, 7:26 pm
> M&M?

That was code for "movie and make-out session."

> Yeah, baby From: DaMan Cell, 7:26 pm

Couldn't wait for that second *M* of M&M.

Since we were still on break, Lucy came to the Midwifery with me on Wednesday, helping clean the toys and organize the books. Around two o'clock, a young woman stepped into the reception area. I hopped up and went to the desk.

"I'm Hannah Bresnick," she said. "I have an appointment with Abra at two."

"Good to have you," I said with a smile. "Congratulations on your baby!"

"Thanks," she said, smiling in return.

"Since this is your first time, we need you to fill these out."

I handed her a clipboard with some forms attached to it. After getting her a glass of water, I returned to the computer to open up her file.

A few minutes later she handed the clipboard back to me. She was about to return to her seat when Abra stepped out of the Gathering Place. "You must be Hannah," she said, holding out a hand in greeting. "Congratulations on your pregnancy. We're so excited and honored to be a part of such a wonderful event in your life."

"Thank you," Hannah said.

"Why don't we get acquainted in here?" Abra gestured to the Gathering Place. "And how would you feel if Katima joined us a little later? She's assisted me during consultations and exams before and is quite capable around the Midwifery."

Hannah looked at me, then back at Abra. "That's great, but I think I'd prefer it was just you. No offense," she said to me.

"No worries," I said. I understood her reluctance. She didn't know me and I was only sixteen. That wasn't what bothered me. What bothered me was what Abra had said. Why had she added "around the Midwifery," like a qualifier? She's capable here but not everywhere—like at someone's birth.

Abra tried to catch my eye before they entered the Gathering Place, but I ignored her. I waited until the door was closed behind them, then joined Lucy at the bookcase to get the books back in order.

31

Buchanan Field Report:
Mitch Lowry's Rockin' New Year's
infamous around the school because:
- alcohol flows freely
- cops show up at least once
- someone always gets naked publicly

I wasn't particularly excited about experiencing any of these things, but if it meant I got to kiss Manny at midnight, I'd do it.

A few days earlier, we'd IM'ed:

DaMan: Cool that you're going to the party.
KatBrat: Christy and Glen, 2. They r v excited.
DaMan: Have fun! Meet me by my car at 11:30. Gotta surprise.

Part of me wished we could be together at the party. But it wasn't a big deal. Most people just mingled anyway, so we probably wouldn't have been together even if we were together. And I couldn't wait to see what Manny's New Year's surprise would be.

> KatBrat: Can't w8!
> DaMan: Hi 5.
> KatBrat: Hi 5.

Glen, who had morphed into Let-Loose Party Boy ever since the invitation, could not stop staring as we stood in the backyard of 878 Fairway Lane. The house belonged to Mitch's aunt and uncle, who had gone to Europe for the holidays. The place was set back on three acres, with the pool and hot tub in the back. Mitch had cranked up both, and they were full of half-dressed, half-drunk people.

"A pool party in January," Glen crowed. "How cool is that?"

"Freezing is more like it," I said. "Stupid, dumb, and asinine also come to mind. And it's still December for another"—I glanced down at my watch—"two and a half hours."

Steam rose in shimmering gray sheets, visible in the yellow glow of the lights scattered around the deck. I watched my breath curl out in front of me. I shivered involuntarily as a boy, naked from the waist up, emerged dripping from the pool. Music was blaring from several speakers, and some girls were dancing, laughing and squealing as boys splashed them with water.

I stepped in front of one of several gas heaters, sighing with relief as the first blast of hot air penetrated my jeans.

"I need a brewski," Glen said.

"Huh?"

Glen had never said "brewski" in his life, let alone had anything stronger than a Coke that I knew of. Christy laughed and squeezed his arm. She was excited, too. "I'll go with you."

"That's okay," Glen said. "Stay with Kat. I'll bring you both back one."

I was about to say no, then stopped myself. I wasn't a big drinker, but it was New Year's Eve.

Glen kissed Christy before swaggering off across the pool deck. Yes, Glen Martin was *swaggering*. He headed for the clump of people huddled in a circle like they were around a fire, roasting marshmallows. The almighty keg.

I engaged my sniper eye, scanning the crowd for Manny.

"There are a ton of people here," Christy said. "You think the cops will come?"

"Probably," I said. I just hoped Manny and I were gone by then.

Glen was back already, one plastic cup dangling between his teeth and one in each hand.

"Thanks," I said, taking a cup from him and sipping. The beer was bitter but I swallowed it, feeling my throat constrict a little. I took another sip. That one went down smoother.

"Hey, Manny." Glen was looking past me.

Christy raised her eyebrows at me and I turned around.

"Hey," Manny said to Glen. "You were at Chili's that one night, weren't you?"

Glen grinned, clearly pleased that Manny had remembered. "Glen Martin, junior. I wrestle and play chess." He took a gulp of beer. "But not at the same time."

Manny chuckled. "Hey, Christy." He turned to me. "Kat."

"Hey." I gulped nearly half my beer, feeling Christy's eyes on us. I had a sudden urge to kiss Manny right there in front of all those people. But something in the way he was standing, half turned from me, held me back. That and my inner chicken.

"Need a refill?" he asked us.

I shook my head. "Nah. But I could use some more heat. Is Mitch out of his mind, having a party outside in the middle of winter?"

"Hey, who're you saying is out of his mind?"

I turned to see Mitch standing next to Manny, a sloppy grin on his face.

"Well, Lowry, I guess that would be you." Manny clapped him on the shoulder, and the head on Mitch's beer foamed over the side like white lava.

"Easy there, Cruz. This is fresh off the keg." He brought the cup to his lips and sucked in the foam before gulping down half the beer. Then he looked at Manny. "You're not here to kiss my woman again, are you, Cruz?"

"You know it wasn't like that," Manny said.

Mitch turned his gaze toward the mass of people filling the backyard. "You seen her?"

"No, bud. I just got here." Manny squinted into the crowd. "She supposed to be here?"

"Everyone's supposed to be here." Mitch raised his cup. "Rock on, Angelini!" We turned in time to see another boy, completely naked, do a flip into the pool.

"Well, that was attractive," I said, looking down at my now-empty cup. I wondered how many beers Angelini had had. I was already feeling a slight buzz. Maybe I'd better cool it or I'd be one of those crazy naked-in-public people.

Mitch looked across the deck. "I'm going to see if I can find her." We watched him shuffle away, exchanging high fives as he wove through the throngs that got thicker, like vines in a jungle, the closer he got to the house.

"I'll get refills." Glen grabbed our empty cups.

"I'll go with you," Manny said, and they were gone.

"So I'm impressed with the way you two handle things," Christy said. "If I didn't know you were together, I wouldn't know you were together."

"Yeah," I said, hugging myself. "We're masters at playing it cool." But I was thinking how cool it was that my boyfriend was going to get beer refills with Christy's boyfriend. Maybe we'd double-date sometime. Maybe we'd—

My thoughts were interrupted by a familiar set of C cups making their way across the deck. And we have a winner, folks. Most Likely to Wear a String Bikini in Twenty-Degree Weather. The patches of cloth barely covered Libby's breasts as she hip-swayed toward the hot tub in her tight jeans, a towel tucked under one elbow.

Glen and Manny strode up then, clutching six beers.

"The line is getting longer," Glen said as we each took one. "You have to stock up."

I took a gulp of my beer and kept gulping. This one was going down even easier than the first, and I felt warmer, too. I glanced back at the Libby Show. She had reached the hot tub and was proceeding to unzip her jeans slowly as three boys in the tub watched, eyes riveted.

"Here we go," Manny said, sighing. "I wonder where Mitch went."

"Manny!" Libby's voice rose above the music. "Come over here for a minute." She was submerged up to her shoulders in the water, poking a lone toe out to wiggle it in his direction.

193

Manny raised a hand in greeting. I liked how he didn't go right over to her. I knew it was because of us, and my heart warmed.

"There's room for one more." Libby raised herself up just far enough for everyone to get a good view of her round mounds before she sank below again. I felt the hair on my arms tingle as she smiled at Manny. Where was a small electrical appliance when you needed it?

A movement caught my eye. Mitch was weaving unsteadily toward the hot tub, a beer bottle clutched in one fist. He smiled at Libby and sat down on the ledge of the hot tub.

"Hey, you." His voice was gentle, soft, barely audible above the music. I saw something like sadness cross her face; then it was gone.

She glanced up at Manny again. Mitch followed her gaze.

"Leave her alone," Mitch said. He placed an unsteady hand on her shoulder.

Manny frowned. "I didn't—"

"Just—go get a beer or something, Cruz."

Manny stiffened. "Later." He strode toward the house.

"Gotta pee," Glen said, taking off.

"Me, too." Christy hurried after Glen.

"I'll be there in a minute," I called after her. I watched Mitch pat Libby on the head.

"Be right back," Mitch said. He glanced at me and jerked his head in the direction of a group of three or four pine trees beyond the deck.

I pointed to myself. *You talking to* me?

He nodded and jerked his head again before standing up and walking toward the trees.

I sighed. What was with Mitch Lowry and meeting me in pine groves? I waited a minute before weaving my way in and around different clumps of people, crunching over snow on my way to the trees.

"Mitch?" The trees cast spiky shadows in the moonlight. I could barely see him.

Mitch wrapped his arms around himself. "I'm freaking out here, Flynn. Libby's trying to make me jealous. She keeps hanging all over Cruz at school and talking to him whenever I'm around. She acts like I'm not there."

How does it feel to be invisible?

"It's driving me crazy," he said. "And she knows it. And that drives me crazy." My eyes were getting accustomed to the dark. I saw Mitch bouncing from foot to foot, rubbing his arms.

"If she's trying to make you jealous," I said, "she still likes you." It seemed logical to me—though, as previously noted, I was not exactly a love expert.

"I know. So why can't she just admit it and get back together with me?" He put his hands under his armpits. "I keep trying to ask her, but she won't talk to me."

"Maybe you should have someone else talk to her."

"I did. She put the moves on him."

"Manny."

He nodded. "She told him she didn't need me anymore. What am I, a used condom?" He dropped to his knees and tossed his head back. Then he let out a howl that curled my earlobes.

I peered through the branches. A few heads turned in our direction.

When he was finished howling, he let out a deep sigh. "What should I do?"

"I don't know," I said. "But maybe you shouldn't howl quite so loud." I crossed my arms against the cold.

He took a deep breath and got up, snow, dried leaves, and twigs stuck to the knees of his jeans. "Right. Okay." He peered through the trees. Libby was holding court in the hot tub, several guys sitting around the edge, talking to her. "She's going away to college," he said. "To one of the brain trust schools."

"What about you?"

He laughed. "I'll go to whatever college will take me within a hundred miles of her."

Mitch Lowry wasn't giving up. I had to admire that. I did admire it. And I would have continued admiring it in the freezing pine grove if I didn't have to pee. Bad.

I punched him in the shoulder. "It'll work out, Mitch." I headed for the house.

When I came out of the bathroom, I couldn't find anyone I knew, so I wandered. Hearing laughter and the crack of a cue ball, I headed downstairs. Two couples were playing pool, moving their beer cups along the edge of the table as they shot.

"Nice one, Heines." The cue ball had jumped before spinning to the left, hitting nothing but bumper. "Scratch."

"Shit," said the guy I assumed was Heines. Everyone laughed. So did Heines as he pulled a solid from one of the mesh pockets and placed it on the table. I laughed, too. I wasn't sure why. Some part of me knew that it was not particularly funny, but I couldn't help laughing. The group glanced at me briefly as I sat down on the couch to watch.

I have no idea how long I sat there, or how the beer in my hand had gotten there. Two other sets of couples played after the first, all equally bad. When my beer was empty, I went upstairs, passing Glen and Christy in the hallway. He was talking to a brunette I didn't recognize. Christy was nodding slightly, sipping her beer. I'd never seen Glen talk to anyone else before, unless he had to. And here he was, talking to another *girl*. Martin was coming out of his shell.

"Where have you been?" Christy asked.

"Downstairs in the game room," I said. "Drunk people playing pool. Fascinating."

She laughed. "Are you going for another beer?"

"I don't know," I said. "I'm kind of feeling it." I was a little hazy around the edges, and it was not unpleasant. "I'm going to walk around."

I spotted Manny in a corner of the living room, talking to a guy I didn't recognize. The music was loud, and I felt my body start to sway without even meaning it to. I loved to dance, but I'd never done it in public before. Maybe it was the beer, but I suddenly didn't care who saw me. I closed my eyes and let the music move through me. Raising my arms over my head, I moved my hips, slowly at first, rotating in a circle. Then I just let loose, arms and hips and head twisting this way and that, totally in synch with the music. People moved back to give me room, some of them clapping encouragement.

"Go, Yoga Girl!"

The name didn't sound mean like it usually did, or maybe I'd just had one too many beers. On one twirl around I caught Manny's eye. He smiled slightly; then his eyes shifted over to the clock. It was eleven-thirty. He looked back at me and cocked his head toward the door. A tingle ran through me. Time to go.

I watched him say something to the guy next to him, his amazing face caught in the light from the lamp on the table next to him. Maybe I should do a Libby, hip-sway over and just kiss him. I could blame it on the beer. Sure. Why not? I twirled in place, then turned in his direction.

But he was already gone. I sighed. Probably a good thing. I would have embarrassed myself and him, and regretted it big-time.

I found Christy and Glen in the kitchen, listening to a drunk guy ramble on about his car.

"I'm heading out," I said. "Thanks for the ride here."

Christy elbowed me in the ribs. "Have fun."

Glen looked back and forth between us. "Is there something going on I don't know about?"

"Always," I said, patting him on the cheek.

32

Manny had champagne chilling in the back of the Range Rover. I caught his excitement as he grabbed my hand and grinned. Then we pulled into the familiar rec center parking lot.

"Are we going to ring in the new year on the smelly weight room mats?" I joked.

Manny laughed and jumped out. "Come on!" He grabbed a sleeping bag and I snagged the champagne and glasses. We raced to the side of the building near the fence and climbed up on the roof.

As we snuggled into the sleeping bag, we had just enough time for a quick swig of champagne before Manny looked at his watch. "Countdown."

We counted together: "Three, two, one—Happy New Year!" We threw our arms around each other and kissed. Fireworks went off and we watched as they illuminated the sky.

"Wow!" I exclaimed as another firework erupted. "How did you know about this?"

Manny smiled, clearly pleased with his surprise. "This is

where my family used to come to watch the fireworks. I've never brought anyone else here before."

I grinned.

We stayed until they were finished, cozy in a sleeping bag with a bottle of champagne between us. We made out and slipped hands in and out of various pieces of clothing and laughed a lot. When we came up for air, I just looked at him, his cheekbone visible in the lights from the building. He could have stayed at the party with all his friends. He could have kissed any girl he wanted. But he wanted to be with me, alone, on New Year's.

Amazing.

We pulled up in front of my house around one o'clock. It didn't look like my parents were home from their party yet. Lucy was at a sleepover, so the house was empty. I had been thinking of inviting Manny inside, but I wasn't feeling too good. We'd finished off the bottle of champagne and my body was hinting that maybe that hadn't been such a good idea.

I pushed open the car door and got out, sucking in cold air. Better. Manny came around to my side just as headlights swept across us. We both squinted in their direction. The car slowed, then pulled up on the sidewalk, barely missing the front bumper of Manny's Rover.

"Ooh." Libby's screech seemed amplified in the cold January night. She sashayed toward us, weaving slightly. She stumbled beside Manny, then squeezed his arms for support before jumping up to sit on the hood of his car. She started to lose her balance. "Whoopsie!"

Manny grabbed her arm to keep her from tumbling into the street. "What are you doing here?"

"Oh, you know, I was in the neighborhood." She waved a manicured hand in the air, her coat billowing behind her. She still had on her bikini top, one breast dangerously close to popping out. "You live here?" she asked me. "I live that way, that way"—I ducked as she waved her arms around—"and over that way." She leaned toward me. "I can't believe we're so close. We should be best friends." She swayed, then righted herself and looked at Manny. "What are *you* doing here?"

I waited, watching Manny.

Manny jerked his thumb at me. "Her ride took off without her."

I smiled at Libby, but inside I felt a little prick of . . . something. A buzzing around in the back of my brain where I couldn't quite catch it. I didn't know what I expected him to say, but I did know I didn't like being just a girl he had given a ride to.

Libby sighed. "Manny Cruz. Always the nice guy." She looked at me. "Did you thank him properly?" Then she raised her hand. "No. Don't tell me. I don't want to know."

"You must be freezing," Manny said, reaching out for her zipper.

Libby took this opportunity to throw her arms around him, pulling his face close so their noses practically touched.

"Why didn't we work out, Manny?" She pouted. "Can't we try again?"

Manny pried her arms from around his neck. "You should try again with Mitch."

"Mitch. God," Libby said. "What am I going to do with him?" She shook her head, blinking to focus. Her skin was pasty in the pale streetlights, her hair messed up, makeup smeared. And even though her flirting with Manny pissed me off, it was kind of pathetic. She seemed sort of . . . desperate.

"I still haven't given you your Christmas present," she said to Manny, unzipping her coat again. "Why don't you send your little passenger inside so I can give it to you"—she adjusted her swim top, capturing the breast about to make its escape—"in private."

"You probably should get home," Manny said.

My stomach started doing gymnastics. I rubbed my forehead.

"Hey, are you okay?" Manny looked at me with concern.

"I'm not feeling that great all of a sudden."

"She's fine," Libby said. "Let her go inside."

He frowned at me. "You don't drink much, do you?"

I shook my head.

"Take some deep breaths," Manny said. "Do you feel like you're going to hurl?"

"It comes and goes," I said, just as my stomach rollercoastered. "Um—"

"Shhh," Libby hissed at me, reaching for Manny. "Come on, Manny."

Uh-oh.

"Hey, maybe you should—" Manny started to say.

But it was too late. I turned and upchucked all over Libby's C's.

33

What a mess. Libby was shouting and Manny was running around and I was trying to find something to wipe off my mouth with. I ended up using my sleeve, which was pretty disgusting. But I felt better.

"I'm really sorry," I said.

"Get away from me!" Libby screamed.

"Maybe you should come inside." I had visions of the neighbors calling the police, reporting a stabbing or something with the way Libby was carrying on.

"No!" She flailed her hands like she was on fire and kept screaming.

Crap. What was I going to do?

I scowled at Manny. "Get her inside," I said. I went in ahead of them and cleaned myself up at the kitchen sink. I started a shower for Libby, then came back down to get her.

"Don't you go anywhere," she said to Manny as I led her upstairs. She seemed to calm down when she entered the bathroom. It was already starting to steam. The shower looked so inviting, I almost pushed her out of the way so I could get in instead. But I was a good host. And I *had* thrown up on her.

"Put your dirty clothes in here," I said, handing her a garbage bag. I set a stack of clothes on the counter. "They're all clean," I said. "I don't have a bra that will fit you, but you should be okay in this." I pointed to an oversized T-shirt.

She looked at my chest and smirked. "Yeah, well." She grabbed the clothes and closed the door behind her. I had a strange sense of unreality. It was almost like this was a movie and I was saying my lines, doing my stage business, because Manny Cruz and Libby Giles would never be in my house in my real life.

I headed downstairs, where Manny was looking out the front door, shifting from foot to foot, his hands in his pockets.

"I'm going to make some coffee," I said as I passed him. The fun and closeness of our time together at the rec center was gone and I didn't know why. It seemed like a long time ago—if it had happened at all.

"I'll help." He joined me in the kitchen. Soon we had a pot going, the warm aroma filling the house.

"Cabinet to the right of the sink," I said. He opened it and pulled down three coffee mugs. I pushed mine away and drank water. My stomach was still queasy, and the cold water felt good running down my raw throat. We sat at the table in uncomfortable silence. Manny kept looking around the kitchen, jiggling his leg.

"Will your parents be home soon?"

I looked at the clock. One-fifteen. "Probably." I could still hear the water running. "Do you think she passed out in there?" I had visions of Libby slumped in the tub, water streaming over her naked body, her glassy eyes staring up as one hand grasped the shower curtain in a last attempt to climb out before she fell back and hit her head on the porcelain.

"She always takes long showers," Manny said. "Once she's in, she doesn't like to get out."

I frowned. Too much information. Now I was having visions of the two of them wrapped in a warm, wet clutch, groping and fondling each other under pulsating shower spray.

"I never took a shower with her, if that's what you're thinking." He gave me a half smile but didn't reach over to squeeze my hand like he usually did when he was reassuring me.

"I wasn't thinking anything," I said.

"Liar."

"Okay, fine. But who wouldn't?"

"You're right," he said. "I'm sorry. It's just that once we were up at this cabin—"

I held up my hand.

"Okay," he said. "Sorry."

I moaned, holding my head in my hands. "Is she done yet?"

Manny cocked his head. "Yep."

The water had indeed stopped. I doubted there would be any hot water left for me. A few minutes later I heard my hair dryer fire up. Help yourself, Libby.

"Body Shop cruelty-free products." Libby stepped into the kitchen, weaving a little as she rubbed lotion into her arms. "Not bad." I couldn't believe it. Sweats and a T-shirt on me looked ratty and comfortable. On her, with her freshly washed-and-dried glow, they looked like a fashion statement. "Pathetic" and "desperate" were gone. Queen Libby was back.

"How do you feel?" Manny asked.

"Better, but the world is still tilting a little." She sipped the coffee as she looked around. "You know, this house is practically identical to mine," she said. "Her bedroom and mine? The same. Just—opposite." She shrugged. "Weird."

And why was this weird? The neighborhood only had about six different models. And why was she snooping in my room?

"Well, time to go," she said, after she finished the coffee. "How about being my DD, Manny?"

Manny stood up quickly, like he was glad to have an excuse to move. Libby snatched her coat from where I'd hung it over the banister and kept walking. She didn't even look back to see if Manny would agree to be her designated driver. She knew he would.

Always the nice guy.

I forced myself to get up and stand on the porch, shivering without my coat. They were standing next to Manny's car. Libby got on tiptoe to kiss him, but he turned and her lips brushed his cheek. He said something to her and she stepped back.

"But she barfed on me."

Manny murmured something else to her.

"Fine," Libby muttered. "Thanks for the shower," she called to me. "But don't ever barf on me again."

"You're welcome," I said.

I watched them drive away in the Range Rover, trying not to picture where her hands might be during the short ride to her house. I thought of following them on foot but felt too crappy. Instead, I cleaned up the kitchen and headed for the shower before popping a couple of Advils and falling into bed.

Fact of Life #403: Never, ever, again.

I was drummed awake by the consistent banging of the vacuum against my door. Groaning loudly, I rolled over, my head feeling like someone was squeezing it in a vise. I blinked several times, squinting at the clock: 4:00 p.m. I pushed myself halfway up. The room tilted and my stomach rolled. I fell back, knocking over my lamp with a flailing hand.

The vacuum stopped. There was a light tap on my door before it opened, and my dad peeked in. "Happy New Year!"

I covered my ears.

"Thank God you're finally awake," he said, stepping inside, one hand behind his back. "I've been vacuuming the same spot for twenty minutes. I think I sucked up all the carpet. It's bald."

I scowled. "Why couldn't you just let me sleep?" My voice was feeble, scratchy.

"Dinner at Uncle Tim's, remember? Family affair, lots of food, drink—" He stopped, looking at me with mock concern. "Hmm. You look a little green. Everything okay?"

He pulled his hand out from behind his back and held up a jar. It was about a quarter full of a yellowish-brown liquid, with blobs of grossness bobbing around in it. It looked like a science experiment gone bad.

"What is that?"

"A nice little gift *someone* left out on our sidewalk."

He scraped up my barf? I rolled over and closed my eyes, wrinkling my nose. "You're a sick, sick man."

"Not as sick as you."

I heard a thunk as Dad placed the jar on the floor.

"How much did you drink?"

The bed lurched slightly as he sat down. "Too much," I said, rubbing my head. "Obviously."

Dad sighed heavily. "Alcohol poisoning is very serious, Kat. People die from it."

"Dad, I know. It was New Year's Eve. There was champagne. It won't happen again. Believe me." I opened my eyes. "Where's Abra? Does she know?"

"She's the one who got the vomit smell out of the kitchen."

I grimaced. "And Lucy?"

"She's fine. She thinks you ate something bad at the party."

He didn't say anything about Libby's car being out in front of our house, so she must have come and gotten it. Or maybe Nice Guy Manny dropped her off, got her keys, and came back to return the car to her house. He'd do something like that.

"I'm sorry," I said.

"So are we." He patted my leg under the blanket. "You've got one hour to get ready."

I moaned, pulling the pillow over my head.

I thought about leaving Libby's clothes—which I had carefully laundered and folded—on her front porch, but didn't want her mother to find them first and start asking questions. Kat Flynn, such a nice, invisible girl. Instead, on the first day back to school after winter break, I gave Libby's clothes to Mitch.

"It's a long story," I said when he raised his eyebrows. "Just give her the clothes and don't ask any questions."

I found the sweats and underwear I'd lent Libby stuffed in a bag near my locker. I almost threw them away, thinking they were trash, since there was no note. I noticed they had not been washed and that my T-shirt was missing.

Thief.

Third Trimester

You're in the final stretch. You will still have to urinate frequently, and your belly will be quite large. You should be able to breathe easier as the baby moves down.

As for Baby, body fat is developing for life outside the womb, peach fuzz appears on the top of her head, and she's starting to turn her head down. She's getting ready for her entry into the world, and you're getting ready to welcome her!

34

About a week after the New Year's Eve Horror, I was dusting the Babies on Parade wall when the door banged open. My eyes nearly popped out of their sockets.

Libby stood in the doorway, staring at me. She looked confused, like she was solving a complicated math problem. *If you find the frizzy-haired girl who stomped on your foot, dissed your dye job, and upchucked on your boobs in a place where you didn't expect her to be, what's the square root of 86?*

"Um, am I in the right place?"

"I don't know," I said. "This is Abra's Midwifery." My eyes flicked to her stomach, and she pulled her jacket around her before tilting her head.

"Wait a minute," she said. "Do I know you?"

What? She hadn't recognized me? I'd barfed on her boobs, for God's sake. She'd been *in my house, using my shampoo.* Yeah, she'd been wasted, but she seemed fairly coherent when she left. Could I be that invisible?

"Whoa," Libby said. "Freak-out here. Did you barf on me

New Year's Eve? Was I at your house?" She shook her head and looked around. "You're totally out of context here."

I flipped the feather duster in front of me, scattering dust. "I work here." I looked down at her stomach again. Was Queen Libby pregnant? Impossible. She was too cool. Too together. Too *prepared*. She must be here for some other reason.

"Okay, so you're that girl and you work here." She began to pace back and forth, swinging her arms. She wasn't wearing any makeup, and her hair was pulled back hastily in a scünci. She wore an oversized T-shirt and a pair of baggy jeans. Giles was going incognita.

"I heard about this Abra lady from someone at my mom's club," Libby said. "She said she was this great person, easy to talk to, could help make decisions. Because I have to make a decision." Libby was talking as if I wasn't there.

"Do you have an appointment?" I glanced at the computer monitor. "Gail Eaton?"

"Yeah." The corner of her lip turned up in a half smile. "That's me."

If she was using a fake name, she was definitely el prego, with a capital Holy Crap.

"But I don't know if I should be here." She tugged at her T-shirt. Wait a minute. She wasn't wearing just any oversized T-shirt. It was *my* oversized T-shirt. The one that was *not* in the bag left near my locker.

I nodded to her. "I'd like my shirt back, if you don't mind."

"I wondered where I got it." She smiled. "Parts of the night are a little fuzzy."

"I'm sure."

She fingered the fabric. "It's really comfortable. Softer than

214

other T-shirts." Glancing up, she gave me the smile she usually reserved for her groupies. "Maybe I could keep it. You know. Since you barfed on me?"

Okay, so a month ago I would have been honored to have Libby Giles not only talking to me but also wearing my T-shirt. But not now.

"I guess," I said.

"Great." She looked at me again. "Do you go to Tabor High School?"

This was humiliating. I'd stepped on her foot and talked to her and passed her a million times in the hallway, and she didn't even know we went to the same school.

"Yeah," I said. "Do you?" So there.

"Well, yeah," she said, as if she couldn't believe I had asked such a question. "Wait a minute," she added. "You do yoga in the halls sometimes. You're Yoga Girl!" She smiled triumphantly, like she'd just answered the winning question on a game show. Her eyes fell on the Zen garden on the bookcase. "It figures."

Before I could say anything, the door to the Gathering Place opened and Abra stepped out. "Gail?" she said softly.

Libby took a deep breath. "Are you Abra?"

Abra nodded. "Would you like to come in?"

Libby looked at me, then back at Abra.

"Well, I—"

I flicked the feather duster against the wall. "I won't tell," I said quietly.

Libby laughed, but she sounded nervous. "It isn't that," she said. "I mean, who would believe you?" She didn't say this in a mean way, but as if she was stating a fact. And she was. No one would believe Yoga Girl. Somehow that stung more than if she was just trying to be mean.

"It's just, well, I guess none of this matters anyway." She stepped toward the outer door. "I need to take care of it."

"You just said you needed to make a decision." The words tumbled out.

"I guess I just did." Libby did not look like she had decided anything. Her eyes darted about like she was some cornered animal, and she kept running her fingers through her ponytail.

"Are you sure you don't want to come in and talk?" Abra asked. She gestured to the Gathering Place. Soft music was playing inside, and I could picture the comfy sofa, the soft chair nearby. "You've got my undivided attention for as long as you need it."

For a second, I thought Libby might do it. She leaned forward as if she were about to take a step toward Abra, her eyes holding a glimmer of . . . what? Hope?

But then she looked at me.

"It's all confidential," I said. Why in the world did I say that? I didn't want Abra helping her. That would mean I'd have to see her here. And this was my oasis, one of the few places I didn't feel like a total bottom-feeder (when I wasn't around Abra, anyway).

"I don't think so," Libby said. She turned quickly, opened the door, and was gone.

Abra and I stood in silence for a moment, the only sound the piano concerto floating out of the Gathering Place.

"Oh, dear." Abra sank into the chair opposite the reception desk, rubbing her forehead with her fingers. "I hope she comes back." She looked up at me. "What's her real name?"

"Libby Giles."

"Giles? Rosemary Giles's daughter?" Abra sat up. "I didn't even recognize her. Poor thing. That woman . . ." Her voice trailed off but she had my attention. Abra rarely spoke badly about other people. She was always pointing out their good qualities. Well, except maybe mine.

"What about her?"

"Nothing," Abra said quickly. "Can you imagine being pregnant at your age?" She stood up. "I hope she comes back. I think she's in a lot of pain."

Libby Giles, Queen of Tabor High School? I didn't think so.

"Emotional pain," Abra continued. "She may not even realize that's what's behind all the confusion and frustration."

Or it could just be that she wasn't expecting to see the girl who barfed all over her breasts at the midwife's office, once she figured out who she was.

Wow. Libby was pregnant. And she had considered keeping the baby. Or at least delivering it. The Buchanan Field Report would go crazy.

"I don't know," I said carefully. "I don't think there always has to be this underlying reason for everything, some deep, dark secret that if we only knew what it was, we could help the person on the road to recovery, to being happy and well-adjusted and normal." I leaned forward. "Why can't she just be confused and frustrated? Why do you have to make it so complicated?"

"I'm not making it complicated," Abra said. "People are complicated. That's just a fact of life."

There was no winning with a woman who believed she had all the answers and was practically perfect in every way.

"So what are you going to do?"

217

"Get her back here, of course." She glanced at me. "We can work through her discomfort with having you here." She tapped her finger on the arm of the chair. "Maybe have her come on your off days." She nodded, then raised her eyebrows. "Or maybe it would be good for you two to be around each other. Maybe that's part of why this happened."

Abra was in full rescue mode. She would save Libby from whatever unknown evils might surround her.

Too bad she wouldn't rescue me.

Abra had tried to get in touch with Libby. She'd left messages on her cell, but Libby hadn't called back. I caught a glimpse of her on Friday in the cafeteria. She was sitting with her groupies, nibbling at a sandwich. Her face was perfectly made-up, her hair gleaming. She said something and everyone laughed.

Let's face it. Libby had thousands of adoring fans, a totally hot and wonderful guy who loved her, another hot guy who was her best friend (and supposedly my boyfriend), and she would go to a great college.

I ask you: Where was the pain?

True, she had this pregnancy thing to deal with. But she would, with her usual Libby coolness. I looked over at her as she laughed and talked with her friends. It was strange, sharing a secret with Libby Giles. You would think it would link our galaxies together somehow, but no. She never looked my way, and it wasn't because she was ignoring me. She really didn't know I was in the same cafeteria as her, let alone just a few tables away.

One of her friends leaned over and whispered something in Libby's ear. Libby smiled and nudged the girl's arm, but she was looking past her toward the doors leading outside. She said something to her friends and stood up. Walking across the cafeteria, she glanced briefly at Mitch before pushing through the doors to the outside. Was she going out to smoke? What about the baby? Part of me wanted to get up and go after her. But if she was going to have an abortion, did it matter? The whole thing just gave me this sucky, yucky feeling deep down.

Mitch walked toward the doors she'd gone out of, leaning against them as he peered through the glass. I felt sorry for him, which surprised me. Why should I feel sorry for Mr. Popular, who could get any girl he wanted? But he liked Libby so much, and she treated him like he was some loser who had a crush on her, not someone she'd dated for half a year and had sex with. She got really uncomfortable around him, avoiding his eyes and shooing him away if he got too close. It had been two and a half months since the breakup, but they both were still feeling . . . something.

"You're ruining your fingernails." Christy nudged me. "What's wrong with you?"

I hadn't realized I was scraping my nails on the jagged edge of the table. I pulled my hand closer to my eyes. I'd torn the top of one nail completely off, and another hung by a thread.

"Nothing's wrong," I said, biting off the hanging nail and spitting it to the floor.

"Nice." Christy scrunched up her nose at me, her eyes flicking to the floor where my nail had landed. "What were you looking at?"

"Nothing." I smiled at her. "How's Glen surviving without his lunchtime breast check?" This semester they'd drawn separate lunches. I was glad Christy and I were still together, though I could have done without Libby and the Popular People.

Christy laughed. "Okay, I guess. He's gotten a lot more

talkative since we went to that party. It's like that whole scene flipped a switch I didn't even know he had." She shook her head. "It's really funny."

"I noticed he's wearing contacts now," I said. "What gives?"

Christy shrugged. "Part of the new Glen. It took me a while to get used to seeing his eyes without each of them being framed with wire, but now I like it." She sighed. "His eyes are really blue, you know?"

I hadn't really noticed, but I nodded.

"You and Manny doing good?"

"I'm meeting him at Starbucks after his practice today," I said. He'd sounded happy on the phone and said he missed me. Maybe all the beer and champagne had made New Year's fuzzy for me, too. Maybe I was making something out of nothing.

"Ooh la la," she said, bumping my elbow. "You'll have to tell me more later. Right now I've got to study for a chem test."

I smiled as she walked away, her gambler's hat tilted slightly on her head. I realized she hadn't pulled out her field notebook. I guess her radar hadn't picked up anything lately.

I decided I wanted to see Manny before we hooked up. Wanted to catch his eye to see if I could tell where he was with us. I lifted weights in the school weight room and then took a shower. After drying my hair, I heard male voices outside the locker room.

"Now she's into yoga, telling me how to breathe and move." Eddie Montero, everyone's favorite center. "It's stupid."

"What about Yoga Girl?" That was Bud Smith, the point guard. "She's always doing that shit in the hallway."

I froze. I heard shuffling and knew he was mimicking one of my yoga poses. Laughter.

"What a freak."

"Careful," said Eddie. "Cruz likes her."

I flattened myself against the wall of the locker room.

"Who's Yoga Girl?" Manny asked.

"You know," Eddie said. "That weird girl who does yoga by her locker in the west hall? By chem?"

I could picture Manny furrowing his brow, pretending like he was trying to picture me. "Oh. I think I know who you mean."

He *thought* he knew?

Manny chuckled his soft, easy chuckle. "Yeah, right," he said. "I like her."

I knew I should leave. I knew I shouldn't torture myself anymore. But my feet were cemented to the floor.

"Wasn't she at Lowry's New Year's party?" Bud said. "Was she crashing?"

"I didn't see her," Manny said.

My pulse throbbed in my ears. This wasn't happening. Not now. Not when I wasn't ready for it. The thing that had been buzzing around the back of my brain had burst out in front. It was stinging, stinging, like a bee trapped and desperate. I couldn't see anything, just felt sting after sting in my eyes, even after I'd scrunched them up tight.

Go away. Make it go away.

"I saw you with her at Starbucks, Cruz," Eddie said. "You've got the hots for her. Skinny ass, no tits. What a catch."

"She helped me study for my final," Manny said. "She's in my Spanish class, numbnuts."

They laughed.

"So after finals it was *hasta la vista,* Yoga Baby?"

Manny laughed. "Yeah," he said. *"Hasta la vista."*

The voices faded away as they entered the boys' locker room. My vision dimmed and I hurled downward, falling into a deep hole with nothing to grab on to. I couldn't breathe. I couldn't see. Then I heard other voices in the hall. Sucking in my breath, I forced my feet to move, to take me out of the locker room, away from them, away from everything.

35

Fact of Life #52: Kat is an idiot.

Stupid, stupid, stupid.

Secret made it special. Secret made it romantic.

WRONG. Secret hid embarrassing girl he's making out with.

What was I thinking? That suddenly Manny and I would be strolling arm in arm down the hallway like all the other couples, talking, kissing occasionally, full PDA?

Well, yeah. I guess I had thought that. Or at least hoped. Someday. Even though I knew we weren't the golden couple, I thought maybe we were silver. Or Teflon.

Stupid.

When I didn't show, Manny left tons of text messages and voice-mails: "Where are you? I waited for a half an hour at Starbucks."

I felt sadness simmering just below the anger, and I didn't want it to break through. I yanked on my biking pants and shoes, glancing at my desk. The pen Manny had given me sat in the corner in its velvet-lined box, all shiny and clean because I always rubbed off the fingerprints after I used it. I stormed across the room, snatched it up, and hurled it into the trash can. I shoved my foot down, pressing the box to the bottom along with yogurt containers, used tissues, and plastic wrapping from a new CD. I stomped until I heard the box crack under my weight. Good. It was broken.

I rode my bike harder and farther than I'd ever ridden before, whipping through "our" tunnel, pushing the memory away as I focused on my muscles, my breathing, anything but him.

When I got home, Manny was walking toward me, down the street. What the hell was he doing here?

"Why weren't you at Starbucks?" he asked. "Didn't you get any of my messages?"

I rolled my bike into the garage and picked it up to hang it on its hook. I missed, dropping the bike with a thud.

Manny reached out, but I jerked the bike away from him. "I can do it."

"Okay, okay."

He stepped back and I could feel his eyes on me. It was all I could do to keep from hurling the bike at him. I set it carefully on the hook and took off my helmet, shaking my hair out. I glanced down the driveway to the sidewalk. I didn't see the Range Rover.

"I parked down the street," he said. "I didn't know if, well, you know."

"Yeah," I said. "Don't park in front of the freak's house." *Wouldn't want to ruin your reputation as an asshole.*

"What?" I couldn't tell if he was surprised by what I'd said or he really hadn't heard. But I didn't care. I just wanted to get away from him. I started for the door.

"So how was your ride? We haven't gone riding for a while. Maybe we should."

"You want to go now?" I asked, yanking my bike back down off the wall. "Why don't we go now, Manny?"

He backed up, his eyes narrow. "What's wrong with you?"

"What's wrong with *you*?" I said. "Why are you here?"

"We were supposed to get together," he said, irritated. "Remember?"

I had to stay angry. If I wasn't angry, I'd cry, and I did not want to cry. "God, Cruz," I said, shoving my bike back up. "Just get it over with, would you?"

This seemed to wake him up.

"Get what over with?" But he wouldn't look at me.

"This," I said. "Us."

He looked guilty, like I'd caught him cheating. Then his face smoothed out, almost relieved. "So you feel it, too?"

I feel like I want to kill you or burst into tears. What are you feeling?

He must have taken my silence as agreement, because he plunged on. "Remember when I said I really wasn't looking to get into another relationship?"

And then you kissed me twice and have been all over me for the last few months?

"And you said you just go with the flow?" He looked out toward the street. "Well, I guess we're back to that." He took a deep breath, then looked at me. "I guess what I'm saying is, I think we need a break. I really like you, Kat, and I have a great time with you, but I'm feeling confused and I don't think that's fair to you."

Oh, please.

"I just feel like I don't know what I'm doing . . ." He paused, licking his lips.

With you. The words hung, unspoken, in the air between us. They twisted together into a sharp point, embedding themselves in my chest.

"Just a little break," he said quickly, "until we figure things out."

"A little break," I said. "No problem. I'm sure *we'll* have it all figured out soon."

He frowned, then looked at me sadly. "You really are the best, Kat."

Please don't say I don't deserve you. I will strangle you with my bare hands if you say I don't deserve you.

But he didn't. He didn't say anything else. So I did.

"I know," I said. "Now get the hell off my property."

36

I could almost hear the blood rushing through my body as I pounded up the stairs. I was so mad, I wanted to scream. And not because Manny wanted "a little break," which meant a forever break, which was bad enough. No, because I'd been wrong about him. I'd wasted all these years caring about someone I thought was different. But it turned out he was just like every other stupid guy—what other people thought about him was more important than what he thought himself.

My heart felt like it had been ripped from my chest, shoved between two weights on the bench press machine, then slammed again and again. I cried hard, the kind of crying where your nose stuffs up so bad you can't breathe and your chapped cheeks sting from where you've wiped the tears away again and again. I had turned my music up so no one would hear me, then pretended I had a headache, skipping dinner because my eyes were puffy and my face blotched.

The TV droned downstairs, and I could picture Abra, my dad, and Lucy sitting there while I was up here, dying. I grabbed my phone, called Christy, and she was at my house in half an hour. I heard her talking to Lucy as she came inside, pictured her giving Luce a hug.

"Thanks for coming," I said when she came up. "I'm sorry I busted up your date."

"It's fine," she said. "Glen was cool about it."

We sat on my bed and I told Christy what had happened.

"He's an asshole," she said, plopping herself down on my bed. "It was kind of cool how it was private and secret, just for the two of you, and I totally got that you both wanted it that way. At least I *thought* you both wanted it that way." She shook her head. "I never thought for him it was because—"

"—he didn't want to be seen with me?"

Christy's eyes narrowed. "Asshole."

I leaned back against my pillows. My whole body felt heavy, like someone had slipped lead beneath my skin.

"So what are you going to do?"

I furrowed my brow. "There's nothing to do, Chris. It's over."

"But do you feel closure? It sounds like it was all about him."

I snorted. "Closure? Who are you, Oprah?" I shook my head. "I knew it wouldn't last. I just wanted to go along for the ride, and I did. And now the ride's over. Fantasy lived. I should feel lucky. Most people don't have their fantasies become a reality."

"Lucky?" Christy practically spit in my face. "You're lucky that he was embarrassed to be associated with you? All that crap about not being ready for a relationship. Give me a break."

My stomach clenched at her words. The thing was, in the beginning it *had* been a secret neither of us wanted to share. We both felt that way. But when someone got too close to the truth, he folded completely.

"You should at least shout a few expletives," Christy said. "Or pop him in the nose."

"I don't want to do anything," I said. "I just want to forget about it."

"Like *that's* going to happen." She joined me on the window seat. "You can't just roll over and play dead, Kat. Stand up for yourself."

I tossed a small throw pillow in the air, caught it, and squeezed. "What's the point?" The truth was, I had no idea what I'd do or say if I stood up to him. Accuse him of being a big fat loser? Tell him he was evil for treating me that way? He'd probably just roll his eyes and laugh, making the humiliation doubly painful. No. I wasn't going to do anything. Just move forward.

"You gave him such an easy out."

I gripped the pillow tighter. I was beginning to regret telling her.

"He got his little fling with you and gets to keep his popular status," Christy said, standing up. "What have you got?"

I frowned. Suddenly the room felt like it was closing in.

"Well, Kat? What the hell have you got?"

"Shut up!" I smashed the pillow against the wall.

"Did you just tell me to shut up?" Christy crossed her arms over her chest. Cocking her head, she raised her eyebrows at me and licked her lips.

And at that moment, I hated her.

Hated the fact that she had a boyfriend who adored her and walked and talked with her and kissed her in public. Hated how cute she looked in her hats when my hair was always a wild mess. Hated how she stood in front of me now, those raised eyebrows making me feel small and stupid.

My anger burned hot, and I stood up so I could look down at her. "At least I'm not completely blind."

She narrowed her eyes. "What's that supposed to mean?"

"What do you think it means?" I said. "You have no idea what's really going on with the 'new Glen,' do you? You think he's getting all spiffed up for *you*? Contacts, working out more. How stupid can you be?" I had no idea where that came from. I was totally making it up. But I knew it would get to her.

"Oh, please."

But I could see the uncertainty in her eyes. I went in for the kill. "You won't put out, so he's finding people who will. And they're all laughing at you behind your back."

"Shut up!" Christy said. "That's not true! You don't know anything!"

"Don't I?"

"You're just pissed because your perfect little Manny Cruz is just another asshole!" Christy yelled. "He couldn't stand to be *seen* with you, Kat. He thought you were a *loser,* a loser he wanted to make out with and feel up. How stupid could *you* be?"

I reached over and snatched her hat off her head and shoved it at her. "Take your stupid, idiotic hat and get out of my house!" I pushed her toward the door. "Everyone thinks you look stupid in those hats, and you do!"

"Bitch," Christy hissed, grabbing the hat.

"You're the bitch!" I yelled.

"I hate you!"

"I hate you more!" I screamed. "Get out of my *life*!"

"Gladly." She turned and marched out of my room.

I heard her pounding down the stairs as I slammed the door. I paced back and forth, my breath quick, my heart pounding. Tears stung my eyes as I stalked to the window.

Christy stood on the sidewalk, cell phone to her ear. She flipped it closed and crossed her arms, looking down the street. Fifteen minutes later, Glen's Jeep pulled up. Before she got in, Christy turned toward my house. She looked straight up at my window, where I thought she couldn't see me but I guess she could.

Because she raised her hand and flipped me off.

I turned from the window and sucked in a breath. Lucy was standing in the doorway, her hand on the knob, a look of complete and utter disbelief on her face. Tears streamed down her cheeks.

I couldn't look at her. "You didn't knock," I said, turning back to the window.

"Sorry," she whispered.

I started to say something but she was gone, the door clicking shut behind her.

37

The thought of seeing Manny in Spanish or Christy in the hall on Monday made me queasy. I almost faked sick but I didn't want to be a wimp, so I went to school.

Everything was the same. There was my locker, still near the chem lab, as Eddie Montero had pointed out. My books were crammed on the top shelf and the empty hook was there, waiting for my jacket. How could it all be the same when everything had fallen apart?

Christy didn't meet me at my locker like she usually did. Not that I expected her to. Or wanted her to, really. But I guess old habits and expectations die hard.

I almost ditched Spanish. I stood outside the door, gripping my books so my hands wouldn't shake. Peeking in, I saw Manny's empty seat. Relief and disappointment washed over me. He wasn't there to see me not be a wimp.

I sat at my desk and stared straight ahead. Maybe he was sick. Maybe he had some horrible disease that only affects people who are complete losers and pretend that secret relationships are special when they are really a way to cover up the embarrassment of being seen with someone.

But then he was there, striding up the aisle, apologizing for being late.

My whole body twitched as Manny sat behind me. Would he say something? Would I?

Neither of us did. But I was aware of his presence behind me the entire fifty minutes, which seemed liked fifty years. I didn't hear one word Señora García-Smith said and forgot to copy down our assignment.

Fact of Life #730: Spanish SUCKS.

When I got home after a run that night, Abra was cooking. "Would you mind making the salad, Katima?" she asked.

"Fine." I started toward the hall.

"Katima?"

I stopped. "Yeah?" I turned and saw her brush a strand of hair off her forehead.

"I was thinking. Maybe you could say something to Libby at school? Ask her if she's gotten my messages? Let her know we care?"

Of course it would be about Libby. And what was this "we" business? "No."

"Why not?"

"Because—" How do you explain to your practically perfect mother that her daughter is less than practically perfect? That in fact, she's so not perfect that she's a total failure as a human being? "Because I never see her at school," I said. "She's a senior. They might as well be in another state."

"Oh." Abra looked disappointed, and I wasn't sure if she was disappointed in me or in the fact that her idea wouldn't work after all. "That's too bad. Do you have her e-mail?"

I groaned in exasperation. "No, I don't have her e-mail." I rolled my eyes. "Abra, Libby and I are not even in the same stratosphere, okay? I can't help you here."

Abra smiled and returned to chopping. "You always exaggerate, Katima." She looked thoughtful. "Maybe I'll send her a letter. I just hate to give up on her. I could tell she really needed someone."

"Libby has tons of friends, Abra," I said. "Tons." *And I don't have any, not that you've noticed.*

"It's not the same thing, Katima. You know that."

"Whatever," I said. "Let me do my homework, and then I can make the salad."

Up in my room, I tried to study for a Spanish quiz but that made me think of Manny, so I pulled out my SAT study guide. Maybe I'd have better luck working math problems.

"Garbage?"

I turned to see my dad standing at the door, holding a large trash bag. Usually this was my job, but he had noticed my SAT books lying around for the last several weeks and wanted to let me "get to it," as he'd said.

"Yeah." I picked up the can next to my desk and dumped the garbage in his open bag.

"Throw something away by mistake?" He pulled out the pen box and handed it to me. The weight burned through my hand. I wanted to throw it back in the trash, where it belonged. But I couldn't. And I hated that I couldn't.

"Thanks," I said.

"You okay?"

"Fine."

He hesitated, then nodded. When he was gone, I let out my breath, not realizing until that moment that I'd been holding it. I lifted the box lid and looked inside. The pen was nestled in the velvet, sleek and shiny, unharmed. I didn't know why I felt such relief, but I did.

KF: Take no prisoners.

It seemed so long ago that we'd played at pen-napping and laughed over donuts and coffee. I held the pen to my chest, letting the tears run down my cheeks. I cried for a few minutes, then wiped my eyes and tucked the pen away in my closet. I went to find Lucy.

She was in her room, listening to music. Her door was open like it usually was. Even so, I knocked softly.

She looked up, her expression unreadable.

"Hey, Luce. Can I come in?"

She nodded slowly, not taking her eyes off me. Maybe she thought I was going to yell at her like I yelled at Christy.

"I'm sorry I couldn't talk to you Friday night," I said, sitting on her bed. "I was just so upset about Christy."

"It's okay."

"No, it isn't. I know Christy's your bud and you were scared and I shut you out." I patted the spot next to me, and when she sat down, I wrapped my arm around her and put my cheek on the top of her head. "I'm really sorry."

Lucy patted my leg. "When are you going to be friends again?"

I sighed shakily, willing myself not to cry. "I don't know. We said some pretty horrible things."

"Mom always says our family and friends are the most important thing," Lucy said. "You can make up."

Did I care right now about what Abra always said? Especially because she didn't walk the talk. She was fully engrossed in Life of Libby. She didn't even know I'd lost my best friend. She wanted to be Libby's best friend when Libby was surrounded by people every minute of the day and I had no one. It pissed me off.

"Maybe if you gave her some candy?" Lucy reached over to her end table and picked up a bag of M&M's. Peanut.

I smiled. "Maybe."

"Katima?" Abra's voice rose from downstairs.

"I have to make the salad." I pulled my arm from around Lucy's shoulders and stood up. "Luce?"

She looked up.

"Thanks for the advice."

38

Manny and I avoided and ignored each other.

Christy and I avoided and ignored each other.

Libby continued to live in her own galaxy, unaware of my existence.

Are we having fun yet?

I purposely arrived late to Spanish third period on Wednesday and sat in the back. Manny was sitting in his usual seat, looking straight ahead the whole time. I shot eye daggers at the back of his head, just above the nape of his neck, and didn't hear anything Señora García-Smith said.

It sucks that life goes on, even if you think it should stop and take a moment of silence just for you.

I threw myself into school, my workouts, my painting, and working at Abra's.

Mitch would say hello and wave at me, but I'd always turn away if there were other people around. Didn't he know I was social suicide? What was wrong with him? Sometimes you have to protect people for their own good.

"What are you looking at?" he asked me in the hallway one afternoon.

"Not you," I said to my locker.

"Libby still isn't talking to me," he said to the water fountain.

"And you're telling me this because . . ."

"Who knows?" he said. "Because you're talking to your locker."

I couldn't help smiling. I wondered if he'd still want Libby if he knew she was pregnant. I thought he would. He wouldn't care. Not like *some* people. But she'd probably already had the abortion. We hadn't seen or heard from her since that one day at the Midwifery, though Abra hadn't given up. I wondered if she'd sent the letter.

"There are other girls, you know," I said to Mitch as I opened my locker.

"Not for me."

The next Friday, I was coming out of the restroom and nearly ran into Christy.

"Sorry," I muttered, looking past her out the door.

"You should be," she said.

"Bitch."

"Bitch."

It barely registered that she wasn't wearing her gambler's hat. Or any hat at all.

On Tuesday, I sat at my desk at the Midwifery, staring at the pile of folders I was supposed to file in the cabinet. Instead, I was leaning back in the chair, staring at the opposite wall, wallowing.

When would it go away? I wanted to stop feeling like I might sink into a hole so deep I could never crawl out. Or that if I didn't beat the living crap out of Manny, I might explode from anger. And then sometimes I felt so numb, I wondered if someone had come during the night and sucked all of my emotions out of me. I bounced from sadness to anger to this strange emptiness—an emotional triathlon that seemed to have no finish line.

The phone rang and I jerked forward in my seat, my heart racing. I had this crazy thought that it might be Manny, even though he'd never called me here. So why would he now? And why would I want him to?

Taking a deep breath, I picked up the phone. "Abra's Midwifery."

"Katima, is that you?" Melanie of the red spike heels.

"Hi, Mrs. Robertson," I said. "How is everyone? How is Ann Louise?"

"Doing well, thank you. But the picture. That's what I'm calling about."

"The picture?"

"The one you drew of our birth experience. I didn't find it until today, because Don took the bags in." Wow. With my life going down the toilet, I'd completely forgotten that I'd tucked the picture into one of the bags they'd had in Serenity Space. "He thought they were all dirty clothes," Melanie continued, "so the bag got thrown in the laundry room, then buried under a mountain of laundry." She sighed, but I could tell it was a happy sigh. "I had no idea one baby could produce so much dirty laundry."

I smiled. A real smile. I hadn't done that for a while. It felt strange.

"So anyway, we love the picture. The red high heels on Ann

Louise? Adorable! And how did you know I was breast-feeding? It was so hard at first, but I love it. And I know it's the best thing for Ann Louise."

Huh. Never thought I'd hear that from Red Spikes.

"Well, anyway, Don thinks you should hire out to do personalized art at other births." She paused. "It's just the most special thing anyone has ever done for us. Thank you, Katima."

"Kat."

"Oh. Yes. Well, Abra always calls you Katima." I heard Baby Red Spikes in the background. "Ann Louise is calling. Thank you, Kat. Really. Thank you."

"You're welcome," I said, setting the phone down in amazement. It must have shown on my face, because when Abra came in, she looked at me funny.

"Who was that?"

"Melanie," I said.

"Is everything all right?" Abra asked.

"Yeah," I said. "She just called to thank me."

"For what?"

"Oh, just a picture I drew of their birth." I tucked both hands between my knees. Why did I suddenly feel like I'd done something wrong?

"You did? Wow." She licked her lips. "You weren't even there."

My chest constricted. I wished I hadn't said anything.

"Well, that's great. Really great," Abra said, but I couldn't tell if she thought it was. "What did it look like? How did you do it? When did you give it to them?"

"It's nothing," I said, feeling assaulted by all the questions.

"You're so modest, Katima," Abra said. "I wish you'd shown it to me. I would have loved to have seen it."

"Sorry," I said. "I didn't think about it."

"Well, I'll have to ask her to bring it when she comes in for a follow-up visit," Abra said. "Oh, and did I tell you? Libby finally called." She looked at me like a kid who had just won the big prize at the carnival. "It looks like she's going to have the baby after all, so she'll be coming in soon. Isn't that wonderful?" She didn't wait for a reply, just bounced—practically skipped—into the Gathering Place.

Yippee ki-yay.

I saw Manny the next morning, hanging out with a bunch of guys, laughing and talking. My stomach clenched. He looked up once and caught my eye. He actually had the gall to give me a little smile.

I just stared at him, stone-faced, until he looked away.

Later I ran into Mitch. "Flynn," he said as I stooped for a drink of water.

"Lowry." I wiped my mouth with the back of my hand.

"So what gives with you and Cruz?" he asked.

I scowled. "Nothing *gives*, Lowry. I don't even know the guy." Absolutely true.

He raised an eyebrow at me. "Want to talk about it? We could meet in the pine grove."

I almost smiled at that. "Talk about what? How I helped him get a B on his Spanish final?"

He stared at me.

I stared back, crossing my arms over my chest. "What are you looking at?"

241

Mitch cocked his head. "Someone who recently joined the I Got Screwed Club."

I looked away, hating how the truth of his words, the compassion behind them, made my eyes sting.

"I'm still the president, because I've been screwed longer," he said as he turned on his heel, "but you can be vice president."

I watched him disappear down the hallway.

Hasta la vista.

39

It was February 20, the first day I could get online and sign up for the Rocky Mountain Women's Triathlon. The parent consent form had gone in, and when I clicked Submit, my hand was shaking. I was going to do it. I was really going to do it.

"Good job," Diane said when I told her. We were sitting in the chairs in the reception area of Abra's Midwifery, going over her birth wish list. Both the tri and Diane were a good distraction, keeping my mind from replaying the breakup with Manny and my fight with Christy in an irritating and agonizing loop. It had been almost six weeks, and I was still doing it to myself.

"Do you have names yet?" I asked, trying to push thoughts of Manny and Christy away.

She nodded. "But we're keeping them under wraps. It seems like everyone has an opinion and they aren't afraid to share it." She sighed. "Once a baby has a name, no one's going to say 'Why'd you name her that?' "

I smiled but felt a twinge. That was why I had liked that no one really knew about Manny and me. No one could tell me if I was doing it wrong. Or dig into details and ask questions I didn't want to answer. But now it didn't matter.

Abra stepped out of the GP and crossed to the Ms. Coffee (she'd scratched out the *r* in "Mr." years ago and written in an *s*).

"Whatever name you pick, it will be perfect." I felt suddenly nervous with Abra in the room. Like I was taking an oral exam and might give the wrong answer at any moment. I pulled a CD out of the drawer. "Here's one possible mix for the first part of your labor," I said, one eye on Abra. "Why don't you and Jeff listen to it and let me know if you like the songs."

Diane took the CD from me. "Okay, but I know it's right the way it is." She grinned. "And the mural's going to be great." We talked more about the mural and music and some possibilities for the atmosphere as Abra went back into the Gathering Place.

"Want to hang with me during the exam?" Diane asked.

"I've got some things on my mind," I said.

"Want to talk about it?"

I shook my head.

She caught my eye. "Whatever it is, I know you'll work through it."

I felt relieved when the door to the Gathering Place closed behind her. I was jittery and irritable. School sucked. I sucked. Everything sucked.

But I didn't know where else to go.

When I got home later, I decided to clean my closet. As I pulled out all the clothes that I'd tossed on the floor, I was surprised to find the drawing I'd done of Linda's birth. I'd forgotten all about it. Sitting back, I traced my fingers along the swirling lines and colors and couldn't help smiling. It was good. It brought me right back to that room, to the sounds and smells and feel of it, without the embarrassment I'd felt. Maybe it would do the same for Linda and Wayne.

After school the next day, I bought a good frame. Then I wrapped the picture in brown paper, taped a card to it, and left it leaning against their front door. It felt like a rebellious act, and I wasn't sure why. But I smiled as I drove away.

When I got home, there was an e-mail from Manny.

From: DaMan@yahoo.com
To: KatBrat@msn.com
Subject: Now what?
I can't handle this. Can we at least e-mail?
M

So he wanted to communicate. I hated that part of me wanted to, too. I wondered if I should just tell him what I'd heard him say outside the locker room that day, how he'd denied he even knew me. But did I really want to relive that humiliation?

From: KatBrat@msn.com
To: DaMan@yahoo.com
Subject: RE: Now what?
Why don't we "see how things go."
K

From: DaMan@yahoo.com
To: KatBrat@msn.com
Subject: RE: Now what?
Fine.

Even though he hadn't written them, I could almost see the follow-up words: *Be that way*.

So that was that.

I checked IM and could see that Christy was online. She had to know I was, too. I right-clicked her name and then clicked Send a Message. What could I say to her?

I stared at the blinking cursor, trying to come up with the right words.

A ping drew my eyes to the corner of the screen.

HatGirl (Away).

I closed the IM window and went downstairs.

40

It was March. I was sitting at the reception desk at Abra's Midwifery, holding a card from Wayne and Linda. I smiled as I reread their words thanking me for the birth drawing, which they'd hung in Claire's room above her bed.

It's amazing how you captured us, the feel of us. We can't thank you enough.

I tucked the card back in the drawer and was logging on to the computer as Libby smacked through the door. She smiled before hanging up her coat. Then she stood in front of me.

"Okay, here's what I'm thinking." She put her hands on her hips.

"Do you even know my name?" I asked.

She looked at me, startled. "What?"

"Do you even know who I am?"

"Well, yeah. You're the chick who barfed on my boobs, you work here, and you're—" She glanced toward the Gathering Place. What was that about?

"My name is Kat."

She frowned, like she wished she didn't know I had a name.

"Okay. So, *Kat*," she said. "Not to be a bitch or anything, but it would be great if you didn't say anything about my 'situation,' you know? And nothing about me coming to see Abra or about me having this baby. I'll tell people when I'm ready. And please, let's leave things the way they've been at school."

I raised an eyebrow.

"You know. You do your thing, I do my thing, and we really don't interact or anything." She smiled, like we were working out a great plan together. "Not that we see each other a lot at school, but I just wanted to make that clear to avoid any, you know, awkward sitches."

"Awkward sitches. Right."

"I think you'll agree that this is the best way to go now that I'm coming to see Abra and you're here, too. Don't you think?"

"Can I pee without your permission?"

She laughed. "You're pretty funny." As she turned to hang up her coat, she smiled over her shoulder at me. "But since we've never hung out or talked before, people would think it's weird and start wondering, you know?"

Well, I wanted to say, *we actually* have *talked—at school, at the Game Zone, and at my house, where you took a shower and used my shampoo and stole my T-shirt—but who's keeping track?*

"Sure, 'Gail.' No problem. We don't want anyone to wonder." Was this secret stuff some kind of popularity disease? Or was it just me? It was weird, because she was actually *asking* me to be invisible—and yet, in a stupid, twisted way, I understood where she was coming from.

She smiled. "Thanks, Kitty Kat. And you can call me Libby if you want."

"Okay, *Libby.* But you can't call me Kitty Kat. No one gets to call me that."

"Oh, okay. Sorry." She sat down in the chair opposite my desk. "So are you really, you know, Abra's daughter?"

That explained her weird look a few minutes ago. Abra must have said something.

"Yeah."

She cocked her head, like she was evaluating a piece of clothing on a rack.

I could just hear the commentary in her head: *Very cool midwife, dorky barf girl. Does not compute.*

"Do you know she called me six times?" Libby shook her head. "Six times. No one has ever called me that much when I didn't return their calls. Well, except for Mitch. He's called me, like, a million times." She rolled her eyes, but a hint of a smile played around her lips. "But six messages from someone like Abra . . ."

I checked the scheduling software. "I don't see you down for an appointment. Did we miss something?"

"Well, I was hoping . . ." Libby's voice trailed off as she looked at the door of the Gathering Place.

"Abra's in there, doing some paperwork," I said. I wasn't going to interrupt her.

"Oh." Libby stared at the door, as if by sheer force of will she could get it to open.

Five minutes later, it did.

"Libby!" Abra couldn't have been more happy if her long-lost sister had been standing in the reception area. If she'd had one. Maybe she'd been missing her long-lost older daughter, since the current older daughter didn't seem to cut it. I'd never seen Abra's eyes light up like that for anyone. I had to look away.

I heard them step inside the Gathering Place, talking together like old friends.

• • •

That night I held my cell in my hands, my finger poised over number 2—Christy's speed dial. One of us needed to apologize, and I figured it should be me, since I was the one who'd started the whole thing. And not having her in my life was excruciating. But what if she started telling me I needed to go give Manny hell?

"Dinner!" Lucy knocked on my door and I dropped my phone on the bed. "Someone named Libby is eating with us tonight," Lucy said as we headed downstairs.

"What?" I stopped at the last step. "Since when?"

"I don't know. I guess she mentioned to Mom that she was going to be alone for dinner, so Mom invited her over."

Great. Just what I needed, Queen Libby sitting across from me, telling me when I could look at her and when I could pass the peas.

"We're so glad you could join us," my dad said as he held out a bowl of pasta to Libby.

"Thanks for having me," Libby said, taking it from him. "This actually looks good. No offense or anything," she said quickly to my dad. "It's just that I've been really nauseous."

"No offense taken," Dad said. "I've been around enough pregnant women to know that eating can be a bit of a challenge."

Libby smiled at him and put a small mound of pasta on her plate before passing the bowl on to Abra. I'm not sure how she ended up sitting between both my parents while Lucy and I were pushed to the other end, but there you go.

"Well, Abra has been great about helping me try to deal with all of this. I'm still not sure I can do the whole natural childbirth thing, but we'll see."

"Whatever works for you, Libby," Abra said. "If you decide to go to the hospital, I can certainly be there to support you."

"Thanks, Abra. I appreciate that." Libby took a dainty mouthful of pasta and chewed carefully. I stuffed a forkful into my mouth and chomped down.

My dad laughed. "Slow down, Kat. It's not a race."

I frowned at him, annoyed with the way Libby raised an eyebrow at me.

"So Lucy's going to teach me how to play dominoes after dinner," Libby said. "Right, Luce?"

"Yeah!"

She was staying after dinner? And where did she get off calling Lucy Luce? That was *my* name for her.

The rest of dinner was agonizing, with Libby sucking up to my parents and them eating it up. Even Lucy was entranced. Libby had once again cast her magic spell over unsuspecting humans, and I was left invisible. In my own house.

I did the dishes, then went up to my room to finish my homework while Lucy played dominoes with Libby. Half an hour later, there was a knock at my door.

Abra poked her head in. "Why don't you join us?"

"I've got a test." I didn't, but I didn't want to go downstairs and feel like an outsider—*in my own house,* my brain repeated.

"Well, if you finish early . . ." Abra closed the door quietly.

I flipped the pages of my math book, not really seeing the problems. They were talking and laughing down there, and it was really distracting. Might as well at least see what was so funny.

When I came downstairs, all four of them were playing dominoes in the dining room, the way we all used to before everyone got so busy. Libby was sitting in my chair, the one opposite the window. They were stacking the dominoes back in the metal box.

"I'm glad I didn't put any money on this game," Libby said, shaking her head. "You really dominated, Luce." She looked at my parents. "And James and Abra are pretty good, too."

James? She was calling my dad *James?*

Lucy grinned up at her, her cheeks pink with pride. "Maybe next time."

"Yeah," Libby said, "maybe next time. I'd like a rematch." She looked up and caught my eye. "I came in fourth place every time." She tugged her jacket off the back of the chair. Finally she was leaving.

Abra laughed, then looked over her shoulder at me. "Kat, why don't you walk Libby home?"

I snorted. "It's three blocks, Abra. I think Libby's a big girl." And who was going to walk *me* back home?

"Of course she is," Abra said. "It's not about safety. I just thought it would be nice."

"For who?" I didn't care if I sounded like a bitch. This whole scene was pissing me off.

"It's okay," Libby said. "I need the alone time to transition." She hugged everyone good-bye except me. She just raised her hand awkwardly. "See you, Kat."

As she opened the front door, she paused to look back, her eyes roaming the room and my family, as if memorizing every detail. Then she stepped out. "Thanks again."

I watched her through the window, walking down the street toward her house. I wondered what she meant by "transition."

"You could have walked with her," Abra said, putting a hand on my shoulder.

"You could have tried not to force us together," I said, stepping away so her hand dropped to her side.

"And you both could agree that it was a great evening and leave it at that," Dad said.

"Fine," Abra and I said.

41

On Monday the word was out about Libby being pregnant. And that she was giving the baby up for adoption. She'd practically held a press conference. Odds were running ten to one that it was Mitch's, but there were several who thought it might be Manny's, or someone's from another school that no one knew about. Of course, I had the hard data. On Abra's recommendation, she'd had an ultrasound, which put conception smack in the middle of Lowryville; due date: end of July.

Everyone oohed and aahed. Libby was using a midwife. She was going to give birth in her own house. She was selflessly giving up her baby to a loving family. It was so cool.

Puh-*leeze*. Only Libby Giles could turn something like being pregnant into a positive thing. If she wasn't careful, all of her groupies would get pregnant just so they could be like her.

I tried to catch Christy's eye in the hall, sure this news would make her want to talk to me again. This was the biggest thing to hit the Buchanan Field Report in years.

But she walked right by, whispering something to another girl, her French beret slung low over her brow. She was wearing her hats again. Somehow that made the distance between us feel even greater. My throat closed in and I turned away, hoping she hadn't seen my face.

Just for old times' sake, and because I was desperate for a latte (I'd switched once Manny had shown his true yellow-bellied colors), I headed to Starbucks after school on Wednesday. I guess part of me hoped Christy and Glen would be there and maybe she'd talk to me, but when I pulled into the parking lot, I saw Abra's moped.

As I reached for the door, I spotted her at a small table near the back. She stood up and moved to the counter to get a napkin. That's when I saw Libby in the chair across from Abra's. She was sipping juice, smiling. She said something and Abra laughed. Abra, who was always serious—Abra, who rarely laughed when I said anything—was laughing with Libby. Again. I stood there, gripping the handle, gaping through the glass.

"Are you going in?"

I glanced up. A man was pointing to my arm, which was blocking his way.

"Oh, sorry." I stepped back and held the door for him. The movement must have caught Libby's eye, because she looked up. Then Abra sat down, blocking Libby from view. I saw Libby's hand stretch out and grab Abra's. She must have said something, because Abra reached over with her other hand and covered Libby's, holding it tight.

Turning on my heel, I stalked back to my car, my body shaking.

I spent most of the evening in the Womb, sitting on the futon with my back against the wall, staring at the mural. I shook my outstretched legs, trying to get rid of my irritation. So they were at Starbucks together. So what? Abra probably met lots of her mothers in different places.

But it was the *way* they were together, talking and laughing. Like old friends, but more than that.

Like mother and daughter.

On Friday, Libby was surrounded by her friends in the hallway. I was standing nearby, checking my homework before heading to class. Her face glowed as she answered questions like a celebrity at the opening of a new movie.

"I thought my mom was going to explode when I told her," Libby said. I was pretty sure I'd seen a hint of satisfaction in her eyes. The girls around her twittered in agreement. Their moms would no doubt go up in a puff of smoke as well. "She really flipped out. But hey, it's *my* thing, you know?"

The girls nodded, then started talking again.

"I can't believe you're not going to have it in the hospital," one girl said. "When I have a baby, I want the drugs." The others murmured their agreement.

"Well, I was planning to do that—just get the epidural and float off—but I met this midwife who is so amazing, she's like a goddess, and she makes a home birth sound really great."

Well, of course you have a great midwife, I wanted to say. *You have Abra.*

"Isn't it dangerous?" another girl asked. "What if something goes wrong?"

"If there's even a little sign that something might go wrong, Abra will get me to the hospital," Libby said.

"But you're giving the baby up," another one said. "Why go through all of that agony?"

Libby looked at her for a moment. "Why not?" she said. She flashed her famous smile, then turned and headed down the hall. Her groupies followed after her. Libby didn't even look back; she just kept walking, hips swaying, hair waving, like she owned the world.

"Is it mine?" Mitch stood in front of me after school that day, blocking my way to the parking lot.

"No," I said. "This is definitely my pen." I held up the Pilot pen Manny had abducted. That seemed so long ago. Like something I'd made up.

"You know what I'm talking about."

I sighed. "How am I supposed to know?" I tried to step around him, but he blocked me.

"Cruz said your mom's her midwife," Mitch said. "You work there. You've got access."

It hardly registered that Manny had been talking about me to Mitch. "It's all confidential."

Mitch stuffed his hands in his pockets, jiggling on his heels. "Come on, Flynn. Spill it."

I shook my head. "You're talking to the wrong person, Mitch."

"I can't talk to her," he said. "She just ignores me and walks away."

"Welcome to the club." I ducked around him before he could stop me.

When I went for a run later, I accidentally on purpose ran by Libby's house, staying across the street. Abra's moped was parked out front. I sucked in my breath and slowed my pace, craning my neck to see through the front window. They were sitting on the couch, Abra's arm around Libby's shoulders.

Where was Mrs. Giles? Why couldn't she be in there with her arm around her daughter? Why did it have to be Abra?

My eyes stung and I turned away quickly, picking up speed until Libby's block was nothing but dust behind me.

Thirty minutes later, I was standing on Christy's porch, my finger hovering over the doorbell. Just as I was about to press it, the door flew open.

"Push it, already," Christy said, leaning out and pressing the doorbell herself. "The suspense is killing me."

I snuck a peek at her. She was wearing her gambler's hat, but her face looked pale, worn. She faced me and our eyes locked.

"I am SO sorry," we said in unison.

I threw my arms around her. "I'm the most horrible person in the world."

"No, I am," she said, hugging me back.

We hugged for a full minute before we broke apart and she pulled me inside.

"I don't even know where to start," I said.

"Me either."

"I'm *so* sorry," I whispered again, tears coming to my eyes. "Glen isn't scamming on anyone. I totally made that up, and it was a horrible thing to say." I sniffed. "And people adore your hats. Everyone loves them. I was just being an idiot."

Christy sighed. "I'm sorry I went overboard with the whole Manny thing. Even though I would go over and kick his butt, that's just not your way and I should have accepted that."

I squeezed my hands together. "No, you're right. But all I can see is him acting like I'm crazy and making me feel stupid all over again. I just can't—"

"It's okay, Kat," Christy said, squeezing my arm. "I know."

We apologized about twenty more times, and then Mrs. Buchanan brought lemonade.

"Thank God you two patched things up," she said. "I couldn't stand another day of her moping."

I looked at Christy. "You were moping?"

She nodded. "I hope you were, too."

"Nonstop." I pulled some peanut M&M's out of my pocket and handed them to Christy. "Lucy said these would help us be friends again."

She laughed. "Props to Lucy."

We munched M&M's and drank lemonade for a few minutes, and then Christy groaned heavily. "Okay, I can't stand it anymore." She ran out of the room and came back, carrying her field notebook.

She pointed her pen at me. "Spill it about Libby." Before I could answer, she started talking. "First of all, I can't believe she got pregnant in the first place. But okay, she did. Second of all, is she really having this baby? It seems so un-Libby-like, doesn't it?" She tapped her pen against her teeth. "I'm sure she'll get an epidural. Or maybe a C-section. That way she can plan ahead and not have to go through all that labor."

"You don't think she'll stick with Abra?" I popped another M&M in my mouth.

"No way," Christy said. "She couldn't handle the pain. Just watch. She'll be crying for drugs at the first sign of a contraction."

I kind of agreed with Christy, except for the Abra Factor. I told Christy how they were all buddy-buddy and Libby had more than enough excuses to come by the Midwifery when she wasn't scheduled. And that was only on the days when I was there.

"Abra hasn't worked with too many teens, has she?" Christy said. "She's probably just trying to make Libby feel comfortable. She's hospital-bound for sure."

"Maybe," I said. I didn't tell Christy she'd been giving Abra gifts—a plant, some incense, and a framed piece of torn paper art of a mountain range.

"Abra loves torn paper art," Libby had told me when she brought the picture into the Midwifery. It now hung prominently behind Abra's desk in the Gathering Place.

"Well, yeah," I'd said, while at the same time thinking, *She does?* How could Libby Giles know something like that about Abra when I didn't? And why didn't Abra have any of *my* art hanging in the GP?

Why haven't you given her any? a smaller voice asked. But I ignored it.

The following Monday I was leaving school, heading to the rec center to swim my laps. As I got in my car, I saw Manny and Libby sitting on the brick wall near the end of the building. They looked deep in conversation. Libby had her hand on Manny's knee and he was nodding, rubbing her shoulder.

I glanced around but didn't see Mitch. It was bad enough I had to witness this. I didn't need him going all ballistic.

Though it might have been fun to watch.

* * *

Christy showed up on my doorstep that Friday night, clutching a bulging duffle bag. "Belated sleepover?" she asked.

I threw my arms around her. "You're the best friend in the world."

"I know," Christy said, hugging me back. "Come on. I've got DVDs of all our faves. If we hadn't had that stupid fight, I would have stayed. You should not be alone after a breakup."

Lucy barreled down the hall, launching herself at Christy, who caught her as Lucy wrapped her arms and legs around her like a monkey. "You're back!"

Christy laughed. "Yeah. I'm back."

Lucy lowered herself and grinned up at her. "I knew the candy would work."

I winked at her. "You are wise beyond your years."

"Can I stay with you guys?" she asked as we lugged our load up the stairs.

"Absolutely, in a little while," Christy said. "Your sister and I have a few things we need to talk about first."

We sat on my bed with snacks and drinks within arm's reach.

"So," Christy said. "How are you doing about the Manny thing?"

I shrugged. "I'm still pissed and hurt." I confessed to obsessively passing by Libby's house, checking for Manny's Range Rover ever since I'd seen them together. "I don't know why I'm doing it," I said. "I just have this feeling he might be with her. But so far he hasn't been, so I guess I'm just a big idiot."

Christy shook her head. "I don't know why we torture ourselves like that, but we do. I don't blame you for still being pissed. But hopefully time will help, and maybe you'll decide you need a little release and go kick his butt after all."

I smiled. "Yeah, maybe." Rolling onto my side, I picked up a pillow. "So how are you and Glen?"

Christy sighed. "I don't know. Things are—weird. He's acting weird."

"Weird how?"

"It's hard to explain. But I think—" She stopped.

I stared at her. "Are you going to break up with him?"

Christy looked down. "I think so."

I was stunned. Sure, he wouldn't have been my first pick for Christy, but they'd been dating for forever. I thought they'd get married and have little Glens and Christys, but name them after me. "Wow."

"I know," she said. "It's so hard, though. Even though it's not right anymore, I don't know how to tell him."

We sat for a few minutes, alone with our thoughts; then Christy got up and called to Lucy to join us for a movie. Before it was halfway through, the two of them were snoring beside me. I got Lucy into her own bed, climbed into mine next to Christy, and stared at the ceiling. I couldn't sleep. Sliding out of bed, I sat on the window seat, my eyes tracking the way to Libby's house.

I glanced down at my shoes and coat, tossed on the floor. It would be easy to put them on, to sneak outside and head down the street, three blocks over, just to check one more time.

It was 1:03 a.m. by my digital watch. Manny's green Range Rover was parked in plain sight at the curb in front of Libby's house. Lights were on downstairs, but the curtains were drawn, so I couldn't see anything. What could I say? Masochism comes in all shapes and sizes, including a tall, kinky-haired girl in torn pajamas.

I turned away, letting the emptiness I felt fill every muscle, every sinew and bone. No anger, no sadness, just . . . nothing.

When I got back to my room, I slipped under the covers, pulling the blankets up to my chin.

"Was he there?"

Christy's whisper startled me. I gasped. Then I took a breath. "Yeah."

I felt her fumbling around underneath the sheets until she found my hand. She squeezed it tightly and I squeezed back. We stayed that way, side by side, hands entwined, until morning.

42

*Fact of Life #673: Sometimes you just have to kick
some butt.*

Monday afternoon I went into the girls' bathroom to check
for zits. As I stepped to the sink, I smelled something musky
but light. Essence of Libby. It was accented with the sound of
upchucking in the last stall, with some spitting and swearing
tossed in.

The toilet flushed and Libby stepped out, wiping her mouth
on the back of her hand. She frowned when she saw me, then
strode over to the sink and closed her eyes, washing her face
with her hands. "Morning sickness, my ass," she mumbled as she
reached out blindly for a paper towel. "It's one o'clock in the afternoon."

"It's kind of a misnomer," I said, using one of my SAT words.
"It can last twenty-four hours a day for some women."

"Great," she said. "That's really encouraging."

"Sorry," I said. "I guess I just believe you should have all the
facts."

She moaned, patting her face dry with the towel I had given her. "Washing your face feels good for, like, three seconds, and then you feel like shit again." She crumpled up the paper towel and tossed it. It missed the garbage can by a good foot, but neither of us moved to pick it up. "God, I could use a cigarette."

I knew from Abra that Libby had quit smoking the second she suspected she was pregnant, which I thought was pretty cool.

"Even though you feel sick?" I asked.

"Yeah," she said. "Weird, isn't it?"

I nodded. It was also weird that even though she was hijacking Abra, and Manny had been at her house at one in the morning, I still felt bad for her. Even I wasn't immune to Libby magic.

"Have you tried the raspberry tea?" I asked.

"Hated it." She pulled a makeup bag out of her purse and dabbed some foundation under her eyes. "I only tried it because Abra recommended it. But it was gross, so no more."

I laughed. "It *is* pretty nasty." I leaned against the wall next to the sinks. "I'm not a big tea drinker, either. But maybe if you think of it as medicine, you can get it down."

She looked at me. "Do you really think it would work?"

I shrugged. "Well, it doesn't work for everyone, but I know some mothers swear by it—"

She cringed and I stopped.

"What's wrong?"

"You said 'some mothers,' like *I'm* a mother."

I bit my lip. "Well," I said, gesturing to her stomach.

"But I'm not," she said. "I'm giving it up."

"Right." Libby was a mother; she would always be a mother, even when she gave the baby up for adoption. But she didn't need to hear that right now.

"That takes a lot of courage," I said quietly. I would have said more, but the door banged open.

"I was wondering where you were." One of Libby's groupies stepped right past me and stood next to Libby. "Are you okay?"

"I'm pregnant," Libby said.

The girl laughed nervously. "Right." She rolled her eyes up and down Libby, from the top of her head to her pale face to her slightly swelling belly. She took a step back, smiling uncertainly. "Well, you look great."

"I look like shit."

"No, really, Libby, you—"

"Please don't." Libby brushed on some blush. "I just can't hear it right now."

The girl's face fell and she took another step back, her heel crunching my toes.

"Ow!"

The girl jumped forward, startled. "When did *you* get here?"

"I was here before you were."

The girl frowned. "If you don't mind, we're having a conversation."

"Oh," I said. "Well, if *you* don't mind, I have to pee." I strode toward one of the stalls and ducked inside.

"We can talk later," the girl said to Libby.

"Sure," Libby said, as if she couldn't care less whether they ever talked again.

I heard footsteps, then the bathroom door swinging open, then closed. When I stepped out of the stall, Libby was still at the sink, applying eyeliner. She straightened up and dropped the eyeliner tube into her makeup bag.

"I guess I shouldn't have brushed her off, but sometimes I get tired of—them."

"I thought she was your friend."

Libby laughed. "I don't have friends, Kitty Kat. I have admirers. Much less complicated."

I ignored the hated nickname, noting that Libby Giles and I were having an actual conversation. "What about Manny?"

"True. We're tight." She stuffed the makeup bag in her purse and flipped her hair over her shoulder. "So I have one friend. And he's a good one." Straightening her shirt over her belly, she looked at herself in the mirror again. "I really wish I'd thought to give him a cool necklace like the one he always wears."

My heart skipped a beat. "He wears a necklace?"

"It's a hawk—pewter or silver or something. It's really awesome. He won't take it off. Says he got it from an aunt who really meant a lot to him." She sighed. "Isn't that the sweetest?"

An *aunt?* I was an *aunt* who had meant a lot to him? I clenched my fists at my sides and pressed my lips together.

"Are you okay?" Libby asked. "Your face is all red."

"I will be." I strode toward the door and grabbed the handle. "Asshole." I whipped open the door and stepped out, nearly running into Mitch.

"Whoa, Flynn."

I glared at Mitch. "Where is he?"

He stepped back. "I assume you mean Cruz, and by the look on your face, if I tell you, I might become an accessory to murder."

I scowled, then caught sight of Manny way down the hall.

"Never mind," I said, pushing past him. "You're off the hook."

"I'll visit you in prison," Mitch called after me.

I marched down the hall toward the jock lock, propelled by pure anger adrenaline. Manny was standing at his locker, his back to me, hanging out with some of the guys from the basketball team. My hands shook and I felt my resolve falter. I had no idea what I was going to do. Was I about to put myself in the Humiliation Hall of Fame?

I breathed in, trying to calm my crazy heartbeat. As Manny turned his head, I caught sight of the silver chain around his neck and my anger surged again.

Manny must have registered my presence, because he closed his locker and hurried in the opposite direction, up the hall.

I followed.

He walked into the boys' locker room. I went right in after him.

"Hey," I said. He didn't turn around.

But everyone else did. Boys were standing around in various states of undress; thankfully none of them were naked.

"Cruz."

This time he turned. He stared at me like I was a stranger, someone he didn't know at all. And I guess he didn't. There was no hint of the guy who had teased me and laughed with me, who had packed a lunch and shared a romantic December day at the Botanic Gardens with me, who had told me once that he was more comfortable with me than with anyone else he'd ever known.

"You're in the boys' locker room," he said. Someone snickered.

"I know."

"Well, maybe you should, you know, leave?" He turned away, shaking his head. The other guys smirked.

Just a little break, Kat. The memory of his voice buzzed inside my head.

I took a deep, cleansing breath and looked around the room. "We don't really know each other," I said to our audience. "So don't hold it against him that he's talking to me." I looked back at Manny, who still wasn't looking at me. "We don't know each other at all."

I walked around and stood between him and the locker, forcing him to look at me. The chain of the necklace glinted in the light. I imagined the hawk at the bottom, pressed against his throat.

"Nice necklace from your *aunt*," I said. Reaching out, I grabbed the silver chain, yanking it toward me. Manny's eyes widened in surprise as two links split apart, making a small popping noise. Opening my fist, I dropped the silver hawk and chain to the floor. They landed at Manny's feet with a dull clank.

"Here's your fucking break," I said. "*Hasta la vista.* Asshole."

So there I was, feeling really great after my big, dramatic parting moment, striding down the hall, thinking that if this was a movie, the theme music would swell right about now and I'd push through the school doors out into the sunshine, fists raised in triumph as I headed to my bright and hopeful future.

But my life wasn't a movie—so I went to AP English. And my hand hurt from yanking the chain. It was all red where the links had dug into my palm.

Later, on my way to PE, I stopped to tie my shoe at a hallway intersection. Then I heard Libby's voice just around the corner.

"A B in an AP class is like an A in a regular class, Mom," she was saying. She paused, tapping her foot impatiently. "I've already been accepted to the college you want me to go to, so get off my back." Another pause. "It's just a few more months. In August you'll be rid of me."

I heard her cell phone snap shut. I skittered backward in case she turned and saw me. But she walked right by, holding up a hand to one of the football players who passed her.

"Wattup, Libby girl?" he said, smacking her hand.

"Wattup." Everything about her seemed the same—hair flowing behind her, makeup perfectly blended, smile turned up to Bright.

But somehow, she looked different.

Apparently, when Yoga Girl decides to make a scene in the boys' locker room, it's pretty big news. The next morning people were pointing at me and whispering behind their hands. Everywhere I went, eyes turned quickly away.

Invisibility shield: out of order.

"Who is this girl who told off Manny Cruz in the boys' locker room?" Christy asked in her announcer's voice, holding the handle of her hairbrush toward my face. We were at my locker, Glen standing beside her with his arms crossed, wearing sunglasses like he was in the secret service or something. A pretty girl walked by, smiling at Glen. He gave her a quick nod. She looked familiar, but I couldn't place her.

"Did she really go in?" Christy said. "What exactly went on? And more important, did she see anything she wished she hadn't?"

There was one group of freshmen standing in a little circle across from my locker, tossing me glances when they thought I wasn't looking. They'd been doing it for about ten minutes, and I'd had it. I stalked up to them and put my hands on my hips.

"You got something you want to say?"

They cringed and shook their heads. As I started to turn, one of them piped up: "Do they have more urinals than stalls in there?"

I stopped and thought a moment. "I didn't notice."

She nodded, big-eyed. "Yeah. I guess you were kind of—distracted."

Later, a couple of Libby's friends were behind me at the drinking fountain. "Does she really expect us to believe she and Manny Cruz were actually *dating*?"

I straightened up, wiped my mouth carefully, and turned around.

"*She* doesn't expect you to believe anything," I said. "In fact, *she* couldn't care less *what* you believe." I stepped around the girl who'd said it and looked over my shoulder. "Oh, by the way. You've got a massive booger hanging from your nose."

I smiled as I heard her huff behind me. "Why didn't you say something?" she whined to her friends.

"We didn't want to embarrass you."

"You're supposed to be my friends."

I just shook my head and walked away.

43

Fact of Life #56: People can be like tornadoes,
destroying everything in their path.

Manny sent some pretty nasty text messages and e-mails after
the locker incident.

   After reading the first text—

   wat the F is wrong w u? From: DaMan Cell
      4:18 pm

—I deleted the rest without looking at them. But there was a
lovely e-mail waiting for me when I got home.

From: DaMan@yahoo.com
To: KatBrat@msn.com
Subject: What the hell?
I can't believe you did that. Are you insane? You
looked like an idiot.

No, *you* did. I noticed he hadn't signed it. Not even "M."
Delete.
Five minutes later, I got another one:

From: DaMan@yahoo.com
To: KatBrat@msn.com
Subject: Why?
Why would you do that? Why would you try to
embarrass me in front of my friends? You
embarrassed yourself more than me. You should hear
what they're saying about you.

Like that could hurt more than what *he'd* said?

You act like you've got your shit together, like you
take things as they come. But you don't. If you had a
problem with me, you should have come to me in
private.

Private. That's how you like it, isn't it?

Don't try to talk to me again.

Believe me, I won't.
Delete.

"As soon as the reservoir is open for swimming, I'm going." I sat
down across from Christy on Friday in the cafeteria, dropping
my lunch bag in front of me. "The open swim is going to be the
hardest."

273

"I thought you said the transition between the bike and the run was the hardest."

"Well, that, too." I sighed. "It's all hard."

Christy laughed. "I'm glad I'll just be on the sidelines, cheering you on as you paddle through all that murky water, where fish and people have probably peed and pooped—"

I wrinkled my nose. "Thanks for that show of support." But I felt good. It was amazing how an angry scene in a locker room and some nasty messages could pump you up. I'd been energized to push myself, channeling every bit of anger and disappointment into muscle power.

I might suck as a birth assistant, I might not be trophy girlfriend material, but I could swim and bike and run. I would rule this triathlon.

I glanced across the cafeteria and saw Libby striding toward the double doors that led to the front lawn. She was followed by two guys who might have been salivating, but it was hard to tell from this distance. True to Queen Libby and her magical powers, the news of her pregnancy hadn't dissuaded a lot of guys from hanging around her.

She glanced over her shoulder. I followed her gaze to Mitch, who was standing nearby with a bunch of his friends. When he looked at her, she quickly turned around, pushing her way outside.

"What's up, ladies?" Mitch Lowry had dropped into the seat across from me, next to Christy.

"You know you're risking your coolness rep by sitting here," I said.

"Would you forget that crap, Flynn? I need to talk to you."

Christy and I exchanged surprised looks.

"Nice move in the locker room, by the way," he said. "Sorry

I missed it." He caught my eye. "He's an idiot, but not a complete idiot, so don't give up on him."

I snorted. I wasn't going to be like Mitch, chasing after someone who clearly didn't want to be with me. We were so over, and I never wanted to see Manny's spineless ass again—do asses have spines?—and that was that. I wanted nothing more to do with Mr. Manny Cruz, wimpy, chicken-livered jerk that he was. I'd said what I wanted to say in front of a group of onlookers in various states of undress. That was enough.

"So can I talk to you?" Mitch's voice brought me back to the cafeteria.

"Is it about the asshole?" I asked.

"No." He looked at me. "Just five minutes," he said. "It's important."

Curiosity squashed my better judgment. "Five minutes," I said.

"What." We were next to the doors Libby had gone through just minutes before.

"I want to be a part of this thing with Libby, but she keeps shutting me down."

Here we go again.

"Mitch, I can't—"

"There she is," he whispered. I moved next to him and followed his gaze through the windows. Libby was standing near the brick wall with the words BABY DOE TABOR HIGH SCHOOL emblazoned on the front. She was chatting with the two guys, using her signature hair flip as she made a point. She tossed her hair again, this time turning her head so she had a clear view of our door. Mitch and I both slammed back against the wall.

"Count to ten," I said, as if I often had to deal with situations where I was spying on someone who made me feel invisible with a guy who was madly in love with her.

I saw his lips move. When he reached ten, he leaned out and looked through the window.

"Oh, shit."

When someone says "Oh, shit," of course you have to see what they are oh-shitting about, so I stepped around him to see for myself.

And wished I hadn't.

Libby was in the middle of kissing one of the guys she'd been talking to while the other guy watched, a stupid grin on his face.

I glanced at Mitch. His breath was coming fast; he was practically hyperventilating.

"Deep breaths, Mitch." I put my hand on his shoulder. "Don't faint on me. I may be taller, but you outweigh me by a good fifty pounds."

"Barely. Taller." His breath came out in ragged puffs.

"Okay, I'm barely taller." Sheesh. He was having an attack of ego at a time like this?

He sucked in fast, like he'd forgotten how to exhale. His cheeks were now drained of all color. If I didn't do something quick, he was going to keel over.

Lowering him to the ground, I squatted in front of him. "Put your head between your knees and breathe."

He did.

"Okay, we're going to do a cleansing breath together now," I said. "Like this." I lifted his chin so he could watch me demonstrate the breathing technique Abra showed to all the mothers.

On the exhale, I pursed my lips as if I were going to whistle.

"Yoga Girl's going to kiss Lowry!" A shout went up behind me, and I turned to see a guy from my calculus class pointing at me from a nearby table.

I scowled. "He's hyperventilating, you idiot. I'm showing him how to breathe."

The boy gave me a knowing look. "Sure you are."

I rolled my eyes and turned back to Mitch. "Breathe with me. Big, deep breaths."

He breathed. Soon it was rhythmic. He closed his eyes and lifted his head, taking in air slowly, then letting it out between his lips in an even hiss. Finally the color returned to his face.

"Now you're ready to push," I said.

His eyes flew open. "Huh?"

"Nothing. So are you feeling better?"

He nodded and stood up. He took another deep breath and smoothed his hair back. "You want to know what I did to make her break up with me and kick me out of her car?"

"Not really," I said, imagining some sordid sexual act gone awry.

He didn't seem to have heard. "I told her I loved her." He shook his head. "She dumped me because I told her I loved her. What the hell is that all about?" He didn't wait for an answer. "Fuck it," he said. "I'm going out there."

He pushed through the doors and strode across the grass to where Libby was still talking to the boys. One of them saw Mitch and said something to the other guy, the one she'd kissed. Both guys started walking quickly away. Libby tossed her head at Mitch and hurried after them.

But Mitch was too fast. He grabbed her arm and spun her around. Her face was twisted with anger, and I could tell they were both yelling. She wrenched herself away from him, shaking her head before stalking away. He shouted after her but didn't follow.

The bell rang. Mitch didn't move. He just stood there, alone, the wind ruffling his hair, watching the place where Libby had been standing as if she was still there.

We had an early dinner—Dad's special whole wheat orzo primavera with artichokes and asparagus as the main course. It was one of my favorites of the meatless dishes. And he'd made mashed potatoes, the one major white carb Abra refused to give up. It was a funny combination, but apparently Abra had professed a potato craving tonight, so he'd obliged.

"Delicious, James, as always." Abra beamed and reached over to squeeze my dad's arm. He grabbed her hand and held it.

"How goes life at the Midwifery?" he asked.

"Oh, good." Abra sighed. "But Libby's really going through a lot right now. Her mother is giving her a hard time, her mother's boyfriend seems to be pushing too hard to be part of the family, and Libby's ex-boyfriend won't give her the space she needs."

"Maybe we should talk about something else," I said. "You know. Midwife-mother privilege and all that."

"It's just that she's constantly on my mind," Abra said. "I really care about her."

Dad squeezed her arm again. "That's what makes them keep coming."

I slapped a blob of potatoes on my plate and set the bowl down with a satisfying bang.

"Katima," my mother said. "Don't take out your bad mood on the stoneware."

"Is the stoneware having relationship problems, too?" I asked. I turned to the brown bowl heaped with potatoes. "Forgive me," I said to the bowl. "I didn't recognize your pain underneath all that mush."

Lucy giggled.

I pushed my chair away from the table. "I'm not hungry. I'm going for a ride."

"Helmet, reflectors, take your cell," Dad said automatically. As I ran up the stairs, I heard him say, "What's with her?"

I paused, but there was silence.

Abra had nothing to say about her oldest daughter.

44

It was the last week of March—spring break. But it felt like winter. I could see my breath as I entered the building to go up to Abra's Midwifery after dropping Lucy off at a friend's house. We'd had three days of overcast skies—very unusual for Colorado—and it was beginning to get to me. I plopped down heavily in my chair and logged on to the computer. As I clicked on the scheduling software, the door opened.

Libby glanced at me before hanging up her jacket. "So, Kat, you're friends with Hat Girl?"

I was startled by the question. Had Libby actually noticed me at school? Was she actually asking about my life? I mean, we'd had the conversation in the bathroom, but that hadn't seemed to put me smack in the middle of her radar. "Christy Buchanan," I said. "Yeah."

"Those hats rock," Libby said, dropping into the chair across from my desk. "But she needs to dump that dude. He's subpar."

"Glen? You don't even know him." Why I was rushing to the

defense of Christy's shadow, I had no idea. Especially because Christy was about to dump him. But it bugged me that Libby thought she knew them and could decide what they should do.

"I know enough to know he's not for her."

"Why?"

Libby picked up a magazine and opened it. "Let's just say some people have an exaggerated idea of their importance in the universe."

"Huh?"

But Libby was done with the conversation.

I glanced at the computer. "You don't have an appointment today, do you?"

Libby shrugged. "I was in the neighborhood."

I looked back at the screen. Abra's Midwifery was not exactly in anyone's neighborhood.

Libby flipped the pages of the magazine, then tossed it back on the table. "Who's that supposed to be?" She pointed to the Fate Goddess. "Tinker Bell on acid?"

The hair rose on my arms. Nobody dissed the Fate Goddess. "She's a fate goddess," I said. "Three days after a baby is born, one of these goddesses flies into the nursery to determine the baby's future." I shrugged. "That's the story, anyway."

Libby snorted. "They must have all been on strike three days after I was born." She pointed to her belly. "Some future."

I smiled faintly. "Abra says the goddesses may determine the fate," I said, "but it's up to people to make good choices about their lives."

Libby turned away abruptly, her eyes skimming the pictures on the BOP wall. The room got quiet, and I continued to work on the computer.

"Why do you call her Abra?" she asked suddenly. "Is it some formal in-the-office thing?"

"Something like that." Like I would tell her the truth. Manny was the only one besides me who knew. I hated that he knew that about me. Knew so many things about me.

The door to the Gathering Place opened and a woman stepped out. "Thanks again, Abra."

Abra smiled widely. "Libby. What a wonderful surprise!"

"Do you have a couple of minutes?" Libby asked.

"For you?" Abra asked. "Of course. How are you?"

They did their little Happy Face Club thing and disappeared into the Gathering Place.

Kat? How are you?

My life sucks, Abra, thank you so much for asking. I wondered what Abra would do if she knew her daughter was such a freak, boys didn't even want to be seen with her.

I finished updating appointments and decided to tidy up the reception area. I was changing the coffee filter when I heard the door to the Gathering Place open behind me. I kept my back turned, waiting for the clink that told me Libby had taken her coat off the hanger, then the thunk of the outer door closing that told me she was gone.

But the hanger didn't clink. The door didn't close. I pulled out the coffeepot and set it on the counter. Still no door. Opening the coffeemaker lid, I saw that the filter was dirty. To get rid of it meant turning around to the trash can, which meant facing the door, and Libby still hadn't left. What was taking her so long? Her coat was right there on the hanger. She just needed to pull it down and walk out.

I looked over my shoulder. Libby was standing there, gazing

up at the Fate Goddess. Her eyebrows were scrunched, her mouth small and tight like she was holding something in. Opening a drawer, I pulled out a playing-card-sized laminated image of the Fate Goddess. "Here," I said, offering it to her. On the back it said *Create your fate*.

"No thanks." She turned quickly, snatched her coat, and was out the door before I could say anything more. Okay, fine. I tucked the goddess card into my back pocket and went back to work.

Later I got a text from Manny:

> Can we meet 2 talk? u name place From: DaMan Cell
>   7:24 pm

My fingers twitched. I pushed Reply.

> How about in the middle of the hall where every1
>   can c u? Will u meet me there?

I didn't think so.

The next day I went for a short run on the High Line Canal trail. I needed to reclaim it after Manny and I broke up. When I got to my car afterward, I turned on my cell phone. Christy had called four times. When I called her back, she answered on half a ring.

"Asshole!" she shouted into my ear.

"What?" Did I do something I didn't know about?

"Why did I wait so long?" Christy said. "Why didn't I dump his ass weeks ago?"

Glen.

"I don't know," I said. "Why didn't you?"

"Because I'm too damn nice, that's why!" she shouted. "I kept trying to find the right time, tried to figure out what to say to let him down easy, and then bam! He pulls this crap."

"What crap?"

"Get over here, Kat," Christy said. "You need to get this story in person."

Ten minutes later, I was on Christy's front porch. She was waiting at the door. The first thing I noticed was that she was hatless. She brushed a hand self-consciously over her bare head.

"I got pissed and mangled it."

No doubt the hat Glen had given her. I held up my duffle of dirty workout clothes and a bag from Blockbuster. "Sleepover?"

Christy threw her arms around me. "You're the best friend in the world."

"I know," I said. "Have DVDs, will travel. Someone very smart and wonderful once told me you should not be alone after a breakup."

She laughed, tugging at my hand as we headed upstairs. "My parents are 'giving me my space.' Dad was ready to go beat up Glen, but I convinced him that wouldn't be necessary." She closed her bedroom door and turned on her CD player, which moaned out a mournful blues song.

"Wrong, wrong, wrong," I said, flipping through her CD collection. I pulled out Alanis Morissette's *Jagged Little Pill*, circa 1995. Christy was into vintage music, in addition to vintage hats. "You need some bitter female empowerment tunes."

Alanis's piercing voice filled the room, and Christy nodded

her head to the music. We both started singing along, then Christy shook her head hard, like she was trying to knock something out of it.

"He's been seeing someone else."

"You're kidding." Now I felt even worse for shouting those things during our fight. I had no idea they might have been true.

"It was that girl he was talking to at Mitch's New Year's party. They were all over each other in the backseat." Click. That was the girl I'd seen in the hallway—the one Glen had smiled at when he was all Secret Service with us.

"I should have known something was up at Starbucks," I said.

"What?"

"Nothing." But Glen was a creature of habit. He always ordered the House Blend. Until two weeks ago. He'd ordered the Arabian Mocha Sanani from the "bold" category. Very un-Glen-like. I just thought he was being adventurous.

Christy sat down heavily on her bed, her hands stuffed in her jeans pockets. "It just pisses me off. Now I'm the poor girlfriend who didn't know her boyfriend was cheating on her instead of the righteous chick who dumped his subpar butt when I had the chance. I hate being that girl."

I looked up, startled. "Did you say 'subpar'?"

"Yeah," Christy said. "Libby Giles said that to me just last week. Can you believe she talked to me? I didn't even think she knew who I was. But right in the middle of me trying to figure out how I should break up with him, she passes my locker, stops, and says, 'Cool hat, subpar guy. Keep it, lose him.' " She looked at me. "Isn't that bizarre?"

"Very," I said, thinking about my own conversation with Libby. And now what she had said back then made sense. "As for Glen the Jerk, some people have an exaggerated idea of their importance in the universe."

"You are so right, Kat. That is the perfect line."

I decided not to give the credit to Libby. Arranging myself against the pillows, I leaned back. "So start from the sordid beginning."

She explained how she went looking for him and ended up at their "spot" at the park. "At first I couldn't believe it. It was like I was watching a movie or something, you know? But then something clicked inside me." She sat up straighter. "I pounded on the trunk." She smacked her hands on the bed for emphasis. "They practically went through the roof." She smiled slightly. "They both turned and stared at me; then she was trying to get her shirt on—"

"No way."

"Mine are much nicer than hers," Christy said, lifting up her breasts in both hands.

I laughed. "Of course."

They both apparently had tried to "explain," but Christy didn't give them a chance. She just started screaming at them.

"I was hurling insults like a madwoman," she said, laughing. "I don't even know if what I said made any sense. I was just so *pissed*. But I did tell him he was a subpar asshole. That I remember." She sank onto the bed. "So much for the all-seeing, all-knowing Buchanan Field Report," she said bitterly. "Why didn't he just break up with me if he wanted to go out with someone else?"

"Ego trip," I said. "It's a disease." I reached over and squeezed her leg.

We ate pizza and watched movies. Around ten o'clock, my cell rang.

"Hey," I said as I flipped it open.

"Your mom told me you left a message that something was up with Christy," my dad said. "Is everything okay?"

"It will be," I said, telling him briefly what happened.

"Good," Dad said. "I'm glad you're with her."

"Me, too," I said. "I'll see you tomorrow."

"Oh, Kat?"

"Yeah?"

"Some guy named Manny called."

45

"Are you going to call him back?" Christy asked as we stood on her front porch saying good-bye the next morning.

I shook my head. "He probably called to yell at me because it would be more satisfying in person than in an e-mail like he's been doing."

"Why wouldn't he just call you on your cell?" Christy asked.

I frowned at her. I'd wondered that myself. "You're the one who keeps reminding me he's a spineless loser. You're not supposed to be encouraging me to talk to him."

"I'm not encouraging, I'm just asking." She jumped down one step.

"So," I said, changing the subject. "You need to promise me that if you feel the urge to set fire to Glen's house or toss rotten eggs through that girl's window, you'll call me first."

"You're no fun," Christy said, and we both laughed. Then she stepped out on the lawn, stretching her arms skyward. "I feel— free, you know? Like I can finally do things."

"Good for you."

"I don't know what I'll do, but I've got all kinds of open days ahead of me, without Mr. Jerk constantly at my side."

"No more turning statements into questions?" I said, imitating him. "No more breast checks?"

She laughed and pumped her fist in the air. "Yes!"

I left her there on the grass, dancing.

When I got home, I went straight to the Womb, stretching out on the futon. I thought about Christy and Glen and why guys could be such unpredictable idiots just when you thought you had them nailed. Like I thought Mitch was a Neanderthal jerk, and he turned out to be pretty decent. And Glen seemed so innocent and shy, and he was feeling up another girl in his car.

And Manny Cruz had called my house when he had never, ever called it before.

But I wasn't calling him back, even though I was practically dying of curiosity.

Forget it, Kat.

I turned my attention to the mural. I still couldn't decide what it needed and hated the feeling that it was somehow unfinished, when I'd thought I'd finished it two years ago.

There was a gentle knock on the door.

"Katima, can I come in?"

"Yeah."

Abra stepped through the door. She glanced at the mural, then down at me. "How's Christy?" My dad must have told her.

"Good."

She nodded. "That's a tough way to break up with someone."

So is having a guy dump you because he doesn't want to be seen in public with you.

"Yeah," I said. "But she was already planning on breaking up. She just hates the fact that people think he dissed her for another girl when she was over him long before that."

Abra smiled. "I can understand that." She looked at the mural again. "But hopefully she'll be able to let go of her anger. Forgiveness is the greatest gift you can give yourself."

"You mean to the other person."

Abra shook her head. "Forgiveness is really about us letting go . . . of anger, resentment"—she paused, smiling—"fantasies of revenge. Those damage *us*, not the person who wronged us."

Okay, this was venturing too far into Lectureland for me. Especially because it made me think about Manny and my own feelings of anger. I picked up my sketchbook.

"So have you seen Libby at school?"

I was relieved she'd changed the subject, but not relieved about the subject she'd chosen.

"Not really."

"Well, how does she seem? How are people treating her?"

Now that Libby was starting to show, it seemed like people had started to keep their distance. But maybe that was just my imagination. Maybe she was choosing to spend more time alone, or with just a few people.

Picking up my sketchbook, I turned to a clean page. "You would know better than me."

"But you're at her school," Abra said. "You can observe her."

"What is she, a science experiment?"

Abra let out an exasperated sigh. "Of course not. I just thought you might have seen something, something that would help me help her."

And why would I want to do that? So you can spend even more time with her?

"Sorry," I said. "I just don't see her much at school."

Back at school after the break, Manny sat behind me in Spanish like he used to.

"Did your dad tell you I called Friday night?"

His question startled me. He wasn't whispering, he was talking in a normal tone of voice that anyone could hear. In fact, the girl next to him, the one who accidentally-on-purpose dropped her papers so he'd help her pick them up, had definitely heard. After glancing up at him, she was now staring intently at her notebook. She couldn't fool me. I was the master eavesdropper. I knew all the tricks. Her eyes weren't tracking, they were staring in one place. She was totally listening in.

I frowned. Was he now talking to me out in the open because his best friend, Mitch, aka Mr. Cool, had been seen talking to me and had not been sent to Loser Island? Did he have to wait for someone else to try before he would?

Is that even fair? I thought, remembering Abra's words about forgiveness.

"Yeah," I said. But that was all. I knew he was waiting for me to say more, to explain why I hadn't called back. But even if I had something to say (which I didn't), I didn't want Ms. Nosy Notebook hearing anything else. Luckily, Señora García-Smith started class and no one could say anything.

That night, I got three e-mails from him:

From: DaMan@yahoo.com
To: KatBrat@msn.com
Subject: I suck

Kat,

I guess I'm really slow but I just realized you must have heard a certain conversation outside the locker room. Where I said some things I REALLY regret. I feel like shit. I am shit. I suck beyond belief. I won't blame you if you never talk to me again but I hope you will. I'm REALLY sorry.

The sucking wonder,

M

Okay, so he had finally acknowledged the conversation outside the locker room. He knew he was shit. He was sorry. I felt a little better. But I still wanted to strangle him.

From: DaMan@yahoo.com
To: KatBrat@msn.com
Subject: Still the sucking wonder

I don't know what to say. But for some reason I can't not write you, even though I know you'll probably delete this without even reading it. Which would be okay because it really doesn't say anything. Except I miss you and I'm totally sorry for being a jerk.

M

And another one.

From: DaMan@yahoo.com
To: KatBrat@msn.com
Subject: A-hole ville
Kat—

Just found out about Hat Girl. He's an asshole. Seems to be something going around. Anyway, I hope Christy is okay. I already know three guys who want to ask her out. Let me know if I can give them the thumbs-up to go for it.

And let me know if you think there is the smallest chance you will ever forgive me or talk to me again.

M

That made me smile. And it was nice what he said about Christy, even if he was a spineless loser.

Why did he have to be so nice?

That night we had a family birthday party for Lucy; she'd have her big bash that weekend with all her friends.

"Happy birthday!" I said, giving her a hug as we gathered around her cake. "You're double digits now, Luce. Unbelievable."

After we sang to her and she blew out the candles—"All ten!" Abra said, clapping—Lucy opened her presents, saving mine for last.

When she ripped off the paper, she gasped. "Oh my gosh! Wow." She opened the wooden case gingerly, revealing an art set with pastels, colored pencils, and markers. "I'll never be as good as you," she said to me.

"You'll be better," I said, squeezing her arm.

Abra and my dad gave her new clothes and some books and music that she wanted, and then we had cake and ice cream.

"I have the best family in the world," Lucy said between mouthfuls.

Looking at her—face beaming, eyes bright—I could almost believe it.

When I got to my car after school the following Monday, Mitch was at Libby's car, moving his arms as he talked. I knew I shouldn't, but I rolled down my window so I could hear better.

"I know it's mine, Libby, and I can't believe you completely shut me out of the whole thing," Mitch said. "I would have been there for you. I want to be there for you now."

"Oh, please." Libby was standing by the open hatch, pawing through what looked like a second closet inside. She had clothes, hair accessories, socks, and different pairs of shoes in there.

"Did you think about me at all? That I'd want to be a part of this?"

She stopped pawing and looked at him. "Why? So you could pay for the abortion and be done with it?"

Mitch pulled back as if she'd slapped him. "That baby is part of me, Libby. Hell, I used to think *you* were a part of me."

She flinched at that.

"You should have told me," he said. "I shouldn't have had to hear it from one of your little pep squad girls."

Libby rolled her eyes, lifting a shirt here, a pair of pants there, before tossing them aside. "Damn," she said. "Where is it?"

Mitch stuck his face next to hers. "You never thought about me, did you?" he said. "It was all about you."

Libby whipped around at that. "I'm the one who's pregnant, asshole."

"And I helped get you that way."

"Oh, God." She brushed her hand at him like he was an annoying fly.

"Forget it." His voice was hard. "You want to go through this alone? Be my guest." Turning on his heel, he stalked away.

Libby dug around for a few more seconds, but her movements had slowed. "Shit," she said, slamming the hatch. She looked up, staring after Mitch, her shoulders slumped. Then she blinked rapidly, wiping her hand across her eyes. As she reached for the door, she looked my way and our eyes locked.

"What are you looking at?"

I bit my lip, then took a breath. "He loves you. He wants to be with you and share this with you. Why won't you talk to him?"

"Shut up." She slid into her car and slammed the door.

Tuesday before school, I stuffed my books in my locker, then reached into my back pocket for a pen. I felt something there. It was the Fate Goddess card Libby had refused to take from me. It was in perfect condition, even though it had been through the wash.

The halls were practically empty as I walked to the jock lock. When I reached Libby's locker, I slipped the goddess card into the grate. I glanced at Mitch's locker, then Manny's, then back down the hall. Funny, this galaxy didn't feel quite so far from my own anymore.

It was barely mid-April. Libby was the last appointment of the day at the Midwifery on Thursday. She and Abra had jumped right into their bonding in the Gathering Place, and I got to work filing and cleaning up the reception area.

Sitting down in my chair, I took a breath, hating the image of the two of them on the couch in the GP, all cozy and friendly. Abra probably wished she could switch me out for Libby, have the daughter she'd always dreamed of. What was wrong with me that I wasn't that daughter? My emotions jumped all over. One minute I felt bad for Libby and thought maybe we could be friends; the next I was pissed at her for spending so much time with Abra, and pissed at Abra for being too clueless to see any of it.

After saying good-bye to Libby, Abra stood next to my desk, looking at the closed door. What? Was she pining away that her darling Libby had left?

"I've invited Libby over for dinner again tomorrow night," Abra said. "Maybe you can join us for dominoes this time."

I didn't answer.

"She's really an amazing person, Katima," Abra said. "Smart and insightful—I think you two could be good friends."

Why? Because you want some of that smart and insightful stuff to rub off on me?

I rolled my eyes. "Libby'll graduate at the end of May with the rest of her class, have the baby at the end of July, hand it over to the adoptive parents, and go on to the Ivy League college of her choice. End of story."

"She'll still be a part of our lives." I heard something in her voice. Desire? Hope?

It made me feel invisible. "What, are you going to adopt her?"

"Oh, Katima, please." She picked up the mail off the corner of my desk.

"And by the way," I said, standing up, "where's Libby going to have her baby? At *her* house, with her wonderfully supportive mother and that dude? I don't think so." I looked right into her eyes. "Oh, wait. Let me guess. Serenity Space."

"We haven't gotten that far in the planning, Katima. We don't know."

"Like hell you don't."

"Katima Flynn!" She stared at me, working her mouth like she did when she really wanted to say something but knew she should say something totally different or nothing at all. She closed her eyes and took a deep, cleansing breath. Then another. And a third. She opened her eyes and stepped toward me, reaching out a hand. She looked like a teacher trying to placate a student disappointed over her grade. Why couldn't she just be my mother?

"Katima, let's be fair," she said calmly. "You don't know enough about her. You don't have all the facts—"

Something inside of me split open. "You want some facts, Abra?" I shouted. "You've made it clear that what I want or need doesn't matter. You think for me and speak for me and want to make me into the image and likeness of Abra so I have no idea how to think or what to say. That's Fact Number One. You're so busy being everyone else's mom that you have no idea how to be a mom to your own daughters. That's Fact Number Two. You expect me to listen to all the trials and tribulations of Libby Giles and be happy that you spend all this time with her and care about her, and you don't even know that I had a boyfriend who thought I was too much of a loser to be seen with in public, and that Christy and I had a big fight. And that Lucy is having friendship problems and wants me to tell her about the 'facts of life,' and not you. That's Fact Number Three. Well, here's Fact Number Four for you, Abra: fuck you."

297

I pushed past her out the door, but not before seeing her reaction, caught forever in my mind like a photograph: eyes wide, mouth open in shock, body bent as if I'd punched her in the stomach.

When I reached the parking lot, I stood stupidly for a moment, unable to remember where I'd parked my car. My eyes, blurred by angry tears, skimmed over the few vehicles left in the lot before coming to rest on a familiar red Ford Escape. Why was Libby still here?

I stormed up to her car and banged on the window.

"Go home!" I shouted. "Quit stalking her."

Libby's face darkened. "I'm not stalking her!" she shouted back through the glass. Then her eyes narrowed. "Did you do something to her? What did you do to her?"

I stepped back from the car. "Would you stop talking like that? You don't own her!"

"You don't deserve her!" Libby said.

"You are not part of our family!" I screamed, nearly choking. "You're not her daughter, and you never will be!"

Libby's voice was loud, clear, through the car window: "I should be!"

And you shouldn't.

She didn't have to say it. It hung in the air, sharp and accusing. I strode to my car and yanked open the door, my whole body shaking as I slumped in the seat.

46

"Kat?" Christy opened her front door, and I stepped past her into the warmth of her house. "What happened? You sounded really crazy on the phone."

"I—I—" I couldn't finish.

"Abra called twice. I told her you were on your way."

Was she worried? Or did she want to scream back at me?

"I can't talk right now," I whispered. "Can I take a shower?" I had to get clean. To wash away the feelings that had seeped up through my skin, pricking at it, making it burn all over.

"Sure, sure," Christy said. "Then we'll talk."

Christy sat behind me on her bed, combing my hair. Her jet-powered blow dryer lay beside us, ready for action.

"I can't believe I said all that to her. It was like someone hit a switch and I couldn't stop talking." I hadn't told Christy about my encounter with Libby yet. It was too raw, too painful. I pulled the blanket she had given me tighter around my shoulders. "You should have seen her face."

"I know," Christy said. "But it had to come out sometime. You were overdue."

I looked over my shoulder at her. "What do you mean?"

She shrugged. "You go along with just about everything when it comes to Abra. It's like you're afraid she'll do something horrible if you don't."

I cringed.

"But lately you've been different. More secure. More your own person."

"Thanks, Oprah."

She smiled and turned on the blow dryer, running her fingers through my hair. I closed my eyes, letting the white noise drown out everything, relaxing under Christy's gentle touch.

We watched two movies before she snapped her fingers. "Oh, I almost forgot," she said, reaching over the side of her bed and pulling out her field notebook. She flipped to a page with a paper clip marking her spot: "Read this."

> *Buchanan Field Report: Mannygate*
> *4/18 1:45 p.m.*
> - *M stops me in hall to ask what he can do to make it up to K.*
> - *I tell him to grow a backbone.*
> - *He says he doesn't want to crowd her.*
> - *I call him a coward.*
> - *He growls at me and stomps away.*

"Did he really growl?" I asked.

"Errrr." Christy imitated him. I giggled.

"Do you think he really wants to give me my space?"

Christy sighed heavily next to me.

"Right," I said. "Coward. No backbone."

"Go to sleep."

But I couldn't. I kept thinking about Abra, then about Libby, then about Manny and back again. I finally fell asleep sometime after 2:00 a.m., but woke up at 6:00 to Abra's face—hurt and bewildered—Libby's face, hurt and angry. I smiled sadly as Christy snort-snored in her sleep and rolled over. Carefully climbing out of her bed, I stood in front of the mirror hanging above her dresser. My eyes were still a little puffy, my hair squished up on the side I'd been sleeping on. I grabbed some of the squished hair and pulled it down, then folded it up next to my chin. Maybe I should cut it all off. Maybe I should shave it off, go bald in penance for my sins.

Nah. Too chicken.

Dropping my hair, I walked to the window and looked out. Early morning sun spread out across the grass; tulips and crocuses bloomed next to the walkway. I had a sudden urge to be outside. I could get in a short run and still make it to school.

Grabbing some of Christy's clothes, I changed quickly, jotted her a note, and headed out the door to my car.

At the trail, I started out too fast, my lungs heaving before I'd even passed the half-mile marker. But I didn't slow down. The burning in my muscles felt good, as if I might burn away all feeling and be left with numbness and peace.

Finally I turned back, slowing to a shaky walk as I peered across the fields to my right, the sun casting a golden glow across the grasses. I saw a hawk circle high, then disappear over the trees. My heart felt heavy.

When I came to a bench, I plopped down, slowing my heart rate with each measured breath. I leaned back and closed my eyes, feeling the cool breeze across my hot, sweaty face.

"Kat. Hey." Manny's voice, though quiet, startled me.

I leapt up. "God, you scared me." I hurried down the path toward the parking lot.

"Kat, please. Wait. Will you just wait a minute?"

I fumbled in my pocket for my keys.

"Look, Kat, I know you're pissed at me and—"

I held up my hand, silencing him. "I can't deal with this right now."

Manny caught up with me. "What happened? Is this about Libby?"

Had she told him what happened in the Midwifery parking lot? Now, *that* pissed me off.

"Not everything is about Libby." My hand trembled as I pressed the button to unlock my car, and I dropped my keys. "Damn."

Manny picked them up and handed them to me. "I've missed you."

I shook my head in disbelief. "Who cares, Mr. Small World. Everything isn't all about you, either." I opened the door.

"If you told me what was going on, maybe I could help."

"It was my screwup," I said. "I have to fix it."

Manny nodded. "I've got one of those, too," he said. "And I'm trying to fix it." Then he held up his hands, as if to ward off a blow. "I know, I know. It's all about me." He smiled. "But it's also about somebody else." He turned around and headed to his car.

I stood against my car for a long time, staring at the trees, feeling as empty as the spaces between them.

• • •

When I got to school, I saw Libby leaning against her car, talking to Manny. They were both laughing, and every so often she would reach over and squeeze his arm. Guilt lay heavy in the pit of my stomach, mixed with anger and jealousy.

Libby looked my way, shaking her head ever so slightly, before turning back to Manny, smiling again. Then he looked at me, his eyes gentle.

I'm mad at you. I'm mad at her. Don't look at me like that.

I ducked my head and went the long way around the building.

47

The DJ's voice woke me up at 4:30 the next morning. After school yesterday I had gone to three movies, and even though I'd gotten home after midnight, managing to miss seeing anyone in the family, it was still a Saturday, swim day. Five in the morning at the pool on a Saturday meant I'd have it practically to myself.

As I started my car, the front door opened. Abra was standing there, framed in the doorway, the lamp in the living room illuminating her pajamas, her arms wrapped tightly around her. She was looking at the driveway, at my car, at *me*. I hesitated. Did she want to talk to me? Did I want to talk to her?

No. I wasn't ready. I switched on my headlights and backed down the driveway. She was still in the doorway when I looked over my shoulder before pulling away.

Fact of Life #22: When you've told your own mother to fuck off, things tend to get a little chilly around the home front.

I stayed at the rec center as long as I could before going home. When I got there, I could hear everyone in the kitchen. As I closed the front door, I could see Lucy walking down the hall, carrying a cookie. She stopped a few feet away and crossed her arms over her chest.

"You made Mom cry."

I let out a breath. Abra had been crying?

"You said bad words to her."

I frowned. "How do you know that?"

Lucy lowered her eyes. "I heard when she told Dad."

I wanted to defend myself, to tell Lucy that Abra liked Libby better than she liked us—or maybe just me—but it sounded petty and stupid, and I couldn't do it.

"Was it something with Libby?" Lucy asked. "She didn't come for dinner last night like she was supposed to."

I couldn't even process that right now. Abra had cried, Lucy missed Libby, and I didn't know which end was up. "It'll work out," I said, tapping her on the head before trudging to my room. The first thing I noticed was Lucy's picture. *Best sister.*

Sighing, I flopped down on my bed, my mind racing with images and thoughts I couldn't seem to stop. I wanted to make it all go away, stop feeling the pain and guilt and anger inside. But I didn't know how.

When I glanced at the clock, I couldn't believe nearly two hours had passed. Hunger drove me downstairs to make a sandwich. I could hear Abra in the laundry room, and practically broke out in a sweat thinking about seeing her.

She stepped into the kitchen, not even glancing at me as she got herself a glass of water.

"Do you have any clothes that need washing?"

Okay. I'd screamed at her and told her to fuck off and she was asking me about laundry?

"I'll check."

I went up to my room to get my laundry and heard my computer chime. There were five e-mails from Manny. Some people just don't give up. You kind of have to admire that, even if they are cowards with no backbone.

I read the last one first.

From: DaMan@yahoo.com
To: KatBrat@msn.com
Subject: What can I do?
Kat,
I want to know what's wrong. Can I help? Did you have a fight with Hat Girl? Is it a family thing?
M
P.S. My dad is pissed at his lawyer, so now he wants me to be an accountant like my mom. I hate math.

I smiled. I couldn't help it. It gave me courage to run my laundry down and face Abra. But she didn't say anything, just took my clothes and started sorting them. I bit my lip and went back up to my room.

"Kat?" My dad's voice was soft outside the door. I didn't want to see him. He must hate me for hurting Abra. I grabbed my iPod and stuck the earbuds in my ears, turning up the volume.

I didn't feel him until he was directly behind me. I turned quickly, startled.

"I didn't mean to scare you," he said. "I had a feeling you couldn't hear me knocking." Ouch. It was just a small thing, me pretending I hadn't heard, but it was a lie and I felt it.

His face looked pained. "So?"

"She asked about laundry."

"It's a start."

I sighed. "I have no idea how to talk to her."

"So tell her that."

"That's lame."

He smiled slightly. "Maybe it would open a door."

I had thought the laundry was a door, but she hadn't said anything when I brought my small load down.

My dad squeezed my shoulders.

"You love each other," he said. "That always wins out in the end."

Yeah, in the end. But when would that be?

48

We were supposed to go up to the mountains the next weekend, but Dad got stuck on a case and Abra didn't want to leave a few of her mothers who were close to delivery. I was relieved. It would have been awkward and uncomfortable, and this way I could keep to my routine of getting ready for the official June tri training session, putting the last touches on Diane and Jeff's mural, and hiding out in my room. Not necessarily in that order.

And of course, I wasn't at the Midwifery anymore. No way. Abra had gotten someone to fill in for me. We never talked about it.

At home, Abra and I talked only when we needed to and nothing more. It was like we were following a dance that someone had choreographed, stepping around each other, avoiding eye contact, the weight of things unsaid hanging like a chain between us. The more time that passed, the harder it was for me to know what to say and when to say it. Maybe it was better to just let it go on the way it was. Maybe it would work itself out without either of us having to do anything.

With Libby, I had decided to take action. A few days ago I'd caught up with her in the hall at school.

"I just wanted to say I'm sorry about what I said," I told her as we strode toward the cafeteria. "I didn't mean it. I was just— oh, I don't know." She didn't respond, didn't even look my way. She kept her eyes straight ahead, until someone she knew passed her. Then her face changed, her famous smile took over, and she said hi to them or nodded.

"You should go back to the Midwifery," I said, unwilling to give up. "Abra's worried about you and I'm not working there anymore, so it's safe." I hoped that would get her attention, or at least a smile out of her.

But it was like I didn't exist. I could see now why it had been so hard for Mitch. If Libby didn't want to acknowledge you, there wasn't a lot you could do about it.

"I'm really sorry," I said again. "I hope you'll go back." I stopped then, letting her continue down the hall without me. She looked over her shoulder and for an instant our eyes met. But her expression didn't change. She just studied my face for a moment, then turned back around and was swallowed up by the crowd.

After school on Monday, I worked out in the school weight room. When I came out to the parking lot, I saw Mitch Lowry standing next to his truck, yelling into his cell phone. The hood was up. Apparently his brother had borrowed his jumper cables and hadn't put them back.

"I've got some," I said, opening my trunk.

After we'd gotten his truck started, I pulled off the cables.

"Thanks, Kat."

I smiled and walked around to the driver's side of my car. "You want me to follow you anywhere?"

"Nah. I'm good." He jutted his chin toward the school. "Cruz is coming."

My heart did a flip, but I kept my expression calm. "Guess I'd better head out."

Mitch raised an eyebrow at me. "Yeah, I know how that is. We know how to pick 'em, don't we?" He put an arm around me. "Maybe you and I should go out."

"Now, there's a good idea." I patted his arm before sliding it off my shoulder.

As I was climbing into the front seat of my car, Mitch grabbed the door. "You should at least talk to him."

"Are you giving me relationship advice, Lowry?"

He grinned. "Thanks again for the jump."

"You're welcome," I said, closing the door tight. I glanced to my right to check for cars. Manny was standing about a dozen feet away. Our eyes locked for a moment. He signaled for me to roll down my window. I hesitated and then thought, *Why not?*

His eyes were soft, but he looked nervous. "She didn't mean what she said, Kat."

Libby. Of course. Did anyone talk about anything else?

"I can't believe she told you."

"She didn't say much," Manny said. "Just that she said you didn't deserve your mom or something like that."

She hadn't told him what I'd said to her. Huh.

"It doesn't matter," I said.

"Sure it does."

Silence followed, with Manny looking out over the parking lot, me staring down at the steering wheel.

"Well, she's now drinking that disgusting raspberry tea because of what you said."

I wrinkled my brow. So poor Libby was one of those with morning sickness beyond the first trimester. What did that have to do with anything?

"I just thought you'd like to know that she actually listened to you." His fingers were on the door, inches from my shoulder. I realized with a pang how much I missed his touch. "She's really going through a lot," Manny said. "That's why I've been spending so much time with her."

"You don't have to explain anything to me, Manny. I know you two are tight."

Manny laughed. "That's her word." His hand moved so his knuckles brushed my shirt. "It's kind of a one-way relationship. She bitches; I listen and try to convince her to go back to Lowry." He glanced over his shoulder. "Speaking of which, what was up with him?"

"Dead battery. I was rescuing him."

Manny nodded. "Got any other rescues lined up?"

"Sorry," I said. "I've filled my quota for the year. One stupid guy every twelve months. That's about all I can handle."

"Sounds like a good policy," he said. "Ever make an exception?"

He was adorable in his baggy jeans and sweatshirt, his hair waving softly around his face. I looked into those eyes, deep and dark. I used to think he knew my soul.

Hasta la vista, Yoga Baby.

I took a breath and let it out. "Sorry. No exceptions."

He tapped the car door lightly before stepping back. "Can't blame a guy for trying."

I pulled away, looking at Manny in my rearview mirror. He had already turned and was walking toward his Range Rover. Was that it? Had he given up at last?

The thought made me heavy with sadness.

49

I was driving home around 7:00 Wednesday night from Diane and Jeff's, where I'd just finished the mural. They had loved it, and the check was tucked carefully inside my pocket. And to make it even more amazing, Diane had asked if she could give my number to some of her friends who had asked about me.

"Really? That is so cool."

So I was feeling pretty good when my cell rang and I saw it was Manny. My heart sped up. Maybe he hadn't given up after all.

"Don't hang up," Manny said when I answered. "I'm not calling you about our stuff."

"Okay," I said warily.

"I can't find Mitch," he said. "We were supposed to meet to shoot hoops at the Y. He didn't show up. He's not home, and he's not picking up his cell."

I frowned. "Where are you?"

"Driving down Colorado Boulevard, trying to spot his truck."

"Okay, I'll go by the school and call you back."

The school lot was empty when I drove by. I stopped at a

light, drumming my fingers on the steering wheel. *If I were Mitch Lowry, where would I go?*

The gym, the weight room, and the Y all flashed through my head.

"Well, duh," I said aloud, flipping a U-turn.

Mitch's truck was parked outside Libby's house when I pulled up. He was huddled in the cab, listening to his iPod. So he wasn't giving up, either.

I rapped lightly on the window.

Mitch rolled it down. "What?"

"She won't be back until nine. She's got her birthing class."

He scowled. "I should be with her."

"Manny waited for you at the Y."

"Crap," he said. "I forgot. Got Giles on the brain." He looked at her house. "I'm freezing," he said, pulling his coat more tightly around him. "Isn't May supposed to be one of the warm months?"

"It's only May 2," I said. "This is Colorado. Why don't you have the heat on?"

"I'm almost out of gas."

I snorted. Kat to the rescue again.

"If you can make it a few blocks, I've got a gas can at my house we use for the lawn mower."

Mitch started his engine. "You live around here?"

"Got to live somewhere," I said, turning back to my car.

I called Manny as I was thawing Mitch out in our kitchen with a cup of coffee and some leftover casserole. My parents and Lucy had gone out to run errands, so he was completely comfortable eating everything in sight.

"He's fine," I said to Manny.

314

"Was he wasted?"

"No."

"Should I come over?"

"Just a minute." I shifted the phone away from mouth.

"Cruz wants to know if he should come over."

Mitch took a big bite of casserole and chewed. "What for?"

"He wants to know what for," I said to Manny.

Manny laughed. "Well, I guess he's in good hands."

"I guess," I said. "Hold on a sec."

I walked out of the kitchen with the phone, lowering my voice so Mitch couldn't hear me. "What should I do about the Libby thing? I think he's going to go over there and wait for her after he finishes eating me out of house and home."

"Let him go," he said. "If she's smart, she'll take him back."

"And if she doesn't?"

"She'll miss out on something really great because of a really stupid mistake someone made and is totally willing to rectify."

Who were we talking about here?

"What?"

There was a pause. "Take care of my boy, Kat."

"Will do, Manny."

It felt good to be doing something nice for someone else. And to be talking to Manny about something besides him, me, or us. I sent Mitch on his way, extracting a promise that he wouldn't stalk Libby any more that night.

Later, I stood at the kitchen sink, looking out at Abra, who was sitting in the meditation garden. I knew we could just let it go on the way it was. But it wasn't working itself out. There was still the weight of it between us, of things unsaid, and I had a feeling it would stay there, no matter how much time passed, until I did something.

Taking a deep breath, I stepped outside, walking slowly toward her so as not to startle her. Then I sat down in a chair opposite her, waiting.

"We should really mulch again this year," she said finally.

"Uh-huh," I said.

She sighed deeply. "I don't know what to do with this."

I didn't know if she was talking about the garden or us. "I'm sorry," I murmured.

She reached down to pluck a dead leaf off the ground. I knew then that she was talking about us. And she really was at a loss. I'm sure there was nothing in her books or in her midwife bible about what to do when your daughter tells you to fuck off.

"I know we're not really talking about the 'incident,'" I said, "but I wanted to say I'm really sorry about what I said. I was upset, but I had no right to say that to you. I'm sorry."

"I know you are." She shifted in her seat. "You gave me a lot to think about, Katima. And I'm still thinking." She spoke so quietly, I wasn't sure she was even talking to me. I waited. I supposed it was about time for the Abra lecture. I deserved it. And it was better than shaving off all of my hair.

She smiled faintly. "You know me. I have to meditate on things and work through them before I can fully deal with them."

"People are complicated," I said.

"Yes," she said, staring back at the garden, "they are."

I shivered and hugged my arms to my chest. Birds chirped and I heard the drone of a lawn mower in the distance. I guessed the lecture would wait.

50

Fact of Life #88: Sometimes people can be . . .
uncomplicated.

I saw Manny several times in the hallway at school the following Monday, which was very unusual. He just seemed to be there, smiling or raising an eyebrow at me, saying hi.

I thought about how it was his birthday next week, and if things had been different, we might have done something together. But things weren't different, so it didn't matter. And that made me sad.

Libby I saw from a distance, but we never made eye contact. Which would have been perfectly normal, except that now it felt like we were avoiding making eye contact, when it used to be that we never made eye contact because she didn't know I existed.

"There's a weird vibe between you and Libby," Christy said as we left school on Tuesday. I was still getting used to the fact that I didn't have to go to the Midwifery on Tuesdays and Thursdays anymore. I was planning to go work out.

317

"Tell me about it." I told Christy how I had tried to talk to Libby but she ignored me. "Maybe she'll come around," I said. "I hope so." I plastered a smile on my face. "But I don't want to talk about that. Tell me about all of these guys who are asking you out."

"Only four," she said, blushing.

"Only four? Gee, I feel sorry for you," I said. "Let's see, I've been single at this school for three years and I've been asked out by how many guys?" I held up my fingers in a circle. "Zero."

Christy opened her mouth, but I stopped her.

"He doesn't count."

She sighed.

"So have you decided who you're going to say yes to?"

"I'm going to say no to all of them for now," Christy said. "I just need some time for me."

I grinned. "Can I interest you in a run?"

Christy smiled. "I'll help you with your tri transitions if you want me to."

"It's a date," I said.

Two nights later, we were out for a family dinner to celebrate my birthday. When I came out of the bathroom, I noticed Libby, her mom, and some guy at a nearby table. The guy was talking to Libby, but she wasn't looking at him, just twirling the straw in her glass and sighing heavily.

"Elizabeth." Her mother's face was pinched. Libby didn't react. It was as if she were at the table all by herself. Like she was trying to invisibilize herself. "People are staring."

"I'm sorry if I'm embarrassing you," Libby said, pushing away from the table. "And I've asked you not to call me that. It's not my name."

318

"It *is* your name," Mrs. Giles said. "I should know; I'm the one who gave it to you."

"It's not what I want to be called." Libby stood up. "I have to go to the bathroom." She tapped the table, then turned and strode away—right toward me.

I stayed where I was, an odd sense of déjà vu flickering through me.

It's not what I want to be called.

I knew that feeling. *I* knew it. And it sounded like Libby Giles did, too.

The galaxy was getting smaller by the second.

"Hey," I said as she got closer. She nodded uncertainly, then looked past me, searching. She broke into a tentative smile and I glanced over my shoulder to see Abra coming toward us, smiling and waving.

"Are you okay?" Abra said, wrapping her arms around Libby. "I've been worried."

"I'm fine," Libby said. "School just got a little crazy. Senior stuff, you know. We graduate in a couple of weeks."

"Of course," Abra said. Then her smile faded as she looked over Libby's shoulder. "Rosemary."

Mrs. Giles was standing behind Libby, her eyes snapping. "Why in the world would you encourage a seventeen-year-old girl to have a baby naturally before giving it up for adoption? What kind of person are you?"

Abra sucked in her breath. Then she did that thing with her mouth that told me she wanted to say something she shouldn't. "Libby made her own decision after a lot of thought and discussion," she said quietly. "She just needs your support."

"Don't tell me what she needs, Abra Flynn." Mrs. Giles spoke

319

through clenched teeth. "You don't know me, and you certainly don't know Elizabeth. She's always been—"

"Mom!" Libby's face was red, and she was close to tears. "Stop it!" Her eyes flitted to the tables nearby, where people were suddenly busy eating or reading their menus. She opened and closed her fists. "This wasn't a big conspiracy to ruin your life, okay? The condom broke."

Mrs. Giles cringed visibly at "condom," like the word itself had jabbed her in the ribs. Libby didn't seem to notice; she just kept talking. "And when I got pregnant, I needed to talk to someone about it, someone who wasn't going to judge me and tell me what to do"—she looked pointedly at her mom—"and I heard about Abra, so I talked to her, and after thinking about everything I decided I couldn't have an abortion. *I* decided. Not Abra, whose last name is not Flynn, by the way. She doesn't have a last name."

Mrs. Giles opened her mouth, but Libby cut her off.

"Can this one thing not be about you, Mom? Just this one thing?" Libby blinked rapidly, then turned and fled. For someone who was almost seven months pregnant, that girl could move. I ran after her, following her out the front door of the restaurant.

"Libby," I said when I caught up with her. "Are you okay?"

"Do I *look* okay?" She was swinging her arms hard, like she was in some kind of race.

"No," I said quietly. "Is there anything I can do?"

Libby's eyes narrowed. "She's just so controlling," she said. "I'm so sick of her thinking she knows more about me than I do. That her way is always the best way and anything I do that goes against it is stupid or idiotic, you know?"

I nodded slowly as we turned a corner and headed down another block. "Yeah," I said. "I know."

She looked at me then, meeting my gaze. "You do know, don't you?" Shaking her head, she stopped walking and leaned against the back of a bench, breathing heavily. "It just doesn't seem possible with Abra. I don't get it." She crossed her arms over her chest. "I mean, when I said that stuff in the parking lot at Abra's, I was pissed about what you had said. With the way she is, I just figured the two of you were—" She crossed her fingers on one hand. "You know. Tight."

"No," I said. "That would be you and her."

"Huh." Libby stared down the street for a moment, before straightening up. She started walking toward the intersection. "I want this whole thing to be over and be out of here. I just want to get away from *her*." She stopped at the corner, looking first one way, then the other.

"Where are you going?" I asked.

"Anywhere but here," she said.

"Want some company?"

Libby shook her head. "I need to be by myself for a while." As the Walk signal flashed white, she stepped into the crosswalk and looked over her shoulder. "Thanks, Kat."

I watched her cross the street and kept watching until I couldn't see her anymore. Then I turned around and headed back to the restaurant.

The third Friday night in May, I found myself home alone. Lucy was at a sleepover, Abra was delivering Diane and Jeff's baby, Dad was out with the guys, and Christy had a thing to go to with her parents. When Diane had called to tell me she was in labor,

I could hardly talk to her. She told me they had a jungle-themed birth. Potted palm trees, an eight-foot plush boa constrictor, silk vines, and plush monkeys everywhere. Even a huge gray elephant. I sighed. I could have been assisting, but Carmen was instead. I couldn't believe I was missing it.

I'd actually considered calling Libby. I had been thinking about her a lot since the scene at the restaurant and our conversation outside. I felt a connection to her I never thought possible. But I didn't call her. I felt like the next step had to come from her.

So I was by myself on a Friday night and I needed comfort food more than athlete food, so I was making pizza. While I was waiting for the oven to preheat, I stood at the kitchen sink in the dark, staring out the window. Rain had been falling for the last fifteen minutes, visible in the back porch light. The refrigerator hummed behind me; the clock on the mantel in the family room was doing its soft tick-tick.

I sniffled just as the oven beeped. Slipping the pizza inside, I poured myself a big glass of iced tea and found a movie on TV.

The movie had barely started when someone knocked on the front door. My heart jumped at the sound, my mind snapping *Who the hell is that?* while at the same time pointing out, *You're alone in the house.*

I tiptoed through the kitchen, leaning around the corner to get a view of the front door. Whoever it was stood directly in front of the door, not peering through one of the frosted windows that flanked either side.

My heart thumped inside my chest. I reached out and picked up the portable phone, pressing the On button. My finger hovered over the 1—our 911 speed dial.

The person on the porch knocked again, louder this time. Everything was silent except for the hum of the refrigerator. I stepped toward the door and peered through the peephole.

What the—?

I unlocked the door and swung it open.

Libby stood on my front porch, her arms wrapped around herself.

"Hey," she said, as if it was perfectly normal not only to show up on my porch but to do so in what were obviously her pajamas. "Thought I'd return this." She held out my oversized T-shirt. "Got any decaf?"

51

I glanced down at Libby's stomach, my midwifery instincts kicking in. "Is everything okay? Because if it isn't, you should really go to the hospital and—"

"Everything's fine," she interrupted, touching her stomach briefly. "Well, as fine as it can be. You know."

"Yeah." I nodded, not sure if she was referring to being pregnant or the scene with her mom at the restaurant or both. We stood there, looking at each other awkwardly. "Um, thanks for bringing my T-shirt, but you could have kept it."

She shrugged, looking down at her feet. She obviously didn't have any plans to leave.

"Abra's not here," I said softly. "I'm sorry. She's catching a baby." Diane's baby. A baby I should have been there to see come out.

Libby looked up. "I'm not here to see Abra."

I raised an eyebrow. "My dad and Lucy aren't here, either."

"Very funny," Libby said, wrapping her arms around herself again. "Come on, Kitty Kat. I'm freezing out here."

I looked at her, shivering in a thin, wet T-shirt that clung to her skin, her breasts and nipples clearly visible. Her pregnant belly bulged in elastic-waisted pajama bottoms, which were tucked into a pair of slip-on boots.

"Jeez, Libby, I'm sorry," I said, opening the door wide. She stepped inside, pulling off her wet shirt and dropping it to the floor, seemingly unaware that her large breasts were bare and exposed in my foyer. I got a towel and blanket and she wrapped them both tightly around her, then walked into the living room and planted herself in a chair next to the picture window. She pulled a curtain back and stared out toward the street.

I grabbed another towel and tossed it on the floor, where her boots were now dripping. She turned and picked up a framed photograph of our whole family skiing last year. She rested her finger in the middle of the photograph, where I knew Abra stood, her smile wide, her face turned slightly toward the glare of the sun. "I've never had an adult treat me the way she treats me," Libby said softly, almost as if she were talking to herself. "Like I matter. Not because I'm pretty or popular or get good grades. Just because—I am." She glanced up at me, blinking several times as if coming out of the dark into a bright place. "She's why you can do yoga in the halls."

I'd never thought about not doing yoga, even though people made fun of me. Had Abra given me that?

Libby placed the photograph back on the table before picking at a thread in the chair.

"I know it's late, but my mom and the boyfriend were on my case again, so I figured it was a good time to exit. And why not come here and hope Kitty Kat is home so I can talk to her about my situation?"

I wiped my eyes and looked at her. "Your situation?"

"I'm thinking I want to have this baby in the hospital," she said. "You know, with the epidural and everything."

"Oh." I took a seat in the chair opposite hers.

"Abra's been so great, but I just don't think I can go through all of that, and my house is not exactly the best place . . ." Her voice trailed off. "Anyway, I think in the hospital—" She stopped, twirling the thread around her finger. "Well, I just think it would be better." She looked up at me. "I hate that my mom was right, but I have to let that go and do what's right for me, you know?"

I nodded. "Absolutely."

"But I'm afraid to tell Abra. She'll be so disappointed." She looked at me expectantly. "What should I do?"

I bit my lip, thinking. "She might be a little disappointed," I said, "but only because she thinks you're the greatest thing since the fetal doppler."

Libby smiled.

"But she can still be at the hospital with you—just not catching the baby."

Libby nodded, her face relaxing. "I knew you'd say just the right thing." She stood up, shivering. "Do you think I could take a shower?"

"Of course! I should have thought of it before." The timer beeped in the kitchen. "Oops," I said. "Pizza's ready."

Libby grinned. "Great. I'm starved." She walked up the stairs, then paused near the top. "And don't forget that decaf."

I smiled. Bossy bitch. "Don't use all my Body Shop stuff!" I shouted up at her.

"I won't!" she shouted back.

I picked up the towel and her wet clothes in the foyer, planning to throw them in the dryer. Something dropped to the floor.

It was the Fate Goddess card I'd left in her locker.

I placed it carefully by her boots and headed to the laundry room, dialing the phone as I went.

I cleaned up the kitchen while Libby scarfed her third piece of pizza, looking Libby-chic in some of my dad's clothes while hers were in the dryer. She'd also downed a full glass of milk, two cookies, and a second cup of decaf. Nothing like a little pregnancy to get that appetite going.

"I've never had sex with anyone except Mitch, you know." Her voice was muffled from the crumbs.

I paused. I was scrubbing the pizza pan, which had crust stuck to it like cement.

"Everyone who goes out with me says we've done it, but we haven't."

I looked back at her.

"I don't know who started it. But one of them said he did, and even though I denied it, everyone believed it. Because they wanted to, I guess. And then, once one guy said we'd done it, anyone else who went out with me had to say it, too."

Apparently Libby didn't need anyone else to carry on a conversation; she did just fine all by herself.

"I got tired of defending myself—no one cares about the truth, anyway." She caught my eyes and held them. "I didn't even do it with Manny."

I turned back to the sink quickly. The relief that washed over me nearly buckled my knees.

"You guys had a thing," she said. "Weird."

My shoulders stiffened.

"Manny told me about it," she said. "About you."

Manny had talked to Libby about me? About us? I still didn't turn around. My emotions were jumping all over the place.

"You have to admit it's weird, but kind of cool in a way."

I sank my hands in the water, making soap fly across the counter. "Hot popular guy dates weird Yoga Girl in secret because he doesn't want to ruin his rep by being seen in public with her. Really cool." I scrubbed the pan harder.

"Okay, so that part was totally uncool," Libby said. "But how much he likes you, what kind of person you are to him—all of that is cool."

Likes me. Present tense. I rinsed off the pan and stuck it in the drying rack. Grabbing a towel, I dried my hands, breathing deeply to slow down my heartbeat. Then I poured myself some iced tea.

"So what's with you and Mitch?" I asked, not wanting to change the subject but also not wanting to talk about Manny with Libby.

She sighed. "Of all the guys I went out with, Mitch was the only one who really loved me." She shifted the cup between her hands. "That's why I did it with him. But that's why I had to cut him loose."

"You broke up with him because he loved you?" Again, I'm not a relationship expert, but this seemed a little backward to me.

Libby laughed. "Well, when you put it that way." Looking down at her coffee, her face turned serious. "I can't explain it," she said softly. "It was like he really knew me. I mean, *knew* me like no one else did. Like I didn't even know myself. Not like my mom thinks she knows me. This was—a deep knowing." She smiled an embarrassed smile. "That sounds like something Abra would say." She sighed. "Anyway, it freaked me out, so I got out." She shrugged, her face tinged with pain. "Besides, I thought he would run away when he heard about the baby, and I would have looked like an idiot."

I rinsed off a plate and set it in the dishwasher. "He wouldn't have run," I said. "You know he wouldn't have."

"Maybe." She stood up and poured herself a glass of water, then looked right at me. "You know, you really should just forgive Cruz and get on with it."

I nearly choked on my iced tea. "You just kind of blurt out whatever's on your mind, don't you?"

Libby grinned. "Pretty much. But you should."

I shook my head. "It's too late." He hadn't tried to talk to me again since we found Mitch. I think he was finally done trying.

"It's never too late," Libby said. "Look at me." She waved a hand around the kitchen. "I've made the only real girlfriend I've ever had just before I graduate high school."

I stared at her. "Well, I'm definitely not one of your admirers," I said.

Libby laughed, a strong, deep laugh from her gut.

Then the doorbell rang.

She raised an eyebrow.

"Could you get that?" I asked. "I want to finish these dishes."

"I didn't invite you," Libby was saying as she and Mitch stepped into the kitchen.

"I'm not here to see you." Mitch turned to me with a grin.

"Gee, I feel so popular." I picked up Libby's dirty plate from the table.

"Why did you call him?" Libby asked. She tried to look mad, but there was a smile twitching at the corner of her mouth.

I sighed. "Because you need to talk to someone who really loves you."

She put an arm around my shoulders. "Are you saying you don't love me, Kitty Kat?"

I laughed. "Will you just talk to the guy? He should totally be pissed at you and he keeps coming back. Doesn't that mean anything to you?"

Libby stood there, hands on her hips, looking undecided.

"You know, for someone who got into two Ivy League colleges, you're acting pretty stupid," I said.

"Three," Libby said, "but who's counting?"

Mitch crossed his arms, staring at her.

"What are you looking at?" Libby asked, pulling my dad's oversized sweatshirt around her belly. "I'm a whale."

Mitch shook his head slowly. "You look beautiful."

"You're so full of it, Mitchell Jonathan Lowry." Her mouth twitched again.

"If you two want some privacy," I said, "you can go back to Serenity Space." I pointed down the hall. "First door on the left."

Libby looked at Mitch. Then she jerked her head. Mitch gave me a thumbs-up and started down the hallway.

"Tell your mom everything's okay," Libby said over her shoulder.

I started. It was the first time she'd referred to Abra as my mother. It almost felt like she was giving something back to me that she'd taken. Or borrowed.

"I will." I watched them walk into the dimly lit hallway, Mitch slightly ahead. Just before they reached the middle, Libby skipped a half step to catch up, taking Mitch's hand.

I was in the family room a few days later, reading the triathlon book Manny had given me, when Abra stepped in.

"So Libby stopped by the Midwifery today."

"Great." I kept my eyes down.

"She said she talked to you and she wants to deliver the baby in the hospital."

I looked up. Her face revealed nothing. Was she angry that we'd talked?

"It's her decision," I said.

"Yes," Abra said. "And it's the right one."

She meant it. I could see that.

"She knows you're with her all the way," I said.

Abra smiled. "Thanks to you." Then she raised an eyebrow. "I knew the two of you would become friends of some kind."

I braced for a lecture on the variety and types of friendships, an analysis of the relationships in her life and mine, a list of suggestions for improving those relationships (in my life, not hers). But she just smiled.

"You're pretty happy with yourself, aren't you?" I said.

"Yes," Abra said, a glint in her eye. "I am. Smart and insightful people should stick together."

I tilted my head. She thought I was smart and insightful?

"We're trying," I said finally. It wasn't like Libby and I had suddenly started sitting together at lunch, whispering secrets. She still had her groupies for that. But she'd been saying hi, and pulling me aside to ask me about her Braxton Hicks contractions or some other pregnancy thing, or even to ask how the tri training was going or when Manny and I were going to stop being stupid and get back together.

Christy was with me in the hall once when Libby came up to ask for advice on her swollen ankles. After I'd made some suggestions, she said, "You rock, Flynn. See you later."

Christy watched her go. "I see Libby's become one of your admirers."

My eyes stayed on Libby, who was walking with a slight waddle down the hallway.

"I don't have admirers," I said. "I just have friends."

Fact of Life #422: Ten-year-old sisters are THE BEST.

I was sittting in the Womb that evening, the painting of Jeff and Diane's birth drying on the floor beside me. They were dancing with the newborn, a monkey wrapped around Jeff's neck. I sighed. I would probably always be drawing birth experiences without having ever been at the actual birth.

I leaned back, staring at my mural, paints and brushes lined up once again. Why did it still feel unfinished?

"Hey, Kat."

"Hey, Luce. Come on in."

Lucy knelt down next to me, looking at the mural. "Do you think Mom will ever go in the water?"

I sucked in my breath. "What?"

"In your painting." She pointed to the woman standing on the bank. "Do you think she'll ever dive in like you? Or will she just stand there, looking up?"

I looked from the mural to Lucy, then back to the mural. Lucy thought *I* was the diver? All this time she'd seen me as the one jumping off the cliff, diving into the unknown waters below, with Abra watching from the sidelines.

I couldn't believe it. I reached over and squeezed Lucy tight. "I think she'll dive," I said. "But what would you say if I added you, doing a cannonball?"

"Really?" She wrapped her arms around herself like she was about to do one. "Awesome."

52

I slipped into my seat in Spanish class early Wednesday morning, feeling lighter than I had in a long time. The seniors were graduating on Saturday and I knew the school would feel strangely empty next week, without Libby to watch or Mitch asking me what I was looking at.

Opening my textbook, I reviewed last night's homework. As I smoothed it out, a piece of paper fell on top of my page. I looked up to see Manny moving past me. He started talking to a girl near the front of the room.

"En español, Manuel. Por favor." Señora García-Smith tapped her pen on her desk as she looked at Manny. *"En esta clase, español solamente."*

"Sí," he muttered, and actually continued his conversation in Spanish.

I picked up the piece of paper and unfolded it. It was a bill from a jeweler's. He'd fixed the necklace.

I waited for him in the hall after class. "So do you want money or what?"

"No," he said, "I just wanted my *aunt* to know I fixed the necklace she gave me."

"Really?" I said. "All of a sudden, your *aunt* wants to break it all over again." But I smiled, and so did he. Then his face got serious.

"I had to fix it," he said. "It was the only thing I had from you. Well, besides the ranger hat." He grabbed my arm, shooting electricity through it. Why did he still have that effect on me?

"I'm really sorry, Kat. I should have stood up for you. For how I felt about you. I can't believe I cared what those idiots thought. If I could do it over again—"

"I know," I said softly, feeling a last weight lift off me. "And I wanted to say, even though it's kind of late, that I'm sorry for that whole dramatic breakup thing in the locker room."

"The fucking break?"

"Yeah. The fucking break."

He nodded. "Yeah, well, you got me, that's for sure. The guys razzed me about it for weeks." He held up his hand. "And I deserved it."

I smiled. "I *am* glad you fixed the necklace." I tapped the chain lightly on his neck.

He reached into his pocket and pulled out a small package. "Happy birthday. You would have gotten it on time, but you weren't talking to me."

I took it, touched that he'd remembered. Unwrapping the package, I opened the lid. Inside was a necklace with a bighorn sheep pendant dangling from it.

"I know you're not a jewelry person, but when I saw it—"

"It's beautiful," I said, my voice cracking. "Thank you." I took a deep, cleansing breath as the bell rang. "Well, I guess I'd better go." I turned and started down the hall.

"Kat."

I kept walking.

He spoke louder. "KAT."

I stopped. There were tons of people in the hall, and they all were looking at me. And at Manny behind me.

"Katima Flynn," Manny said, as if he were making an announcement. "Foot-stomper, hair police, stopwatch finder, barf girl."

I turned around slowly. "Did you have to mention the barf thing?"

He smiled and walked toward me. We stood toe to toe. "Person who made me better than I was."

I swallowed, embarrassed.

He looked over my shoulder, at the crowd I knew was gathered behind me.

"This girl rocks," he said to them. "I love this girl."

"You don't need to do this," I said. "You don't have to prove anything."

"I know," he said. "But I want to." He raised an eyebrow. "It's all about me, you know."

I smiled.

"Can I kiss you?"

I glanced around at the crowded hallway. "Do you think that's a good idea?"

"Probably the best I've ever had." He pulled me toward him.

Because I was only three inches shorter than him, we were practically eye to eye. Nose to nose. Lip to lip. He took my face between his hands. He leaned forward. Without even thinking, I leaned in to meet him and our lips said hello in a very intimate way. The kiss was long and slow and exploring, sending tremors through my entire body. And then I was deep inside my body, or inside his body—it was hard to tell. It was like we'd gone somewhere warm and dark where only the two of us existed. Time had stopped. Sound had ceased.

We came up for air slowly, as if we were ascending from the bottom of a pool. Our eyes opened at the same time, then caught and held each other. Our lips pulled away gently.

I could barely hear the clapping and cheering around me. I was still lost in that kiss.

"Hey, Cruz," somebody yelled. "What do you call that?"

I looked at Manny.

"That," Manny said quietly, looking right in my eyes, "was Rescue of Stupid Guy Number Two."

Labor and Delivery

This is it—the moment (well, often the hours) you have been waiting for! You're feeling strong contractions, your water may break or be broken for you, and Baby is ready to enter the world! Your life is about to change forever . . . and so are you!

53

In June I stepped tentatively out onto the grass for the first meeting of the Rocky Mountain Women's Triathlon training group. School was out; summer and the tri had begun. It would be eight weeks of training up to the day of the race next month. My heart pounded as I sat down next to a young woman in her twenties. Her calves were tight, the muscles looking as if they were carved beneath her skin. I glanced at my own calves, which were toned but not rock solid like hers.

"I'm Amy," she said. Her voice was high, not fitting the solid body that accompanied it. "First tri?"

I nodded. "I'm Kat. You?"

"Third," Amy said. "It's always scary, but the first time is the hardest, not knowing what to expect." She looked me over. "How old are you, anyway?"

"Seventeen."

She whistled low. "I remember those days."

"Like you're a senior citizen," I joked.

She laughed. "Twenty-eight. But sometimes I feel a lot older."

We sat quietly while the coaches told us about how the training would progress, handing out papers showing our schedule and what we would do each week. During a break, Amy nudged me. "Seventeen, that hottie over there has been staring at you for twenty minutes."

I glanced over. Manny was leaning against a tree, his solid arms crossed over his chest. "Oh, jeez," I muttered, jumping up and running over to him.

"Hey," he said.

"What are you doing here?"

"Just checking out your competition." He nodded, clearly liking what he saw. "You've got it made, Kat. All those old ladies? No problem."

I looked back at the mix of athletes, many of them forty- and fifty-year-old women. "Some of those 'old ladies' are Ironman competitors," I said. "They're going to kick my butt, which is why I'm not competing in the elite race. Just against others in my age group."

"I still think you could take them all," he said.

I smiled.

"So how's it working so far," he said, cocking his head and smiling his heart-melting smile, "with me giving you your space?"

After the Big Kiss in the hallway, we'd agreed that I needed some time to sort through everything, though we were IM'ing, texting, and talking on the phone.

"You're not giving me much space right now."

He backed up about two inches. "How's that?"

I shook my head, but couldn't keep from laughing.

"Got her to laugh. That's good." He raised his eyebrows. "So any movement toward a date? Semi-date? An un-date?"

342

A whistle blew behind me. "I've got to get back," I said. "You're not staying, are you?"

"Why? Am I embarrassing you?"

I narrowed my eyes at him. Was that a sick attempt at humor because *he'd* been embarrassed by *me*?

"Yes," I said. "As a matter of fact, you are."

"I don't want that," he said softly, touching my arm. "I'll call you later."

The training was intense. My own running, biking, and swimming felt like nothing compared to the sprints and laps we did in the training course.

"You're doing good, Seventeen," Amy said during one particularly brutal set of sprints. She slapped my back as she passed me.

"You're doing better," I gasped, my lungs heaving.

She just waved a hand and laughed.

I went home after each session exhausted and woke up so sore I could barely walk.

"Are you sure this is good for you?" Abra asked as she saw me limping into the kitchen the day following a biking session.

"It'll get better," I said. I'd been working out in between the actual training sessions, and at the moment the thought of moving my feet faster than a shuffle seemed humanly impossible.

"But you might still be growing," Abra said. Somewhere along the line she had morphed into Mother Hen, worried about everything. "How are your knees? Do they feel all right?"

"I can't feel my knees," I said, looking down. "Are they still there?"

Abra laughed ruefully.

It wasn't like I was going to quit. I knew the first week or two was the worst.

And I was right. By the third week, the soreness following a workout was almost gone. In the fourth week at the end of June, they ratcheted things up, trying to help us increase our endurance.

"You're looking like a rock in the water, Seventeen," Amy shouted as she stood on the edge of the pool.

"Jump in here and say that to my face, Old Lady," I said as I turned to finish my laps.

Little by little, I felt myself getting stronger. My lungs seemed to have expanded; my legs glided more easily during a run. My swim stroke had improved tenfold, and I could tell I was moving in a more streamlined fashion through the water.

"Just wait till they get us out in open water, Seventeen," Amy said when I dared suggest I'd improved in my swimming.

"That's what I like about you, Old Lady," I said. "You're always encouraging me."

"That's my job, Seventeen," Amy said, before diving into the pool.

On the last day of training, I threw my arms around Amy and cried into her shoulder.

"Oh, jeez, Seventeen," she said. "Don't go all sloppy on me."

"You really pushed me," I said, pulling away from her. "I couldn't have done it without you."

"Sure you could," she said. "It just wouldn't have been as fun." Her face turned serious and she smacked my arm with her fist. "You are ready, girl," she said. "You are so ready to dominate."

I grinned. She was right. I knew she was right. I could feel it in every bone and muscle and sinew in my body. "See you on Sunday, Old Lady?"

"See you on Sunday, Seventeen."

54

I got up much earlier than the five o'clock alarm on race day. I was so excited and nervous, I'd hardly slept. And when I did, I dreamed that no matter what sport I was doing, I did it as if moving through mud.

Rolling out of bed, I stretched my muscles, peering through my window into the darkness. Then I reached for my unitard, one I'd bought especially for the race because I didn't want to wear a wet suit in the water, then have to take it off for the bike and run. The unitard would dry quickly, and I could wear it for all three events. It would carry me all the way across the finish line.

I grinned, hearing Amy's voice in my head: "Move it, Seventeen! We don't have all day." I changed quickly, then grabbed my duffle with all of my tri stuff. I dropped the duffle by the front door and went into the kitchen to drink the special "prerace liquid meal" Abra had prepared for me the night before. She'd consulted several experts and felt this was the best thing for me, in addition to slamming a few glasses of water.

I'd just finished my second glass of water when the doorbell rang. Insistently.

"Who could that be?" my dad muttered, pounding down the stairs. My heart sped up as I had a vision of a police officer standing on our front porch, face grim as he readied himself to report some horrible news about Abra, who had left after dinner last night to catch a baby.

I hurried down the hall as my dad opened the door.

"Libby!" I shouted as she fell heavily into my dad's arms.

"She's having the baby," Mrs. Giles said, her face pinched in the pale porch light. "We were on our way to the hospital when she starts shouting at me to turn around and come here." She took a breath and let it out. "I stopped quickly at the house to pick up a few things we'd forgotten, made two calls, and now we're here."

"It's early," I said, to no one in particular.

"Abra's not here," my dad said. "She's delivering another baby."

"No," Libby moaned, clutching her stomach. "She needs to be here."

"What's going on?" I asked. "I thought you were all set to go to the hospital."

"She was," Mrs. Giles said. "But then she changed her mind." Her lips pressed together in a thin line. "I wasn't going to force her if she didn't want to go."

Libby looked at her mom, then back at me. "I just wanted to be with people who—in a place where—and I want Abra to deliver it."

"Okay," I said, not quite sure what she meant about the people and the place. "Call her, Dad." I wrapped my arm around

Libby. "I don't know if she'll be here in time," I told her. "I think you should go to the hospital like you planned."

"NO!"

My eardrum practically split in two. "Or not," I murmured.

My dad strode out from the kitchen, grinning. "It was a boy! Abra said she can be here in about two hours."

"Two hours?" Libby moaned. "I need her now." Her eyes glazed in pain. Her grip on me tightened, and I winced as her nails dug into my skin. She had reached the peak of the contraction. I waited, counting in my head until her grip relaxed and I knew she was coming down.

"Okay." Her voice was ragged. "Take me back to Serenity Space."

"But I can't check you!" I said. "I don't know how far along you are. You could be minutes away from having this baby."

"I'm not," Libby said. "These feel like how Abra described First Stage, even though they hurt like hell." She glanced at me. "Take me back."

I looked at Mrs. Giles.

"I wish you'd let me take you to the hospital, Elizabeth," she said.

"Don't call me that."

Mrs. Giles sighed, then looked at my dad. "She was at both the OB and Abra's yesterday. Everything was fine. Head down, perfect position." She looked back at Libby. "I called your OB to tell her you were coming here . . ." Mrs. Giles stepped back. "But if you change your mind . . ." She glanced around, her eyes stopping at the living room. "May I wait in there?"

"Of course," my dad said. "Can I get you anything?"

"Coffee would be wonderful."

"Wouldn't you like to come back with her?" I asked. It wasn't just because I thought Libby should have someone with her besides me. *I* wanted someone with her besides me.

"I think we'd both prefer if I waited out here," Mrs. Giles said, and Libby nodded beside me. "And she'll have plenty of support."

"You bet she will." Mitch Lowry stood on the front porch, peering through the screen door. His eyes were trained on Libby.

"Mitch." Libby reached out for him and he stepped inside, pulling her into his arms.

"Your mom called me," he said, answering the question on her face.

Libby looked at her mom. "Huh," she said. "Thanks, I guess."

"You're welcome, I guess," Mrs. Giles said, shifting uncomfortably.

Mitch turned to Libby. "How are you doing?"

"It hurts like hell, but I'm okay."

"Has your water broken?" I asked.

Libby shook her head. We walked through the kitchen, Mitch on one side, me on the other. I grabbed a notebook and pencil from the counter and wrote down the time and what had happened so far.

I looked at Mitch. "Follow her lead. Sometimes she'll want you to touch her, sometimes she'll want to throw sharp objects at you."

"That's what I need," Libby said. "Some scissors. Or a dagger."

"Funny," Mitch said.

When we got to Serenity Space, Libby and I stepped inside, but Mitch hung back. "You want me inside or outside?" he asked.

Libby looked at him. "Where do you want to be?"

"With you," he said.

Libby smiled, then glanced at my dad, who had followed us back.

"I'll be just down the hall if you need me, Kat."

I nodded. "Make yourself useful," I said to Mitch. "Get her some ice chips." I pointed to the small refrigerator/freezer in the corner. Then I opened the cabinet and started laying out all the things Abra would need when she arrived.

Libby lay down on the bed, and Mitch patted her forehead with a damp cloth. She fell asleep almost immediately, her chest rising and falling. Then she tensed and woke up.

"Oh, God," she moaned. "Here comes another one."

I checked my watch. They were about eight minutes apart.

She was clenching again, her whole body tight against the contraction.

"You've got to breathe, Libby."

"Quit telling me what to do."

Why couldn't I be like Abra, who seemed to calm women and get them into a breathing rhythm as if by magic?

She stood up. "I can't decide if I want to stand up or lay down," she said. "Either way, I can't get away from it." She shuffled around the room, one hand on her belly, one hand on her back. Several minutes later, she grimaced and I knew she was about to have another contraction.

"You don't want to get away from it," I said. "You want to get inside it."

"Fuck you!" she shouted, face twisted in pain. "What do you know?"

I looked away. What *did* I know? Who did I think I was?

Abra? No. I wasn't Abra. But that didn't mean I couldn't help. "I don't know a lot," I said. "But I do know you need to breathe."

She grabbed her belly and started pacing. "I can't do this," she said. "I thought I could do this, but I can't. It hurts too much. I think I'm dying." She panted heavily through the contraction, gripping my arm so hard she nearly touched bone. I winced but didn't pull away.

"Then let's go to the hospital," I said.

Libby shook her head like she wanted to shake it right off, then flopped onto the bed.

Two minutes. Three minutes. Four minutes. I watched them tick by. At eight minutes, her face contorted and her eyes filled with tears. "Oh, God, here comes another one." She let out a wail so loud and anguished I cringed. "Oh, God, make it go away! Make it go away!"

She rolled back and forth on the bed. "Don't hold your breath," I said softly. "Go with the pain, don't fight it."

She kept moaning.

"I know that sounds impossible, but the pain is what's helping the baby come out," I said. "The more you fight it, the longer it's going to take."

"Shut up, would you?" Her voice was ragged. She clutched her belly and sucked her breath in and out, finally letting out a deep sigh as she came down from the contraction.

I wondered if anyone ever told Abra to shut up. Somehow, I doubted it. "You're going to hyperventilate," I said. "Mitchell knows all about hyperventilating."

"Shut up," he said, but he was smiling.

Libby clutched my wrist. "Okay, Kitty Kat," she said, "help me breathe."

351

55

"Let's try some prana breathing. It's breathing we do in yoga." I leaned closer so Libby could see me. "Breathe in deeply through your nose—one continuous breath, trying to fill your lungs from the bottom up."

"Huh?"

I knew that having to focus on this new breathing technique would distract her in addition to calming her. I continued explaining, watching her and making suggestions as she practiced.

"Do you have your birth bag?"

Libby shook her head. "It's in my mom's car."

"I'll go get it." Mitch turned toward the door, but Libby grabbed at him.

"No," she said, "I want you here."

"That's okay," I said. "We'll improvise for now."

I grabbed some matches and tossed them to Mitch. "Light the candles and dim the lights." I pulled out some incense. "Sandalwood? Lilac? Ocean breeze?"

"Any," Libby said. "My back hurts."

I lit some incense and came to the bed. "Lay on your side," I said, then turned to Mitch. "Press on her lower back with the heels of your hands," I said. "Hard." I positioned myself to counter the pressure.

Mitch knelt beside her and pressed.

"Harder," Libby said.

Mitch leaned his weight into her while I held her hands, breathing with her as she rode the contraction. We did that for a few more contractions; then she wanted to walk again.

I gently squeezed both of Libby's shoulders. "Look in my eyes. I want you to listen to me and do what I tell you, okay?"

She nodded.

"Open your mouth. Groan, growl, howl, whatever you need to do. Mitch could probably help you in the howling department."

"Shut up," Mitch said.

"You want to open up that cervix," I said. "Opening your mouth will help you do it."

She gritted her teeth.

"Open your mouth, Libby! Bite my head off if you have to, but open it."

She did. And let out a sound that came straight from her gut.

"Good. That's it. You're doing it."

She kept it up—one loud, long groan stretching across the room, wrapping around the corners and shooting out the window.

"Picture your cervix opening to make room for the baby. See it in your mind. Make it happen."

Libby closed her eyes. Her voice cracked and she gasped, so I knew she'd reached the peak of her contraction and was coming back down. Slowly the blood returned to her face.

"You were awesome, Libby. Amazing."

We all stood quietly, honoring the moment. Then Mitch reached out and stroked her cheek. "God, you're beautiful," he said. His voice was rough, full of emotion. Libby turned to him and he kissed her full on the mouth. They both closed their eyes and kept kissing. It was the sexiest, most sensual thing I'd ever seen. If we'd been anywhere else, I would have been embarrassed to witness such an intimate moment. But here in Serenity Space, enveloped by sweet incense and burning candles, I wasn't a witness, I was part of it.

"Wow," I murmured.

There was a light tap on the door. When I opened it, my dad was standing there.

"How's it going?"

"Pretty good," I said. "But I wish Abra would hurry up."

"I'm sure she'll be here soon." He squeezed my shoulder. "You're doing fantastic, Kat. I'm so proud of you."

My eyes pricked with sudden tears and I smiled.

"You know," he said, "if you want to make your wave, we need to leave soon."

The race. The tri. The thing I'd been training for and dreaming of for weeks and months. I'd forgotten all about it.

"Go," Libby said behind me. "I'll be okay."

I turned to look at her. "I can't leave you."

"Sure you can," she said, smiling. "I've got Mitch and your dad, and Abra will be here any minute."

"Just a few more minutes," I said to my dad. "We can still make it. Would you mind getting Libby's birth bag out of her mom's car?" I turned to Libby. "Let's get the tub going while we try the birthing ball."

After I turned on the tub, I rolled the ball in front of her. She knelt on the floor with her arms around it and I helped push her forward.

"That's much better," she said after she'd finished her contraction over the ball.

"How about some music?"

She nodded. I cued up the first disc to "Deer Dance." Libby shifted her eyes to me at the first sounds of the flute. Then Joanne Shenandoah's voice floated in above the flute, sing-chanting in Iroquois, a language neither of us could understand. And yet we understood it perfectly.

"Wow," Libby murmured, before scrunching her eyes up as another contraction hit. I went to turn off the water in the tub before coming out to be with her.

"Breathe deeply," I said, dropping my voice a notch so that it took on an almost singsong quality. "Let it out as you come down from your contraction. Open everything up."

Libby followed my instructions, relaxing her muscles and opening her mouth and letting out a long, steady *uhhhhhh* as the contraction subsided. Her eyes opened, she looked at me—

—and threw up all over my unitard.

"Nice shot," I said.

"Oh, God! I'm sorry!"

I smiled. "Now we're even."

She smiled back wanly and moved to the bed. I cleaned myself up as best I could, then pulled some towels from the closet. Mitch was patting Libby's face with a damp cloth when we heard a light knock at the door.

Mrs. Giles stood there uncertainly, Libby's birth bag in her hands. She held it out and I took it from her. She glanced at

Libby, who was breathing heavily next to the bed, her eyes closed. Libby didn't seem aware that her mother stood looking at her. Mrs. Giles pressed her lips together and blinked rapidly.

"Do—do you need anything else?"

I shook my head. "Would you like to stay?" I motioned to a comfortable chair in the far corner of the room.

Mrs. Giles shook her head. "I can't," she said, her eyes full of pain. "It's too hard." She looked up at Libby, whose eyes were now open. "I'm sorry." She turned on her heel and left.

My eyes met Libby's, and she smiled faintly. We pulled her iPod out of her birth bag, and Mitch cued up the music while I grabbed some massage oil she'd packed and set it by the bed.

"Can you get one of my hair clips?"

I pulled one out and combed her hair back away from her face, securing it near the top of her head. Then she gripped her belly and powered through the next contraction like a pro.

"Can you bring her closer?" She pointed to the bronze Fate Goddess sitting on a shelf across from the bed.

"Sure." Taking the goddess down, I carried her back and placed her carefully on the end table next to Libby.

"I wonder what she said about me when I was born." Libby reached out and ran her finger down the back of the goddess.

"You will be the most popular girl in school and marry a guy who howls," I said in a spooky ghost voice.

Libby laughed, then looked at Mitch. "What's up with this howling thing?"

"Nothing," he said, shooting me a look. "Kat's just weird."

Libby labored in the tub, and after she got out, rode out a few contractions walking around. I relit some of the candles while Mitch massaged her back.

Then she gripped her belly. "Oh, shit."

"Oh, shit" was right. That was less than five minutes, more like three.

I turned to Mitch. "There's some plastic floor covering in that cabinet. Lay it on the floor on the right side of the bed. Spread it out and pull back the bedspread." Mitch went to work, and I grabbed some extra pillows from the closet.

I called Abra, but she didn't pick up. Where was she? "Mitch, go get my dad."

Taking a deep breath, I put my hands on Libby's shoulders. She wrapped her arms around my neck, looking me right in the eye. I started with her shoulders, working my fingers into the knots that were there. I moved down to her arms, continuing to massage and speak softly. I opened my eyes. I watched her face relax, her eyelids flutter, her breath even out.

"That's it," I said. "You're there."

My arms hummed with her contraction. I couldn't believe what was happening. It was like Libby was transforming before my very eyes. Like I was giving her a part of myself and she was giving right back. Like we were one person.

As I turned to help her to the bed, I noticed Abra standing in the doorway, ignoring her own rule about knocking before entering the birth space. Mitch was behind her.

"How long have you been there?"

Abra's eyes flicked to Libby, then back to me. "Long enough to see that you don't really need me." There was a strange catch in her voice.

"Abra." Libby's voice was quiet, as if it had become part of the room.

Abra hesitated, glancing at me as if looking for permission.

357

I gave Libby a hug and stepped back. "Libby needs you," I said to Abra.

It was over. My shoulders sagged, and I felt incredibly tired all of a sudden. Abra would handle things from here. I could go to my race, knowing Libby was in good hands. My eyes pricked with tears. "I guess you met Mitch."

"I'm glad you're here," Abra said to him. She strode over to Libby, wrapping her arms around her on the bed. Libby sobbed into her shoulder. Abra stroked her hair and murmured softly in her ear. Then Libby moaned and looked over Abra's shoulder at me.

"Breathe," I mouthed, pointing to my nose and sucking in deeply. She nodded, closed her eyes, and breathed.

"Let's check your dilation and see if Baby's in a good position." Abra reached for a pair of sterile gloves from the box I'd set out earlier.

"Her water hasn't broken," I said, handing her the notebook. "You may need to deal with that."

Abra took the notebook from me. "Great work, Katima."

"Thanks." I looked down at the top of my unitard, soggy with Libby's sweat, the faint smell of her vomit wafting up through my nostrils. I'd been training for over a year for this tri. I was going to rule this tri.

Abra looked up at me. "I'm really sorry I'll miss your race."

I reached for a cloth to wipe Libby's forehead. "I'm really sorry I'll miss it, too."

Three sets of eyes turned to stare at me.

"Manny said you've been training like a maniac for this race," Libby said.

I shrugged.

Libby's eyes glistened. "You'd miss your race for me?"

"What are friends for?" I said quietly.

She squeezed my hand, then released it. "Okay, Kitty Kat," she said, back to her old self. "But don't start bitching if this turns out not to be worth missing that triathlon for."

56

Libby was now ten centimeters dilated and one hundred percent effaced. She was breathing heavily, sweat pouring down her face and between her breasts. Mitch grasped her hand, kissing her knuckles. I slipped my hand in her free one, feeling her clench as she breathed and moaned through the next contraction. I wiped her forehead with a damp cloth, breathing deeply, my heart beating in time with the pulse I could feel in Libby's neck. It was like everyone in the room was a single being—one breath, one beat, one mind focused on a single purpose.

"You're close," Abra said. "That's it."

Libby smiled. "Um, Abra? Do you think Kat could—" She looked at me. "I mean, would you like to—you know. Help catch the baby?"

My mouth dropped open. "But you waited for Abra," I said. "Abra's the midwife. She should—"

"We can do it together, Katima," Abra said. "You were the one who got her this far."

"But you've been with her since the beginning," I said. "You were the one who—"

"She wants you to help, Katima," Abra said, "and we need to—"

"Excuse me," Libby said. "I really hate to interrupt." Abra and I both looked at her. "But I'm about to have a goddamn baby! Kat, get your ass down there and catch it before it falls out. I feel the urge to push."

I scrambled for a new pair of surgical gloves before dropping to the floor, shaking my hands to get rid of my nervousness. Abra scooted out of the way.

"I'm just helping," I said to her.

"No," Abra said, a faint smile on her face. "I think you've got this one."

I caught my first baby—with a little help from Abra—on a hot July morning during the transition between the bike and the run at the Rocky Mountain Women's Triathlon. Well, not exactly during the transition, but that's where I would have been if I'd been competing in the triathlon instead of kneeling in Serenity Space, bringing Libby's baby into the world.

I sucked in my breath when I saw the baby's head. Libby pushed a few more times and the baby began to emerge. I supported her as she slid out, overcome with the strangest sensation, as if my mind and body had separated and all that remained were raw emotion and the feel of her warm, slippery wetness against my skin. Time stopped, suspending the baby and me in a moment of pure joy where sight and sound and taste didn't exist— only touch. The electric touch of skin, heart, and soul.

The spell broke when Abra used a bulb syringe to suck the mucus from the baby's nose and mouth and Katherine Abigail Sullivan let out her first healthy cry.

"Do you want to hold her?"

Libby shook her head vigorously. Then: "Yes. Please." She reached out, and I placed Katherine gently on her breast. Libby cried silently as she cradled the baby in her arms, stroking her small back. Mitch had his arm around Libby and was crying, too, his hand covering Katherine's tiny one.

I didn't realize tears were running down my cheeks until one dropped on my arm. I brushed it away and sniffled. Out of the corner of my eye I could see the Sullivans in the doorway, their arms around each other. They had arrived fifteen minutes before Katherine. They were her adoptive parents. Mrs. Giles stood stiffly near the wall, her damp eyes fixed on something across the room. She didn't look at Libby or Mitch or Katherine; she just stared ahead, her lips pressed together.

Libby, Mitch, and the Sullivans had agreed on the name—Katherine for Mrs. Sullivan's grandmother (and for me, Libby told me later—something that stunned the pee right out of me), and Abigail for Libby—that was her middle name.

"What if it had been a boy?" I asked Libby.

"John Mitchell," she said immediately. Mitch looked away, biting his lip.

It would be an open adoption, so Libby would hear about Katherine growing up, Katherine would know her birth mother, and they would get to visit each other.

I sat on the edge of the bed, watching Libby stroke Katherine's back. Mitch stepped out to call his parents.

Libby turned to the Fate Goddess: "I guess she'll visit Katherine in her new home." She looked at the Sullivans and started to cry again.

"Take as much time as you need," said Mrs. Sullivan softly.

"Yes," said Mr. Sullivan. "As much time as you need."

"We don't have that much time," Libby said, sitting up straighter in the bed. She held the baby out to me. "Can you clean her up and get her ready to meet her new parents?"

I nodded, but took my time getting to her.

"I hope she doesn't hate me." Libby's arms curved as if Katherine was still nestled between them.

"No one could hate you as much as I do," I said, my voice catching as I handed Katherine to a waiting Abra, who could clean a baby better than I could.

Libby smiled tiredly.

"You're brave and strong and amazing," Mitch said.

I nodded. "And she'll know you with this open adoption, right?"

"Right," Libby said, sounding far from convinced. I saw tears well up as she turned her head away. "I shouldn't have held her," she whispered, and I gripped her hand. "I didn't think I'd love her right away. I'm so tired, and it hurt, and I knew she wasn't really mine." She took a deep breath, then exhaled slowly. "I just didn't think I'd love her."

She looked up at me. "Geri Border didn't have any problem giving hers up." Geri was a senior at Tabor High last year. She and Libby had hung out together sometimes. "She acted like she was handing off a piece of furniture she wasn't using anymore. It was no big deal." Her eyes filled with tears. "Abra told me I'd be sad and I should be ready to grieve, but I didn't believe her." She reached out and took my hand and I squeezed it. "Why am I so sad?"

I squeezed her hand in reply. "Because you're not Geri Border," I whispered. "You're someone totally different."

And she was.

• • •

While Libby rested and the Sullivans oohed and aahed over Katherine, I went upstairs to change out of my sweaty, barfy unitard. I threw on some shorts and a tank top and caught myself in the mirror, hair mussed, face slightly freckled, with a zit saying hello on the side of my nose. I wondered how I could look so ordinary on such an extraordinary day. I had just picked up my sketchbook when there was a gentle tap on my door.

"Come in."

Abra stepped through, looking tired and worn. "Do you have a minute?"

I really wanted to go outside and sit by myself for a while, but she looked like she needed to talk.

"Sure." I sat down on my bed.

Abra sat on the end so there was space between us. We stayed that way for a few moments, listening to the faint hum of my computer and the muffled rumble of a lawn mower in the distance outside.

"You were absolutely amazing with Libby, you know," Abra said finally.

I shrugged. "I just did what you would do."

"No," Abra said. "You did what *you* would do, which is much better."

I smiled.

"Is that Libby's birth picture?" She glanced at the sketchbook behind me.

"It will be. I haven't started it yet." I sighed. "I don't know if she'll want it, though. It might be too hard for her."

I waited, expecting Abra to offer some advice, some perspective or observation. She didn't.

"You'll know what to do when the time comes," she said. She seemed distracted as she pulled a piece of paper from her pocket. "I have something I'd like to say."

Oh, no. Lecture time. And she had *notes*.

She opened the paper, smoothing it on her leg. "I'm nervous," she said, shaking her head. "Isn't that the craziest thing?" She took a deep breath. "I think it would be easier if I read this part, if that's okay."

"Okay." My pulse quickened. This was way worse than waiting for a Buchanan Field Report.

"Fact Number One," she read. "What you want or need *does* matter to me, but sometimes I get caught up in other things—or other people." She paused and tugged at her hair again. "I guess in some ways I was trying to get you to be like me because I knew I could relate to that. Then you were becoming someone I wasn't sure what to do with." She sighed. "It's funny, but it's always been easier for me to get close to people who don't really know me. But with you—well, sometimes I think you know me better than I know myself. You scare me sometimes."

I nearly fell off the bed. *Me* scare *Abra*?

"You are really amazing and wonderful, and I love you for who you are," Abra said. She smiled. "In spite of everything I did, you still managed to be yourself, to be Kat."

I looked up, startled by the nickname. She didn't even seem to notice that she'd said it.

"I was nowhere near as perceptive as you are at your age." Abra sighed again. "You are good at so many things that I'm not. You should celebrate those things. And so should I."

I felt my cheeks warm and looked down. I thought about how I made Diane laugh, how I'd talked to Mr. Robertson about

Melanie going to the hospital, how thrilled Melanie and Linda were with their birth pictures, how I'd become friends with Mitch and gone out with Manny.

And how Abra, for all her perfection, hadn't done any of those things. How she'd misread Melanie and couldn't be for Lucy and me what she could be for other people.

I looked at her, her hair slightly graying, but her eyes full of light. Maybe she was trying to find her way, just like me.

She folded and unfolded her paper. "Fact Number Two: I guess I haven't had much left to give to you and Lucy." She looked up. "I'm really sorry for that. I'm not sure what to do except try harder. And differently."

I looked away, not wanting her to see my eyes, which I knew were glistening with almost-tears.

"I'll try harder, too, Mom," I whispered, testing the word on my tongue. It felt a little strange, like drinking milk when you were expecting to taste Coke.

"That's all we can do," Abra said. If she'd noticed what I'd called her, she didn't show it.

I stood up and crossed to my desk.

"I was going to wait until your birthday to give you this," I said, "but maybe this is a better time."

I sat down again, handing her a picture I'd drawn. In it, Abra was standing in a meadow with her arms outstretched, surrounded by children. I'd put myself and Lucy front and center, Abra's eyes on us. I was holding Lucy's hand and Libby was on the other side of Lucy, holding her other hand.

"Oh, my goodness, it's beautiful, Katima." She blinked quickly. "Thank you. I know just where to hang it at the Midwifery." She smiled shyly and looked at me. "I—I don't suppose you'll come back?"

366

"I don't know if that's a good idea right now."

She nodded, looking at the picture again. "It's remarkable, Katima. Truly."

I blushed and looked down, feeling a movement beside me.

I turned then and saw she'd closed the space between us. I found myself in her arms, the same arms that had wrapped themselves around Libby so many times, the arms that had hugged so many women at the Midwifery while I watched and waited and wondered what it was like.

The arms that, in this moment, felt like the arms of a mother around her daughter.

Postpartum

Your body goes through a lot of changes now that the baby has been born. Allow yourself to ease into these changes. Be gentle with yourself. And enjoy!

57

Fact of Life #31: There are no facts of life.

The hot sun beat down on my face as I sat on the top step of our front porch, my journal and the pen Manny had given me resting beside me. I smiled, feeling strangely cool in the sun, wrapped in a cocoon of quiet within myself, still on a high from having caught Katherine a few hours before. I felt vast, grand, invincible. Able to leap small potholes in a single bound. I was part of the earth, the sky, the sun, the very air that was filling up my lungs and swirling around me.

I ran my fingers over the pen, thinking of Manny's text from last night:

> U will kick butt in the tri I'll be at the fin line
> w the go, kat, go sign From: DaMan Cell 8:14 pm

Christy had called Manny to tell him I wouldn't be racing, that I was with Libby. His text this morning said:

I glanced down the street, trying to figure out why things looked so different. The VW bug was parked in front of the Larsons' house like always. The streetlight still stood tall between the Mahers' and the Duffords' houses, and Libby's house was still three blocks away, tucked around two curves, where I couldn't see it. Nothing had really changed, and yet everything had.

I pulled out the Fate Goddess card I'd given Libby. She'd handed it to me for safekeeping after the birth. I traced my finger over the goddess's face. Abra had once said I'd "know in time" what the Fate Goddess might have whispered in my ear three days after my birth. I didn't know if that time would ever come, but I did know what I hoped she'd seen in me, what vision of the future she thought I might fit into, the difference I might make.

I opened my journal again.

There are no facts of life, only expectations, assumptions, and a whole lot of trying. Only experiences that you try to make sense of, try to pull meaning out of, like a baby at the breast. And sometimes, when your eyes are wide open, you get lucky. You get it.

I closed the journal and pulled out my sketchbook. I had nearly finished the picture of Libby and Katherine, with Mitch snuggled beside Libby, his hand wrapped around Katherine's small fist. I had actually been at this birth. I think it made a difference.

I still didn't know if I would give it to Libby. It might make her too sad. I thought I'd ask her about it. Maybe I'd even ask Abra for advice. Wouldn't that blow her mind.

Abra. I didn't expect us to have heart-to-heart talks all the time, or even lots of hugging and laughing over shared jokes. But maybe there would be an ease between us, an understanding that we'd never had before. It wouldn't be perfect, but it would be something.

I pulled out my cell phone. Christy had sent two text messages. The first said she was sorry about the race and asked if Libby had had her baby yet.

I felt a little tug in my chest about the triathlon. But there would be other races. There wouldn't be another Katherine Abigail Sullivan.

Her second text was short:

```
Well? From: HatGirl Cell 3:12 pm
```

I smiled. I'd call Christy. I just had to make another call first.

"Hey," I said. "It's a girl."

I could actually feel Manny's smile through the phone.

"And guess what?" I said, feeling my throat close up with tears. "I caught the baby. She asked me to."

"Good for you," Manny said. "Good for her." There was a pause. "I'd like to come over."

"I think she'd like that." I took a breath. "We both would." I heard Manny suck in his breath. "And maybe later tonight we could go out. Flipflops, Chili's—hold the crazy cousins."

Manny laughed. "Is this a date, Katima Flynn?"

"Yeah," I said. "It is."

He sighed. "I thought you'd never ask."

We hung up and I called Christy, making a plan for her to come over to see Libby and the baby. Then I turned off the phone, content just to sit on my porch, looking down the street for a familiar green Range Rover that I knew was on its way, my heart light in spite of the heavy heat surrounding me.

Looking up, I watched a wisp of cloud drift slowly across the deep blue sky, reminding me that there was something much bigger and better than myself, an entire universe that was doing its thing . . .

. . . with, maybe, just a little help from me.

Acknowledgments

I'm deeply grateful to my sister, Cheryl Vega Ryan, and her husband, James Ryan, for inviting me and our other sisters to be a part of the births of their sons, and to their home birth midwives, Lisa Afshar and Tracy Ryan. I was changed by these sacred experiences and will always remember them—especially since Alexander decided to be caught by his capable father before any of us arrived at your house!

Thank you to my own nurse-midwives, Pauline Connor, who caught my babies in the hospital, and Kate Dykema, who takes care of me today—you are amazing in every way. Thank you also to my completely centered yoga instructor, Robin Secher, who helps keep me sane twice a week in my yoga practice. I also owe so much to my critique group, who loved this book and gave me their usual excellent advice on how to make it better. Thank you, Wild Folk . . . may the guacamole celebrations abound for all of us.

And major thanks to my agent, Wendy Schmalz, who believed in this book and found the perfect home for it at Knopf.

Speaking of which, big Rocky Mountain thank-yous to my editors, Michelle Frey and Michele Burke, who are beyond incredible. Our vision of the book was completely in sync, and I cannot thank you enough for your keen eye and astute insights. I had so much fun revising with you and really grew as a writer.

I'm also indebted to the copy editor, Susan Goldfarb, who saved my you-know-what more than once with her incredibly detailed review of the manuscript. Thanks also to Michael Storrings for the great cover art, and to Sarah Hokanson, who designed the most perfect cover ever. My gratitude to everyone else at Knopf for supporting Kat and her story. And finally, hugs to my amazing extended family, who are always there for me, no matter what.